Praise for *Heart-Shaped Bruise*:

'This book creeps up on you as more of the story is revealed . . . I became fascinated with the girls' relationship, constantly trying to guess how things would end up – but I'm impressed to say I got it wrong' *Woman*

'Dark but addictive' *Look*

'A tense, emotionally complex study of love and hate' *The Sunday Times*

'Punchy and raw . . . the engrossing and fast-paced narrative proves Byrne to be a consummate storyteller' *Red*

'An addictive, thrilling read' *Cosmopolitan*

'Intrigue and brilliant writing . . . a first rate debut' *Sun*

'Byrne is a talented writer with attitude and a fresh, original voice' *Daily Mail*

'Gripping' *Telegraph*

'Intriguing and utterly addictive' *Woman's Own*

'Gorgeously dark and twisted . . . impossible to put down' *Image* (Ireland)

'Punchy, gripping and completely compelling' *Glamour*

'Compelling and clever. We loved' *Company*

'A compulsive and moving novel' *Stylist*

'Raw and gripping with a wholly unexpected final twist' *Guardian*

'Intriguing and compelling' Sophie Hannah

Tanya Byrne was born in London and studied in Surrey, where she still lives with her cat who goes by several names, none of which he actually answers to. After eight years working for BBC Radio, she left to write her debut novel, *Heart-Shaped Bruise*. She has a weakness for boys with guitars, drinks far too much tea and even though her mother tells her not to, she always talks to strangers.

Tanya is currently working on her second novel.

TANYA BYRNE

Heart-Shaped Bruise

headline

First published in 2012
by HEADLINE PUBLISHING GROUP

First published in paperback in 2012
by HEADLINE PUBLISHING GROUP

1

Cataloguing in Publication Data is available from the British Library

ISBN 978 0 7553 9305 3 (YA)
ISBN 978 0 7553 9606 1 (Adult)

Typeset in Goudy by Avon DataSet Ltd,
Bidford-on-Avon, Warwickshire

Printed and bound in Great Britain by
Clays Ltd, St Ives plc

Headline's policy is to use papers that are natural, renewable and
recyclable products and made from wood grown in sustainable forests.
The logging and manufacturing processes are expected to conform to the
environmental regulations of the country of origin.

HEADLINE PUBLISHING GROUP
An Hachette UK Company
338 Euston Road
London NW1 3BH

www.headline.co.uk
www.hachette.co.uk

For Jacob. Reach for the sky.

Last year, the psychiatric unit of Archway Young Offenders Institution was closed. A notebook was found in one of the rooms. The contents are as follows . . .

Juliet,

I know you've been waiting three months for this letter, but I have to start by saying that this isn't an apology. I'm not sorry. I'm not. If I have to spend the rest of my life crossing that word out of every dictionary I find, I will. So, if that's what you've been waiting for me to say, why you keep writing to me, stop reading now.

This is the only letter I'm going to write you, and the only reason I'm writing it is because you keep asking me why I did what I did. I guess you don't believe them when they say that I'm out of my mind. I don't know. I might be. My normal and everyone else's normal isn't the same any more. Mine is out of time, like I'm a record playing at the wrong speed or something. That's why I'm letting them do this to me, why I swallow their

3

pills and sit here, scratching my sins into the walls.

But that's not why I did it. You must know that, otherwise you wouldn't be asking. So, okay, you want to know why? This is why: you stabbed my father. That's it. What don't you understand? China shop rules, Juliet: you break it, you pay for it, and you broke me. You got what you deserved.

Now leave me alone.

Emily

That was the only thing I was supposed to write in this note-book. When Doctor Gilyard gave it to me yesterday, she told me to write the letter to Juliet and give it back when I was ready.

I was going to, but, earlier, while I was hiding a cigarette on top of my wardrobe, I found a letter to someone called Will. I know I shouldn't have, but I read it and – *my heart*. I didn't think it still worked, but I felt it again, all hot and red and heavy in my chest.

I don't know why the letter is still here; it's in an envelope with the address on it and everything. Maybe the girl who wrote it – Sonia, who loves Will, and slept in this bed before me – forgot to take it with her when she left. Or maybe she was too scared to send it. I'm not. That's the first thing I'm going to do when I get out of here, because Will, whoever he is, deserves to know how much he's loved.

God knows, no one will ever love me like that. Not now.

So I found Will's letter on top of the wardrobe and you found this notebook there, too, and that's the way it should be, I think. Everywhere I go I try to leave a piece of myself behind. I'll never be lost because there are bits of me scattered all over London; compliments written on the back of Starbucks receipts, secrets scribbled in public toilets. It's like I'm everywhere, all at once. Waitresses will think of me and smile. Bathroom walls will remember me. I'll live for ever.

You should try it – leave something on top of the wardrobe before you go. If there's something you want to say to someone but you can't, write it down and leave it behind for someone else to read. That's why I'm writing this now. It's easier this way, kind of like how you can tell the stranger sitting next to you on the bus all of your secrets, but you can't tell your best friend because best friends never forget.

So, here we go, I'll be me and you be the stranger on the bus.

This isn't a journal. I'm eighteen; I don't have the patience for journals any more. I don't have the patience for straight lines, either. I tend to avoid them. So don't expect this to be all this-happened-then-this-happened-then-this-happened because my brain doesn't work like that. You'd be bored anyway.

As for what you do with this notebook, that's up to you. Tell the nurses, tell Doctor Gilyard. I don't care. You can even put it back on top of the wardrobe and pretend you never saw it if you want. But I need to say this, to be rid of it. I can't keep carrying it around with me; I'm buckling under the weight of it. I look at myself sometimes, at the broken lines across the palms of my hands and the creases in my elbows, and I can see myself coming apart at the seams.

Like today, with Doctor Gilyard. I never speak first. Never.

I've seen her once a week since I got here and I haven't said a word without being prompted. But this morning, I sat down and before she even opened her notebook, I said: 'I know what you think of me.'

It came from nowhere, I swear. For a moment I thought I meant it, that I'd turned the corner she'd been dragging me towards. But then she took her glasses off and as she did, I saw her fingers flutter and I realised that I did that to her – I did that – and some imbalance in the universe tipped back in my direction.

'What do I think of you, Emily?' she asked, but it was too late, the moment was gone; I'd faltered, but I'd still scored the first point.

It was cruel, I suppose. She must have thought it was a breakthrough because I watched her cheeks go pink as she waited for me to respond. I wonder if she was holding her breath, hoping that I would finally collapse into a broken, sobbing heap at her feet. But I turned my face away.

'It's okay, you can say it.'

'Say what, Emily?'

'You know what.'

'What's that, Emily?'

'Why won't you say it?'

'Why won't *you* say it, Emily?'

Always a question with a question.

My fingers curled around the arms of the chair. 'Can I smoke?'

'Do you have any cigarettes?'

She knew I didn't have any cigarettes. The nurses have them

and we're only allowed four a day; one after breakfast, one after lunch, one after dinner and one before bed. I was furious about it when first I got here, but it's for my own good, apparently. That's what this place is about, *establishing routines*. I get up at the same time, shower at the same time, eat at the same time, go to bed at the same time.

My life is a song I listen to on repeat.

I think I'm supposed to find it comforting, the consistency of it all. This is normal, I'm told. This is what normal teenage girls do – they sleep for eight hours and take their make-up off every night. They don't call their mates for a chat at 3 a.m.

That's all normal is, you know, a habit I have to relearn.

Crazy is a habit I have to break.

'You used to let me smoke.'

She did, when I first got here and we would sit in her office for hours – hours and hours – suffocating on the silence. She would put the box on the coffee table between us and she wouldn't say anything, but I knew that if I said something, I could have one. So I would tell her things, tiny things. Cigarette-long confessions to distract her from the things I didn't want her to write in that notebook of hers.

'I don't have any cigarettes, Emily.'

I stood up then. I do that a lot, walk around her office. It's as though I have to see everything, touch everything. Trail my fingers along her desk and over the books on her shelf as though I'm counting each one.

'Is this what's wrong with me?' I asked her during our first

9

session, plucking a textbook on adolescent schizophrenia off the shelf and holding it up. 'Am I mad?'

When she didn't respond, I put it back, next to a textbook on sleeping disorders before moving along the row. 'How about this?' I said, pulling out another and looking at the cover. '*Personality Disorders: A Practical Guide.*' I glanced across the office at her, but she just lifted her chin, her shoulders perfectly still and straight.

I began flicking through the book, stopping at a chapter about borderline personality disorder. 'This could be me,' I told her as I read the symptoms. 'My emotions go up and down, don't they? Me and every other teenage girl. I guess we're all nutters.'

When I turned to her with a smug smile, she nodded. 'Why don't you read the rest?'

I looked down at the page – *difficulty in making and maintaining relationships . . . unstable sense of identity . . . taking risks without thinking about the consequences* – and snapped the book shut. 'Nah. It's boring. Got anything with vampires in it?'

Doctor Gilyard just smiled. And she just smiled today as I walked over to her desk and began opening the drawers. There was nothing in the first one; a few Biros, a neon-pink highlighter. There was a silver tube of hand cream in the second one and I stopped and stared at it. I couldn't picture Doctor Gilyard doing something as normal as using hand cream. In fact, I don't think I've even seen her stand up. In my head, when I leave her office, she sits there until I go back in the following week. She doesn't leave. She doesn't walk or eat or worry about what to wear in the morning.

The half-empty box of cigarettes was in the last drawer and I took one out and lit it with the lighter that was in the drawer next to it. I closed my eyes and inhaled deeply. It tasted disgusting – I didn't even want it – but when I went back to my chair, smoke trailing behind me, a scoreboard somewhere registered another point.

'What was it that you wanted me to say, Emily?' Doctor Gilyard continued as though those last few minutes hadn't happened. She just stepped over them.

I looked at the end of the cigarette and blew on it. 'That I'm evil.'

'Are you evil, Emily?'

'Isn't that what they say about me?'

She took off her glasses and looked at me. 'Who says that you're evil?'

'Everyone.' Juliet. The police. The newspapers. The girls I barely know from school who sigh and shake their heads on the six o'clock news and say they always knew there was something not quite right about me.

'Is that why you won't talk about what happened, Emily, because you think I already know what happened?'

'You do know what happened.'

She put her glasses back on and scribbled something in her notebook. I wanted to lean over and rip it from her, to read what she was saying about me. She has one for each of us, apparently.

I imagine them sometimes, lined up in a row in a room, all of these secrets sitting on a shelf like dusty jars of jam.

'You know everything about me,' I told her.

She looked up again. 'Do I?'

'What you don't know, you can Google.'

'Is that who you are, Emily, what other people say about you?'

'That's all any of us are.' I shrugged and took a drag on the cigarette. 'The person people remember when you leave the room. You can't be any more than that.'

'So what do I remember about you, Emily?'

'What I did.'

'What did you do?'

'You know what I did.' I tried to control the tremor in my voice but we both heard it. I was furious with myself. She does that every time. It's like she wants me to keep saying it, over and over, as though if I keep saying it, I'll believe it. I'll be sorry.

'I know what you were arrested for, Emily.'

I tapped the ash from my cigarette on to the floor. 'What else is there?'

'You tell me.'

My gaze edged towards hers again. 'Why do you want to know?'

Her eyes dipped to the notebook. 'I want to help you understand why you did what you did, Emily.'

'I know why I did it.'

'Okay.' She nodded. 'Why did you do it?'

I could have given it to her then, the letter to Juliet. I could

12

have told her that Juliet made me do it, that I used to be like every other teenage girl, that I was stubborn and restless and melodramatic and said the wrong thing sometimes and broke mirrors and misheard lyrics, but I still sang, even though the words were wrong. That I threw coins in fountains and made wishes at 11.11 because I thought that if I wanted something, all I had to do was ask for it. And I asked, not for world peace or money or good health or any of those things other people wish for. I asked to be special. I wanted to be the sort of girl boys wrote books about, the sort of girl boys sang songs about.

I think I could have been, but then Juliet stabbed my father and I couldn't be me any more. I turned into someone else, into this hard, angry, *miserable* girl who did the most terrible things. Things that made people take a step back when I walked into a room.

That's what you won't find on Google, I wanted to tell Doctor Gilyard today. *Who I used to be.*

But I didn't because she'd never get that, would she? She'd never get that sometimes we do things that are so big – so awful – that they just become who we are. It's like you do it and *BOOM* everything is blown to bits.

I guess if you're here too, then you know how that feels.

I'm laughing now, as I'm writing this, because I don't even know who you are but I think you understand me better than anyone else I know. After all, isn't that why we're here, you and me? Because we're broken?

Saturday. Art therapy. We had to paint how we were feeling so I balled up my piece of paper and threw it at the therapist. I'm not allowed to have a cigarette for the rest of the day.

Saturday is also Visitors' Day so Naomi (17, schizophrenic) is having her weekly shit fit. I'm writing this from the TV Room because there aren't enough nurses to deal with Naomi's histrionics and keep an eye on us too, so we've been corralled into the TV Room to watch a film like we're two years olds. I half want to wander into the corridor weeping about how it isn't worth it any more just to see how they would react.

The new girl, Lily (16, anorexic), keeps looking at me with this sad little smile as though she's waiting for me to tell her that it's going to be okay, but I won't smile back because why should

I be the one to tell her that it won't be? If she doesn't know that already, being in this place, then I can't help her.

If you can't read the tail end of that sentence, it's because Naomi just broke something – something glass – and we all jumped. I say *all*, Val (17, bipolar) didn't budge. She just sat there, staring at the television. But that's Val; once she sits in front of the telly, she doesn't move. You can go over to her and slap her across the face and she won't notice, but turn it over when *Deal or No Deal* is on and she'll pull you apart, bone by bone.

Naomi's just broken something else. She does this *every time* her boyfriend comes to visit; she sees him, feels her heart again, and thinks she's better. Then when it's time to take her meds, she screams blue bloody murder. That's why I won't let anyone visit me. Not that there is anyone to visit me; Dad's in prison and Mum's – well, I don't know where Mum is. Wherever she is, she isn't thinking about me, so I won't waste any more ink on her.

Naomi just roared, 'I'm fine! I'm in love, I don't need drugs!', so it won't be long until she threatens to kill herself and they sedate her, which is good, because we're having spag bol for dinner. I don't do much willingly here, but I'm first in the queue for spag bol.

I just had to stop writing because the new girl approached me.

'Are you her? Are you Emily Koll?' she asked, her eyes wide.

I'm not wearing my YES, IT'S ME, EMILY KOLL T-shirt today so I nodded.

She took that as her cue to sit next to me and as she did, I looked at her, at the gold crucifix around her neck and her unbrushed brown hair. She looked so fragile, as though her clothes were the only things holding her together, but she was bold enough to sit next to me without being asked, so I had to give her that. She's braver than most of the girls in here.

'You're not what I expected,' she told me with a whisper.

I made a show of rolling my eyes and snapping this notebook shut because what could I say? It wasn't a compliment, was it?

'You're blond.'

I am blond. That's what surprises people the most when they come here. They expect to meet the red-lipped, red-haired girl they've seen in the papers. But they find me – tiny, blond, doll-faced me – and they stare at me as though they've been betrayed. They want the wild redhead. Tiny blonde girls don't do what I did.

'Is it true? Did you really do that to that girl Juliet?' she asked.

She was breathless and I love and hate that, how people are in awe of me and terrified of me, all at once. So I smiled at her. 'Don't believe everything you read.'

You shouldn't either, by the way.

Emily Koll. Slipped that one in, didn't I?

I probably should have told you that straight away, on the first page. I wasn't trying to trick you; if I procrastinated, it's only because I know what people think of me. I've read what they say about me in the newspapers, that I'm wicked, that I'm so rotten my bones are the colour of bitten-down apple cores.

But there's more than one side to a story, and this is mine.

First, the facts:

Yes, my father is Harry Koll.

Yes, Juliet's father is Jason Shaw.

Yes, my father is one of London's most notorious gangsters.

Yes, Juliet's father ran the police investigation to take him down.

Yes, my father broke into his house and shot him in his bed.

Yes, Juliet stabbed my father when he tried to shoot her too.

No, I didn't know. About any of it. That Dad was a gangster. That he could just shoot someone like that. The dad I knew put me on his shoulders at Arsenal games and read me *Goodnight Moon* when I couldn't sleep and came to all my cello recitals. All of them. So I don't know who that man is, the one who sells drugs and kills men in their beds.

I don't suppose it matters what I say now. You can take this notebook and tear it to pieces. You can burn it and let the ashes float away like dirty confetti, because all you'll remember is that my father murdered her father. If you ask Juliet, she'll tell you that's all you should remember. Maybe you should. Call me mad, call me wicked, but I'm under no illusions – I know how easy it is to pick sides here – her father was the big brave policeman and my father is the gangster who shot him. He got what was coming to him. I did too, I suppose. But I told you – *I didn't know.* I need you to remember that while you're drawing that line between Juliet and me. And that's fine, draw it. Go on. I'll stay on my side of it if you remember that I didn't know.

Here's another fact for you: yes, I went after Juliet. That's why I'm here. Why most of the girls here are too scared to sit next to me. But don't believe everything you read in the tabloids, there was no vendetta. When I found out what Dad did, my instinct wasn't to go after Juliet. I reacted like anyone else would have; I was horrified, ashamed. For months I tried to ignore it, to wash the taste of it from my mouth with cheap vodka and cigarettes.

But it wouldn't go away.

Doctor Gilyard says that's when it started – the crazy – but it felt more like grief. It was like this blackness that crept into the corners of my life until everything was grey and dirty. My insides felt burned out, like if you cut me open, all you would find would be smoke. No heart. No bones. There was nothing left, just the anger. It followed me everywhere. It sat on my bed and watched me sleep and when I had to eat, it looked at me across the table.

So I gave into it, rolled around in it, swam in it, deeper and deeper, until it pulled me under. When I emerged, I had only one thought: Juliet. It was her fault. *That*'s how it started, the day I traced that line back to the night she stabbed Dad and everything fell apart. So I suppose I don't always avoid straight lines.

Sometimes I run across them.

Sunday. Music therapy.

As a group, we don't agree on much in here, but we are united in our hatred of music therapy. I actually *like* music, so it shouldn't be such an ordeal. But if Her Majesty's Prison Service is trying to teach me that violence isn't the answer, they really shouldn't make me do music therapy with Kim, an over-eager Australian girl who insists on playing ABBA songs as though we can dance the crazy right out of us.

She's twenty-two, so I guess we're supposed to relate to her, but she's *so* happy. Happy happy happy, all the time. Happy when Halina (16, Post-Traumatic Stress Disorder) wets herself. Happy when Reta (17, schizophrenic) starts bickering with the aliens sent to earth to protect her. Happy when Val refuses to stand up, let alone take an instrument from the box. Happy happy happy.

She's clearly the maddest one here.

Once, I asked Doctor Gilyard what the point of it was.

Of course she responded with: 'What do you think the point of it is, Emily?'

'It's clearly a form of torture,' I muttered. 'If that lunatic plays "Dancing Queen" once more, I'm writing to Amnesty International. I'd rather be waterboarded.'

'Which lunatic?'

I huffed, but I suppose you do have to specify in this place.

'Kim! Get her in here,' I said with a wave of my hand. 'Ask her about her mother. She's off her nut if she thinks that banging a tambourine is going to stop Reta thinking that she's BFFs with the High Priestess of Maladoth.'

'You don't think it helps?'

'Of course not!'

She took off her glasses and looked at me. 'So it wouldn't help to play the cello?'

I'd been waiting for that. Waiting.

'It's impossible to play along to "Dancing Queen" on the cello,' I told her with a smug smile, but I still felt my heart in my throat.

She can't.

She won't.

She won't.

Doctor Gilyard started our session this week by asking me if I often lose my temper.

That's all she ever does: ask questions. Questions. Questions. Questions. If the sun slants into her office at the right angle, you can see all the question marks floating in the air. Question marks and dust. I try to catch them on my tongue sometimes, as though they're snowflakes. I can't, of course, but it's fun to see the look on her face as I try.

The first time I did it, she looked so worried that I don't know how I didn't laugh. Now she knows me well enough not to flinch when I do stuff like that. She just closes her notebook and when she puts her pencil on top of it, I stop because what's the point of giving her what she wants if she isn't going to write it down?

I swear I wouldn't do *half* the stuff I do if someone wasn't paying attention.

But I guess she's learned a trick or two over the last few months, which is why she didn't tell me about Juliet's letter today. Usually, she would try to hand it to me and I'd huff and puff and refuse to take it. But today she just put the envelope down on the coffee table in front of me and sat back in her chair.

There was a ceremony to it, to the way she turned it over so that I could see my name and the address written neatly across it. And I looked at it, then at her, and when she picked up the pencil again, I felt the silence roll out between us like a red carpet.

I didn't say anything for the rest of the session and it actually hurt not to. There was this pain – this ache – in my stomach as I looked at the letter. She usually reads them out to me so I waited and waited, but she didn't. She just let it sit there, on the coffee table, while she waited for me to give in and reach for it.

I almost did because I'm desperate to know how miserable Juliet is. That's the only thing keeping me going right now, knowing that even though she's out there while I'm stuck in here, I'm the one who's free. But I didn't reach for it and Doctor Gilyard didn't read it out, so I guess I'll never know now.

I'll never sleep again, wondering what's in that letter.

I think Lily has started smoking because of me. I've never seen her smoke before, but now she sits with Naomi and me whenever we're having one. Naomi says she has a crush on me. I don't know about that, but if she does, she has exceptional taste.

Today after breakfast, Naomi was with Doctor Gilyard so it was just us. I watched as Lily tried to skin up, her forehead pinched and her tongue poking out of the corner of her mouth. It was funny at first; she was concentrating so much it looked like she was trying to disarm a bomb. But after a few minutes, her hands started to shake. When the tobacco began to spill from the ends of the thin paper I took it from her and rolled the cigarette with a few quick flicks of my wrist.

When I gave it back to her, she didn't light it.

'Homesick,' I said, picking my roll-up back out of the ashtray.

She looked at her feet. I saw her toes curl in her shoes. 'I don't want to talk about it.'

'I wasn't asking.'

It was a statement, not a question. There are words you can't say in here; you don't ask why, you don't ask how, you don't ask about tomorrow and you never ask about home.

It's one of the only rules I observe here without protest.

I don't know what Naomi and Lily did to get put in here. I know what they were *charged* with, but I'm not writing it down. I want you to know them for who they are, not what they've done. When they get out of here, that's all they'll be. That's all any of us in here will be, right? What we've done. You must know that, being in here, too.

At school they drummed it into us that God will forgive us anything if we ask him to, but that isn't true, is it? Forgiveness is useless if other people still remember what you did. Sometimes I wonder if I'll ever shake off my mistakes or if I'll just carry them around with me for ever like a bunch of red balloons.

Our don't ask, don't tell rule isn't one Doctor Gilyard pays much attention to.

'Tell me about the day you found Juliet,' she said to me a couple of weeks ago.

I ignored her but she pushed on because she's as stubborn as I am. One day, one of us will win. I'm looking forward to finding out which of us it will be.

'It was three weeks after your father's trial, right?'

Silence.

'Juliet was in Witness Protection. How did you find her?'

Silence.

'It was your Uncle Alex, wasn't it? He told you where she was.'

Silence.

'What did you go there to do, Emily?'

I didn't speak to Doctor Gilyard for the rest of our session, but when Lily asked me if I ever get homesick, I told her that I didn't. I don't know why; there's just something about her sad little smile and fragile fingers that makes something in me soften.

'Why not?'

'I don't have a home,' I said between puffs of my cigarette.

She lifted her chin. 'How come?'

I shrugged. 'When you go to boarding school home stops being one place.'

I guess that's why it doesn't bother me, being in here. I'm used to it, to eating when I'm told, to sleeping in a room that isn't mine, in a bed that isn't mine.

'When I think of home,' I said, almost to myself, 'I think of the flat I was born in.'

'Where's that?'

'On the Scarbrook Estate in Finsbury Park.'

She thought about it for a second or two. 'Is that a council estate?'

I smiled. Most people think I was born in Surrey because that's the story they tell in the papers. They print pictures of our house and Dad's fleet of vintage cars (it's not quite a *fleet*, but four doesn't sound as impressive, I suppose) so people think I'm a proper princess. And yeah, it's true, I did go to a £30,000-a-year boarding school and we had a villa in Puerto Banus and I drove a Mercedes and wore dresses made of kitten hair and I had a baby unicorn.

Yeah, yeah, yeah. It's all true.

But I was also born on a council estate.

'So when did you move to Godalming?' she asked.

I sat back and smiled. She knows I live in Godalming. She's not that naïve.

'When I was three,' I told her. 'When Mum left.'

'Where did she go?'

I tensed. As sweet as Lily is, there's a line and her toes were on it. 'I dunno.'

'What? She just left and never came back?'

I had to stop because it was like Lily had my heart in her hand and she was squeezing it hard enough to leave a bruise.

So I stood up and she watched me carefully as I stubbed my cigarette out. She probably had a dozen more questions, but she pressed her lips together and for once, she didn't follow me when I walked away.

I haven't said a word to Doctor Gilyard since she wouldn't read me Juliet's letter. It's become a battle of wills now. I don't even know what I'm fighting for any more; I just know that giving in first feels too much like breaking.

'I'd like to go back to the day you found Juliet,' she said this morning, like that was actually going to happen. Like I was just going to say, *Okay, Doctor G*, and spill my guts.

I snorted and crossed my arms.

'You didn't do anything, did you, Emily? You followed her to London in August, so why wait until you both started college in September to speak to her?'

She waited for me to respond, but I looked away.

Doctor Gilyard's office is almost bare. There are only a few bits of furniture – the chairs we sit on, the coffee table between them, a bookshelf, a desk and swivel chair, but that's it. No plant in the corner of the room, no framed diplomas, no paintings of calm country scenes.

It's an empty, hopeless room, but if I have to ignore her, there are still half a dozen things I can distract myself with. A ring on the coffee table. A loose thread on my chair. Recently I've been focusing on a crack in the wall. It's nothing, just a thin line in the plaster that looks like someone's brushed past the wall with a pencil, but I've been staring at it for weeks. It's bigger than it was when I first noticed it, I'm sure of it. I've convinced myself that if I keep staring at it, it'll get bigger, and if it does, a crack will become a gap and a gap will become a hole and I'll be through.

'Why didn't you confront her, if that's what you went there to do?' she persisted.

When I didn't respond, I heard her scribble something in her notebook.

'I went back to Juliet's interview transcripts yesterday. She says that she doesn't remember seeing you before you met that morning at the college, is that right?'

Juliet doesn't remember seeing me because I made sure I wasn't seen. For a month we moved around each other. I followed her everywhere; across bridges, down escalators. I trailed behind her at the supermarket, watching as she sniffed peaches and read the backs of cereal boxes. Once, I even sat in the row behind hers at the cinema. I can't remember what film it was, I just remember looking at her – looking and looking – waiting for her to do something, to laugh, to cry, to fall asleep. Anything. It was as if my life had become a reaction to hers. If she had run out of the cinema that afternoon, I would have run after her. If she had stayed and watched another film, I would have stayed and watched her.

By then, I knew her routine. Every morning she bought a green tea from the café on the high street and drank it in the bookshop next door, sitting on the floor of the poetry section with her back against the wall. She would emerge an hour later with a half-read paperback between her fingers, then head to the park to watch the office workers sitting on their jackets eating Pret A Manger sandwiches in the last of the summer sun. In the afternoons, I followed her around art galleries or watched as she picked through the clothes rails at charity shops. Some afternoons she would just sit on the top deck of the bus and ride it until the end of the line, then get off, cross the road and get another bus home.

I guess it became my routine too, because when I got back to the perfect but hollow flat Uncle Alex had found for me, the only thing that made those long, long nights bearable was knowing I'd see her the next morning, walking out of that café with a white paper cup.

But she never saw me. Not once. And I was surprised because I expected her to look up every time someone got on her carriage on the tube or sat on the bench opposite hers at the park. But she'd be too distracted by a book or she'd be sketching something in the black Moleskine she carried with her everywhere. I was desperate to see what she was drawing. I wanted to cross everything out, write, *I KNOW WHO YOU ARE* on every page.

Three Wednesdays in a row she met a man at a café near Euston station. The café was always frantically busy. Tourists chatted excitedly while men in dull-coloured suits swept in and out, in and out, each of them barking into their phones, then at the baristas, then at the tourists for leaving their backpacks on the floor. So neither of them noticed each week as I sat at the next table, pretending to be engrossed in *The Catcher in the Rye*. They were distracted, I guess. He was her counsellor. Sahil, a quiet, elegant man with long fingers and hair the colour of poppy seeds. He was a lot like Doctor Gilyard; they both have that poise, that smoothness I want to disturb. Juliet told me later, when we were friends, that she'd been seeing him since her parents died and when she moved to Islington, he continued their sessions.

'Why did you want to meet here, Nancy?' he'd asked her that first Wednesday.

I wonder if he had to tell himself not to call her Juliet.

When she didn't respond, he crossed his legs and looked across the small, round table at her. 'What makes you uncomfortable about meeting at UCL like we usually do?'

I lifted my eyes from my book then but she didn't respond. She just shrugged and continued to trace the rim of her coffee cup with her finger.

That's how it was every week; she didn't say much and she never said Dad's name. Never. She just said *him* whenever she had to mention him. It was like he didn't exist, like it never happened. Maybe that's why she wanted to meet at that café instead of the hospital, because she thought she was better.

After all, she'd taken a match and thrown it over her shoulder. She was Nancy Wells – she never had to say Dad's name again. But each time I heard her say *him* I wanted to take a handful of her hair and pull until she said it.

I know she couldn't sleep, that much she told him. She said that she woke up most nights gasping, the sheets sticking to her skin. She had tablets for it, but when Sahil asked why she wouldn't take them she said that she didn't need to, that not all the dreams were bad. She said sometimes she dreamt she was standing on the edge of a cliff, looking at the sea.

When she described it – the blue of the sky, the blue of the sea – it made me think of that cottage in Brighton where we took Nanna Koll every summer before Gramps died. There was a tree not far from it and I would climb it and look across at the sea claiming everything I saw as my own; the birds, the hills, our postcard-perfect cottage with the red-painted shutters. So when Juliet said that standing on the edge of that cliff in her dream was so beautiful that she threw herself towards the sea, I knew why.

Sahil asked her if it was scary, falling like that, but she said that it wasn't, that it made her feel light and strong, all at once. But then she said that before she hit the water, she realised she had wings and started to fly.

I'd stared at her then. I couldn't help it, because when he asked her what she thought it meant, I knew what he was trying to do: he was trying to make her think that she saved herself that night, from Dad. It made me so angry that I wanted to fly across the table at him, remind him that she wasn't the only one who'd lost everything.

But as I was about to, Juliet shrugged. 'Sometimes you just dream about flying,' she said, dipping the tip of her finger into her latte, then licking the froth away.

That night I had the same dream, that I was falling – falling and falling – but I had no wings. I still have that dream, and every time I do, when I hit the sea, it swallows me whole.

'Emily,' Doctor Gilyard said then, and the shock of it was like tripping up a kerb.

When I recovered, I sat a little straighter and turned my cheek towards her. 'Have I ever told you about my cat?'

She looked at me for a moment too long, then said, 'Your cat?'

'Yes, *my cat.*'

'Okay, Emily.' She nodded. 'Tell me about your cat.'

'His name's Duck.'

'Duck?'

'Yes.'

She took a deep breath, then smiled. 'You have a cat called Duck?'

'Yes.'

'Okay.'

'That's his real name. I'm not making it up.'

'Okay, Emily. Tell me about Duck.'

'I've had him since he was a kitten,' I told her, twirling a strand of hair around my finger. 'Dad came home with him one afternoon, out of the blue.'

'When?'

'When I was three—'

'Before or after your mother left?' she interrupted.

'After,' I said too quickly, charging on before she could ask any more about it. 'He let me name him, hence Duck. It was my favourite word at the time.' I grinned at the memory and it felt kind of nice, even if the muscles in my cheeks felt ancient. 'Uncle Alex was mortified. He tried to get me to call him something more fitting, like Charlie or Tigger, but Duck stuck.'

'What's Duck like?'

'He's not like other cats. He doesn't climb trees or sit by our pond, swatting at the koi carp like the other cats on our street.'

'Does he chase birds?'

'He doesn't even notice them; they just strut around him, pecking at the grass while he sleeps in the sun. But he's fascinated by squirrels,' I told her with a slow smile. 'He has no idea what to do with them, though. He chases after them, then stops. It's as if his instinct is to go for them, but he doesn't know what to do next. So he just stands there, looking at them as they scuttle over the garden fence.'

I sat there for a moment or two, smiling to myself, but when I heard Doctor Gilyard write something in her notebook, the corners of my mouth drooped. 'What?' I asked, sitting forward. 'What are you writing?'

She stopped and looked up at me. 'Why does it bother you so much, Emily?'

'Because I didn't say anything worth noting. I didn't tell you *anything*.'

She closed the notebook and put her hand on top of it. It made my heart throb like a fresh bruise. 'These sessions aren't just about what you say, Emily, they're also about how you react to what I say.'

I flew out of my chair and paced over to her bookcase. My hands were shaking so much I had to reach out for one of the shelves.

'I didn't tell you anything,' I wanted to shout, but it came out as a whisper.

'You told me rather a lot, actually.' I heard the leather notebook creak as she opened it again. 'You told me about your cat, a cat your father brought home not long after your mother left, presumably as a way of consoling you or distracting you from asking where she was. A cat who instinctively chases squirrels but then doesn't know what to do with them.'

'So?' I glared at her across the office. 'What does that have to do with anything? It's just a stupid story. It doesn't mean anything.'

'But it does, Emily. The things we reach for when we're trying to avoid talking about something else sometimes mean as much.'

'What? That's ridiculous!' I took a step forward then, my fists clenched.

But she just lifted her chin to look at me. 'You were thinking of Duck because when you found Juliet you didn't do anything. You're Duck and Juliet is the squirrel.'

I stared at her for a moment, then turned and retreated to the bookcase. I looked at a textbook but the title on the spine was out of focus. 'Why are you doing this to me?'

'Why are you doing this to yourself, Emily?'

Always a question with a question.

Thursday. Poached eggs for breakfast. I hate poached eggs so Naomi ate mine. And Lily's. And Val's.

'Want those?' she asked the new girl who must have been admitted after we went to bed last night.

It was the first thing anyone had said to her, but that wasn't unusual. There are only fifteen beds in this unit, which isn't nearly enough given that there are seven hundred girls in Archway and everyone here must be a bit unbalanced to have done what they've done.

We're all craving something. Mourning someone.

But seven hundred inmates into fifteen beds doesn't fit, so this place is more like a sick bay; girls come, they cry, claw and scream, then they sleep and when they wake up, they're sent back to the main wing. That's why the unit is set up the way it is:

fifteen cells, ten on the ground floor and five on top, all of them facing the nurse's office. In the main wing, they eat on tables in the space between, but we have a separate room, which is next to Doctor Gilyard's office, in case one of us loses it. That way they can lock us in until it passes.

The ten cells on the ground floor are for the girls who won't be here long. Plus, there are two cells with glazed doors for the ones on suicide watch. That's where Lily was when she got here last month. Naomi and I were fascinated by her; most of the girls on suicide watch are too drugged-up to move, but Lily flitted around the cell, from corner to corner, wall to wall, like a butterfly trapped in a room.

It was kind of beautiful.

If you found this notebook, you must be on the top row like me. Naughty girl. Right now it's me, Naomi, Val, Reta and a sociopath called Ruth, who hasn't been around much recently because she's been going back and forth between the Old Bailey for her trial. We're the lifers. We're not going anywhere. We're all on remand, but we'll come back here after we're sentenced, because Archway is the only young offenders institution in London with a psych unit. We're also the ones who pose a threat to ourselves or the people around us. I haven't laid a finger on anyone since I got here, but I'm Emily Koll, so that's earned me the middle cell.

I'm queen of the fucking castle.

'Erin needs to finish her breakfast,' a nurse said when Naomi went for her plate.

Another anorexic, like Lily.

I must have been staring, because she stiffened.

'What you looking at?' she spat. 'I ain't scared of you, Crazy Koll.'

'No. You're just scared of carbs.' I rolled my eyes, but it stung, I won't lie. I haven't been called that in a while. The *Sun* was particularly fond of that nickname, if I recall.

'Emily,' the nurse said, approaching the table.

'What? She started on me!'

'Be the bigger person.'

'I wouldn't be here if I could be the bigger person, would I?'

That earned a titter from the table. Even the new girl's face softened.

'Do you have a happy place?' Naomi asked as soon as the nurse walked away.

'Maladoth,' Reta piped up with a wistful smile. 'It's so beautiful. The sky's burnt orange and the citadel is enclosed in a mighty glass dome that shines under the twin suns. Beyond that, the mountains go on for ever – slopes of deep red grass, capped with snow.'

Whatever. 'I think she just described Gallifrey,' I told Naomi, lowering my voice.

She frowned. 'Galli – what?'

'Gallifrey. You know? *Doctor Who*.'

'Don't listen to anything she has to say; she's as mad as cheese.'

'How's that schizophrenia thing working out for you?'

'Great. I just need a happy place. What's yours?'

'The Electric Ballroom,' I told her, inspecting my nails.

'No, a happy place,' she said, mopping up the yolk on her plate with a piece of bread. I wanted to vomit, so Lily and the new girl must have been ready to faint. 'Somewhere you go when things go all woo-woo in your head.'

I stared at her. 'Woo-woo? Really, Naomi? You've been here six months and the best you've got is *woo-woo*?'

She shrugged. 'It's woo-woo.'

I turned to Lily for support, but she shrugged too. 'It's better than doolally.'

I was appalled. 'Is this what it's come to? Saying woo-woo because it's better than doolally? Isn't a woo-woo a cocktail?'

'You'd know, alcy,' Naomi said with a smirk.

A lesser soul might have kicked her under the table. I just knocked my tea over the rest of her breakfast. 'Oh, how clumsy of me!'

'Fucking hell, Ems!' she gasped, jumping back.

I feigned horror. 'Ladies don't say fuck, they say pardon.'

'They teach you that at your fancy school?'

'That and an unyielding sense of entitlement.'

She called me something I won't repeat as the tea spilled over the edge of the table, on to her lap. I cackled, but Lily looked confused. 'I don't have a happy place.'

'Doctor G seems to think we need one,' Naomi huffed as the nurse wandered over and handed her a wodge of paper napkins. The nurse gave me a look that told me I was on nicotine smackdown again, then wandered off again.

'But where?' Lily asked. 'Somewhere safe, like a forest?'

'Forests aren't safe,' I snorted, and her little face folded. 'Read a book, Lil; they're full of vampires and werewolves.'

'She's winding you up, Lil,' Naomi said, wiping the tea my way across the table. 'Forests are perfectly safe. Especially the ones in your head.'

'Why do you wanna know about our happy place, anyway?' I asked, grabbing a napkin and wiping the tea Naomi's way again.

'Doctor G asked me about mine in our session yesterday, and I don't have one. Do I need one? I can't stop thinking about it. I didn't sleep a wink last night!'

'You got a happy place, Val?' I asked with a laugh, but I was seething.

So when I saw Doctor Gilyard this afternoon, I let rip.

'This is so unfair!' I spat, pointing at her. 'You make me talk about Juliet and Dad and Uncle Alex and—' I couldn't say his name so I stopped for breath, my heart shuddering. 'And you sit here talking to Naomi about her happy place? What is that? Why can't we talk about stuff like that?'

She nodded. 'Would you like to talk about stuff like that, Emily?'

'No,' I told her, crossing my arms.

'Do you have a happy place, Emily?'

I ignored her, determined not to tell her a thing after the last time.

'Is it the cottage in Brighton?' she asked, and my heart stopped. The woman is a witch.

I'm not allowed to have a cigarette for the rest of the day because I told one of the nurses to get fucked in art therapy this afternoon. We were making a card for Val who's in court tomorrow and won't be back. Naomi overhead Doctor Gilyard saying that she'll probably get a suspended sentence because she is 'too vulnerable' for prison and would benefit at an out-patient facility, which is Doctor Gilyard for *too mad for us*.

I didn't object to making a card, but when I was confronted with a pair of childproof scissors and a tube of glitter, I kind of lost my shit. Hence, the nicotine smack-down. (With hindsight, I guess that's why they give us childproof scissors here.) So Lily let me have her cigarette after lunch in exchange for blasting me with questions.

'What was the college like? Was it nice?' she asked, all but bouncing. 'I'm going to college when I get out of here.'

I scoffed. 'It was a shit-hole.'

I wish there was a more delicate word to describe it, but nothing about the College of North London is delicate. My old school, St Jude's, is delicate. It's a neat, long building with ivy bubbling over its walls. There's a sundial on the front lawn and a statue of St Jude by the entrance to the library, his brass toe worn down because it's supposed to bring you luck if you rub his foot. It's a good school. A small school. Four hundred girls living under its sloped slate roof, each of us pretending that we didn't miss home as we taped photographs to the walls next to our beds.

The College of North London is a beast in comparison. It's a wide, low building that squats in the middle of the high street, its glass front reflecting the buses and cars that roll by like smudges of crayon. There are no trees, no lawn, no elderly rose bushes like at St Jude's, just a car park, a cash machine and a few worn benches, the wood split and the varnish brittle.

Lily looked crushed. 'It can't have been that bad.'

'It was! It's one of those grim, 1970s buildings. Kind of like here.'

I looked up at the chewed chewing gum-coloured walls, then down at the cracked floor tiles and realised that I wasn't being melodramatic, for once.

'And nothing worked,' I told her. 'The lifts. Toilets. Everything was old and grey and broken. It would be *weeks* before anything got fixed, if it got fixed at all.'

She winced and I smiled playfully, thrilled that she didn't know I was teasing her.

'But I loved it,' I said and she perked up. 'There were eight thousand students, Lil. *Eight thousand*. St Jude's was so quiet. It was all glossy and gilt edged. But the College of North London was a mess. There was always someone in your way and it was so noisy! Phones and music and voices *everywhere*.' I threw my hands up. 'It was *alive*! There was always something going on. You'd turn a corner, and there'd be a couple kissing; you'd turn another and two girls would be screaming at each other. And people laughed, Lil, *out loud*. You'd be walking down the stairs and you'd hear this great BOOM of laughter that would make your bones rattle.' I shook my head. 'No one at St Jude's laughed. They chuckled or they giggled, but they didn't laugh.'

'Do you miss it?' she asked when I stopped to take a drag on my cigarette.

'Of course.'

'Would you go back?'

I thought about that for a moment and my heart turned to pulp.

'You can't go back, Lily,' I said with a small shrug.

I waited for her shoulders to fall, but she just smiled. 'That's why you can't take anything for granted. You don't know what you have until it's gone.'

She looked so proud of herself that I smiled back, even though I don't believe that. We all know what we had, don't we? We just never thought we could lose it.

Naomi's boyfriend didn't visit today, so she was first in line for her meds. I've been itching to tease her about it all day, but as I was about to, Lily pulled out a drawing.

'What's that?' Naomi frowned as Lily held it up.

'It's my happy place.' She grinned, her shoulders back. 'I drew it in Art.'

(She always says it like that – Art – as though it's a lesson, not an attempt to kill us slowly.)

'Here are the trees,' she said, pointing to the brown lines with the green scribbled blobs on top of them. 'And the wild flowers and the babbling brook.'

'Hey non nonny,' I sang, but they ignored me.

'. . . and here's the treehouse where you can sleep.'

Naomi blinked at her as she handed over the drawing. 'Me?'

'Yeah. You've been so sad. I thought you might like to borrow it.'

I have to remind myself that Lily is sixteen sometimes. Regression, Doctor Gilyard calls it. It's a defence mechanism, she says. A lot of the girls in here do it to avoid dealing with whatever landed them here. Me, I've gone the other way; I feel ancient sometimes, like an old woman sitting in her favourite chair telling tales of her misspent youth.

'Don't get too close to the babbling brook,' I warned Naomi with a wink.

I expected her to laugh, but she burst into tears.

I turned to Lily, horrified. 'Wait. What? What's that?' I asked, pointing my roll-up at Naomi. 'What's she doing? Has she gone woo-woo?'

'She's crying, Emily,' Lily said, stroking Naomi's hair.

'Why?'

'Because I'm not dead inside!' Naomi roared. 'Comfort me!'

I tried to take the drawing from Naomi, but she wouldn't give it to me. 'Stop it, Emily!' she hissed. 'No mocking the happy place.'

'I'm not going to mock it, I just want to show you something. See?' I pointed at a space between the trees. 'Look who's in the happy place?' They both leaned forward, peering at the drawing. 'It's Jake Gyllenhaal.'

Naomi pressed the drawing to her chest. 'I need some alone time in the happy place.'

I turned to Lily to ask if she would mind if I borrowed her

happy place next when her eyes widened. 'Who's that?' she asked, nodding down the corridor.

Naomi and I turned to look over our shoulders to find one of the nurses leading a tall girl with pink cheeks towards the office.

'That's Cara,' Naomi said, lowering her voice.

I stared at her. 'You're having an existential crisis and you still know about the new inmates?'

She tapped her temple with her finger. 'Knowledge is power, my friend.'

'Who is she?' Lily asked, lowering her voice too.

'Eighteen. Schizophrenic. On remand for stabbing her mum, apparently.'

I tutted. 'You schizos are so stabby.'

'You can talk.'

'Touché.' I nodded slowly.

'She's looking this way,' Lily said, blushing like a schoolgirl.

'She's looking at Emily.'

She was, so I smiled sweetly and waved. The new girl looked at her feet, mortified.

'You're a rock star, Ems,' Naomi snorted.

'Yeah. I'm the Kurt Cobain of the criminally insane.'

Naomi winked at me. 'Courtney Love, more like.'

I kicked the leg of her chair.

'She looks so scared. We should let her sit with us tomorrow at breakfast,' Lily suggested, and I rolled my eyes.

'Let's see how she goes. She might be a complete nutter.'

Turns out I was right to be wary, because an hour ago she just woke us all up doing . . . okay, I'm not going to tell you what she did because that's not fair. Honour among thieves, and all that. Let's just say she won't be around to sit with us at breakfast tomorrow morning.

I haven't spoken to Doctor Gilyard since the happy place incident. I thought our session this week was going to be painful, but she was feeling particularly brave. I don't know if she does that to you, too, but she leaves me alone for a week – sometimes two – then BANG, she hits me with a question that would be enough to knock me off my feet if I wasn't already sitting down.

Like today, she opened with: 'I'd like to talk about your decision to befriend Juliet.'

The audacity of it made me forget that I was ignoring her. 'I'm sure you would.'

'Why didn't you just kill her?'

The audacity of *that* made me smile. 'Should I have?'

'Your uncle went to great lengths to find where the Witness

Protection team had sent her to live,' she said, not missing a step. 'Then finally he found her—'

I interrupted with a snort. 'Yeah, the bloke he paid to find her was the same bloke the Witness Protection team paid to hide her. And they question my morals.'

She ignored me. 'He finally found her, living with foster parents in Islington – on his doorstep, in his manor—'

I interrupted again. 'Did you just say manor?'

'Why did he send you to get her?'

I laughed. 'Who do you think my uncle is? Don Corleone? He didn't *send* me to do anything. I overheard what was going on and went.'

'He didn't know?'

'Of course not.'

'So how did you get away from him? From Puerto Banus?'

'I just left,' I told her with a shrug. 'Every Sunday we went for lunch at this seafood restaurant on the front line, right by the beach. I told Uncle Alex I wasn't feeling well, then waited for him and Nanna Koll to go, packed a bag and left. Daddy gave me a credit card for emergencies so I put it all – the flight, the hotel in London, everything – on that. I was getting off the plane by the time they got back to the villa.'

'Okay.' She nodded. 'But why wait? You were obviously as desperate to find her as your uncle, so why didn't you just end it then, the day you found her?'

I shrugged. 'What was I supposed to do?'

'What would your father have done?'

'I'm not my father,' I said before I could stop myself, and she wrote it down.

That fucking notebook. I'm going to set fire to it.

'Why the theatrics, Emily?' She took her glasses off to look at me. I turned my face away. 'Why pretend to be someone else, befriend her, endear yourself to her foster parents, go to her college? It's a tremendous amount of effort.'

I had had the same argument with Uncle Alex. He said I was out of my mind when I told him what I wanted to do, that I was nuts, that I was doing what Dad did and making it more complicated than it needed to be.

'This is easy,' he told me when I called asking for his help. 'In, stab-stab-stab, out. Done. Danny's on his way there now. I'd do it myself if the police weren't on me.'

I remember the panic, how it bubbled up in my stomach. I can feel it now, as I'm writing this, like milk boiling over in a pan.

'No. Don't,' I told him. 'It has to be me.'

'You know her foster dad is ex-CID, right? That isn't a coincidence, Em. He won't let you near her.'

'Exactly. This is the only way, by being her friend.'

'Forget it, Emily.'

'I have a better chance of getting to her than Danny.'

'Don't be ridiculous. Just come home and let me handle this.'

'This is nothing to do with you, Uncle Alex!'

'Except you're ringing me asking for money and a flat and a fake identity and fake GCSE results so you can get into her college, on to the same courses, and be her friend.'

'I'm sorry!' I said, dripping contempt into the phone. 'Is that a problem? Or are you too busy shooting people and selling drugs to half of London?'

I thought he was going to roar back, but he just waited for my breathing to settle, then sighed. 'Ems, listen to me. Leave it. Just *leave it*.' I shook my head even though he couldn't see me doing it. 'We have to be careful. That little bitch told them everything. As soon as they get something on me, too, they'll be on the next flight out.'

'It's fine – they think I'm in Spain with you and Nanna Koll.'

'Exactly. Let's keep it that way.'

'The police aren't watching me, Uncle Alex. They're watching you.'

'Which is why I'm not there now. You'd be halfway to Stansted with me if I was.'

I bristled at that. 'I'm seventeen. Stop treating me like a kid.'

'Stop behaving like one, then.'

'I don't expect you to understand.'

'You don't think I understand?' he said tightly. 'Juliet Shaw is a fucking grass. She stabbed my brother and destroyed everything we've ever worked for. I want her dead, too, but I'm not stupid enough to do it myself.'

'Then you don't understand.'

'What is it with the Shaws? First your dad, now you. They'll lead you both to hell.' He sighed and I remember thinking he sounded exhausted, but I still bit back.

'I'll see you down there.'

'Don't do that, Emily. Don't take the piss. This isn't funny,' he said and it made my cheeks sting. 'I told your dad not to go after Jason Shaw. He was a detective superintendent, for fuck's sake. What did he think would happen?'

He never swore in front of me so I knew he was livid. The tops of my ears burned.

Dad and Uncle Alex and their 'rules'. They never swore in front of me, never raised their voices, never talked about work at the dinner table. I used to think it was because they were old fashioned, but it was because they didn't want me to find out who they really were.

I guess Uncle Alex didn't have to bother any more.

I waited for his breathing to settle this time. 'Please. I know you're trying to protect me, but you have to let me do this my way.'

He wouldn't listen. 'Do you want to end up in the cell next to your dad's?'

'Of course not.'

'Then listen to me. *Hear* what I'm saying: This will eat you up if you let it.'

I shut up then because it already had. But I couldn't tell him that, could I? I couldn't tell him that every day I felt it eroding my insides like rust because he'd make me go back to Spain while Juliet was in London, going to college and living her life like nothing had happened. Like the world didn't have a dirty great crack down it.

'You're doing what your dad did, Emily,' he told me. 'Just stop.

Don't get involved. I'll handle it, I swear. In a few hours this will all be over.'

'That's not enough, Uncle Alex.'

'How? How is her *death* not enough?'

'Because I want to break her, like she broke me!'

That was the first time I'd said it, out loud like that. It felt like I screamed it from a hole inside of me, a filthy black hole. Even writing it now is making my hands shake; then it scared me so much I started to cry. I put my hand over my mouth so he wouldn't hear me, but I know he did. Alex Koll hears everything.

'She took my dad away from me,' I told him with a small sob.

'He isn't dead, Ems, he's in prison. He'll be back. You'll get him back.'

I wiped my cheek with my fingers. 'That's not what I mean.'

'What do you mean, then?'

'There are things I'm not supposed to know about,' I said, stopping to suck in a breath. 'Things Dad wouldn't tell me. Things I couldn't even *ask* about, like what happened to Mum. And that was fine because I trusted him. But now.'

I stopped to suck in another breath, but I couldn't say it. So Alex waited – waited and waited – as I thought about what Dad had done. I fell asleep most nights thinking about it, about gunshots and blood on white sheets.

'I don't know who he is any more, Uncle Alex.'

I remember the silence that followed after I said it, that week-long silence as I waited for Uncle Alex to say something, to defend Dad like he always did. When he didn't, it was worse. He

60

didn't tell me that it would be okay and he didn't ask me to trust him like he did the night it happened, when he called me at St Jude's and told me to pack a bag. And I did trust him; I packed a bag and waited for him in the House Mistress's office like he told me to. And when I climbed into the back seat of his car to find Nanna Koll sitting there, a scarf over her curlers and her blue leather vanity case on her lap, I didn't say a word, even though a voice in my head screamed and screamed all the way to Folkestone.

But when we got off at Calais and he finally told me that Dad had been stabbed, I was hysterical. I begged him to take us home, to Dad, but he just drove, drove and drove while I cried myself to sleep in the back seat, my head in Nanna Koll's lap as she stroked my hair.

I don't know if that's ever happened to you, if you've loved someone, loved *who* they are, then found out they're not that person after all. It doesn't just break your heart, does it? It breaks *you*. Then you're not who you thought you were, either.

'Did he go in there?' I finally asked. The thought had been like a splinter in my heart since it happened.

'In where?'

'Into Juliet's bedroom?'

'Of course not.' Something in the universe realigned and I let go of a breath. 'She wasn't supposed to be there. She was out with her boyfriend but they had a row or something and she came home early. She heard her dad and Harry rowing, that's how she could give evidence like that; she heard everything. So she called the police and they told her to get out of the house, but she took a bread knife from the kitchen and went upstairs. Your dad didn't hear her. She stabbed him in the back.'

I laughed at that, loud and bright. I hated her. I still do. I probably shouldn't say that if I want to endear myself to you, but I'm not trying to endear myself to you. Like me, don't like me, I don't give a shit. So yeah, I hate her. I hate her so much that every time I think about her, I can feel the white peeling off my bones. But the truth is, if that was me, and I came home to find someone hurting my father, I would have done the same thing.

I had to give her that.

'Do you know what's funny?' I told Uncle Alex with another laugh.

'What, Ems?'

'I get it now, why Dad did it. I never understood how he could want to hurt someone like that, but I do now.' When Uncle Alex didn't respond, I shook my head. 'But he never wanted that, did he? He did all of this – *God knows* what he did – so I could go to a good school, be whatever I wanted to be. But now I'm the one thing he never wanted me to be.'

'What's that, Emily?'

I closed my eyes. 'Him.'

I'd love to say that being in here without the distraction of the Internet and mobile phones elevates each of us to some heightened state of awareness where we can see the error of our ways and repair ourselves, but we just talk about rubbish. Nothing real, like who we are and how we got here and why we do the things we do. I suppose it's the only time we don't have to talk about those things, when we're together.

'When I get out of here, I'm getting a tattoo,' Naomi announced today while we were having our post-dinner cigarette.

I snorted. 'Why?'

She ignored me. 'Right here.' She showed us her wrist.

'What of?' Lily asked, wide eyed as always.

'Not your boyfriend's name, I hope.'

She ignored me again. 'A bird flying out of a cage.'

I rolled my eyes.

'Better than Hello Kitty on my arse!' she snapped.

I almost choked on my fag. 'Who has Hello Kitty tattooed on their arse?'

Lily looked confused. 'Who's Hello Kitty?'

Naomi and I stared at her for a moment, then Naomi sighed. 'At least it means something.'

'True.' I nodded. 'I like my dad's tattoo. That means something.'

Naomi sat forward. 'What is it of?'

'Just words: *Ou Theoi, monon Anthropoi*.'

'What's that, like Latin or something?'

'It's ancient Greek,' Lily interrupted.

We stared at her again, then Naomi looked at me. 'What does it mean?'

'*No gods, only men.*'

Naomi sat back in her chair. 'That's deep.'

'My dad is pretty deep,' I told them. 'When he's not shooting people.'

I don't know how much longer I can do this. Doctor Gilyard is finding a way in. The threat of it is like a storm – I can feel the nearness of it. So I've been running around closing windows and locking doors but she's getting closer and closer and I don't know what to do.

Today, she put something on the coffee table between us, but I wouldn't look down at it to see what it was.

'What's that?'

Silence.

'Is it another letter from Juliet?'

Silence.

'I told you, I don't care what she has to say. Why did you bring it?'

Silence.

'Fine.' I sat back in my chair and crossed my arms. 'You want to do this?'

Silence.

'I can do this.'

Silence.

'I *invented* this.'

I stared at the crack in the wall so that I wouldn't look at the coffee table, but my gaze kept flicking back and forth – back and forth, back and forth, back and forth – between the crack and the coffee table, like the pendulum in the grandfather clock at St Jude's.

I've only tried to give up smoking once, after my friend Olivia's grandmother died of lung cancer. I didn't think I smoked that much, but I only lasted three days before I broke and bought a box of cigarettes from the girl who used to sell them out of her room. I felt useless as I locked myself in the bathroom and smoked one, and that's how I felt today when my gaze finally settled on the coffee table – useless.

It was just for a moment, but it was long enough to see that it wasn't a letter; it was a photograph. It was folded in half and when I saw the curve of Juliet's smile, her cinnamon-coloured cheek pressed to a paler one, my heart began to ring like a bell.

I knew that photo. I was there when it was taken.

I stared at Doctor Gilyard. 'Don't,' I warned, my hands balling into fists.

She knows. That's the first thing I told her when I got here. I told her that she could ask me anything – anything – but she couldn't ask about him. And I'll give her that, she hasn't; she's poked and prodded me for months, but she's never even said his name.

I shook my head as she leaned forward to pick up the photograph. 'Don't,' I told her as she began to unfold it. 'Don't. I'm not ready.'

If I had any control over myself, I would have snatched it from her, ripped it into a million pieces. But my hands don't do as they're told any more – my hands, my head, my heart – so I could only watch as she put it back down on the coffee table.

Fear licked my palms, and when I was brave enough to look at it, I almost collapsed into a boneless heap on the floor.

It wasn't him in the photo with Juliet – it was me.

If I could still cry, I would have.

The photograph was Doctor Gilyard holding a gun to my head and telling me to talk.

So when she asked to see me again today I talked.

'Tell me about the day you first approached her, Emily.'

I started to shift in my chair and told myself to stop. 'It was September third.'

There are only a few dates I remember for sure; everything else is a mess. Weeks knot together and some days feel like tiny holes in my memory. But I remember that day – 3 September – the day I met Juliet Shaw.

'They had a freshers' thing at the college the week before classes started, so I met her then.' I tugged on the loose thread on my chair. 'We applied late so we missed enrolment and had to enrol then. I went up to her while we were waiting to have our photo IDs done.'

'Had the Witness Protection team done anything to change her appearance?'

I nodded. I only had one photo of her that I used to take everywhere like a prayer card. In it, her hair was straight and smooth and it spilled over her shoulders like Lyle's black treacle. But the first time I saw her in London, it was curly and just brushed the line of her jaw. I hope she cried when they cut it. Reading that back, that sounds awful, but it's true; as I picture her sitting on a chair with chunks of it at her feet I smile. It's those little things that kept me going. It's like every time she broke, I got a bit stronger.

'What did you think when you saw her?'

'She was prettier than expected,' I admitted. 'And her skin was browner. I know she's mixed, but it looked like she'd caught the sun.'

'Why did that bother you?'

I bristled. 'I didn't say it did.'

Doctor Gilyard didn't respond; she just looked at me, and after a few minutes, I gave up and said, 'It pissed me off a bit that she had a tan, that's all.'

'Why?'

'Because I could just see her, sitting in the garden reading a magazine like she didn't have a care in the world, while I—' I stopped.

Doctor Gilyard finished my thought. 'While you were alone.'

I shook my head. 'Don't.'

'Don't what, Emily?'

'Don't feel sorry for me.'

'Why shouldn't I feel sorry for you, Emily?'

I turned my face away. 'Will you just stop?'

'Stop what, Emily?'

'Just *stop*!' I slapped the arms of the chair with my hands. 'I keep drawing these lines, and you keep pulling me across them.'

She wrote that down and if my hands weren't shaking so much, I would have grabbed the pencil from her and snapped it in half.

'Okay. Let's go back to the morning at the college: what did you say to her?'

'Nothing,' I told her with a huff. 'I just stood behind her in the queue and said hello.'

'What did she tell you her name was?'

'Dad Stabber.'

I smirked, but she didn't miss a beat. 'What did she tell you her name was?'

'Nancy Wells. Stupid, huh?'

Doctor Gilyard frowned. 'Stupid how?'

'Nancy. It's a stupid name. Nancy's an old lady's name.'

'Does it matter?'

'Of course it does,' I scoffed. 'Why didn't the witness protection team give her something normal? Like Jo or Sarah or something?'

Doctor Gilyard wrote that down and I groaned. 'What now?'

'I just think it's interesting that you're so fixated on her name.'

'God, you're so melodramatic sometimes. I'm not *fixated*, I'm just saying.'

Doctor Gilyard looked up at me with a smile. 'If you say so.'

I knew what she was getting at, but I refused to take the bait.

So she carried on. 'What did you tell her your name was, Emily?'

'Rose Glass.'

'Why Rose Glass?'

I shrugged. 'I don't know. Uncle Alex sorted all that.'

'What did he sort?'

'Everything. A name, a flat, everything.'

'Like what?'

I groaned and tipped my head back. 'You're worse than the police.'

'Humour me, Emily.'

'A passport, birth certificate, GCSE results, references.'

'That's very thorough.'

'Uncle Alex used to be a Scout.'

'You said you were a year younger, right? So you'd be sixteen like Juliet.'

'Yeah.'

'How did it feel to start again? You were halfway through your A levels when your father was arrested and you went to Spain, right? Was it strange, studying again?'

'I guess.'

Realising that she wasn't getting anything out of me, she moved on. 'What was Juliet like?'

I turned my face away. 'She was *fearless*.' It came out as a whisper. 'It was the first time she had to be Nancy Wells; you'd think she would have been nervous.'

'Were you nervous, Emily?'

I smiled to myself. 'A bit.'

When I looked at Doctor Gilyard again, I could tell that she was trying not to smile too. Given that I now tell the most epic, Tolkien-esque lies, the irony was kind of beautiful. 'Do you think she was just being brave?'

I shook my head. 'No. No way.'

Anyone else would have been terrified. Not Juliet. She held her head up. I've always loved and hated that about her – how, even after everything she'd done, she could still look the world in the eye.

'So what did she say?' Doctor Gilyard asked, looking up from her notebook.

'Nothing. I said hello, and she said hello back.'

I remember how hard my heart was beating as I sat next to her. I felt each beat like a punch. I was sure I'd find a heart-shaped bruise the next morning. But she didn't even hesitate. And that's another thing I'd come to love and hate about her: she's a beautiful liar.

Who do you think I learned it from?

One of the girls who was in my room before me scratched LET IT BE into the wall next to my bed. I lie here staring at it sometimes and at night, when I can't sleep, I search it out with my fingers, tracing the letters over and over until sleep finally pulls me under.

That's how I fell asleep last night and today, in Doctor Gilyard's office, I kept writing it in the palm of my hand with my finger. Over and over.

LET IT BE. LET IT BE. LET IT BE.

'Are you ready to talk about—' she said, finally.

I looked away before she finished the sentence.

'I know we're edging towards when he—'

I had to say it out loud then. 'No.'

She nodded and opened her notebook. 'Last week, we spoke

a little about the day you met Juliet. I'd like to go back to what you said about her not being what you expected.'

I groaned. 'Can't we just go back to talking about my cat?'

'In what way was she different?'

'I don't know. She was just different.'

'Emily.'

I groaned again. 'She was quiet.'

'Quiet?'

'Yeah, *quiet*. She didn't say much.'

When I looked up again, Doctor Gilyard was writing something in her notebook and I rolled my eyes. 'What are you writing now?'

'I just think it's interesting that you expected her to be more amiable, Emily, given everything that had happened to her.' She looked up from her notebook. 'She was in Witness Protection and you were a stranger; I think her reaction to you was entirely appropriate. But you seem disappointed.'

I snorted. 'I wasn't disappointed. I knew she wouldn't be all over me.'

And I did, I knew she wasn't going to be one of those chatty, chatty girls like Lily and Naomi who have to tell you everything in endless, breathless detail. But I didn't think she'd be so quiet, so sweet. And there was a fragility to her that I wasn't expecting, either. Her hands were small, the bones in her wrists delicate.

'What were you expecting, Emily?'

She stabbed my father. I expected nothing but sharp edges and swagger.

When I didn't respond, she moved on. 'When did you approach her again?'

'The Monday classes started, in English Lit.'

'What happened?'

'Nothing. I just said hello and sat next to her.'

'Did she remember you?'

I smiled to myself. 'Not straight away.'

'Your hair?'

I nodded. I went to touch it, but told myself not to in case Doctor Gilyard saw my hand shaking.

'Why did you dye it, Emily? Granted, Juliet wouldn't have known what you looked like; you were under eighteen when your father was arrested so the newspapers couldn't print your photograph.' Unlike now, I thought when she said it. Now my picture is on the front fucking page. *Emily Koll: Schoolgirl Psycho.* 'But you were still trying not to draw attention to yourself,' Doctor Gilyard went on. 'So why dye your hair red?'

She was being kind; it wasn't just red, it was *red* red. Skittles red. The sort of red that ruins towels and bathroom tiles.

Juliet gasped when I approached her that morning. The way her face lit up made me wonder if she'd always been that quiet. Maybe she wasn't as okay as I thought she was. I like to think so because that would mean something had changed. Something real, not just her name and where she went to school and whatever else the Witness Protection team changed, but something *about* her. Some small part of her that would never be the same again.

I needed that. She stabbed my father and ripped up my world as though it was a letter she didn't want to read. I needed her to not be okay with that.

'I don't know,' I told Doctor Gilyard with a shrug. 'A moment of madness, I guess.'

'Did it make you feel more like Rose, having red hair?'

I guess it did. I guess that's why I wasn't worried that Juliet would find out who I was, because I wasn't me any more – I was Rose Glass. That's the only way I could do it, if I took Emily Koll, wrapped her in tissue and left her in a drawer somewhere for a while.

It was easier that way.

'New start, new me,' I'd goaded Juliet that morning as I twirled a strand of red hair around my finger with a wicked smile.

It worked, because as soon as I said it, I saw a tiny tremor in her chin. Everything went quiet then. I couldn't hear the chatter in the classroom any more or the buses rolling by outside, all I remember is white noise. I can't even remember what the classroom looked like. There were windows along one side, I think. The desks were grey. White, maybe. That's all I remember. It's as though my whole world narrowed to that one point, to that tremor.

That's when he walked in.

'Can we stop?' I asked Doctor Gilyard, standing up and looking at the door. My heart was beating so hard I thought it was trying to come through my ribs.

She nodded and closed her notebook. 'If you'd like to, Emily.'

But I was gone before she finished the sentence.

Lily has been giving me her laxatives so I missed my session with Doctor Gilyard this week. My 'tummy bug' should have given me a reprieve until next week, but Doctor Gilyard just swept into my room with a chair. She didn't say anything, just sat by my bed.

I considered pulling the blanket over my head, but I sat up with a sullen sigh and crossed my legs. 'I'm fine,' I told her, but my voice sounded old. Rusty.

'Glad to hear it,' she said with a tight smile. 'Where were we?'

I blinked at her. 'Excuse me?'

She reached into her bag for her notebook and it made the hair on my arms prickle with panic. 'Can't this wait until our next session?'

'When will that be, Emily?'

'I told you, *I'm fine*.'

'You'd rather take laxatives than say his name. That isn't fine.'

I turned my face away and looked at the lines scratched into the wall by bed.

'Look at me, Emily.'

I shook my head. Everything in my skull felt loose. 'I can't. It's too hard.'

'Who said it would be easy?'

'I don't get this.' I looked down at the blanket and started tracing the weave of the cheap wool with my finger. 'It's done. Why do we have to keep talking about it?'

'This is what the judge decided, to send you here.'

I looked up at her then. 'But you can tell them. You can tell them I'm okay.'

'So you'd rather *go to prison* than say his name?'

I looked back down at the blanket. When I didn't respond, I heard her sigh. 'You can't go into the main wing, Emily. You're too vulnerable.'

I scoffed at that. 'I'm Harry Koll's daughter. No one would touch me.'

'Prison isn't just about surviving, Emily, it's about *rehabilitation*. You won't get better there.'

'I'm evil,' I told her with a slow smile. 'There's no pill for evil.'

'You're not evil, Emily, and you will get better.'

'How?'

'By talking about it.'

'I can talk. I can talk about Juliet until my last breath.' I lifted my chin defiantly. 'She's a fucking bitch and I hate her. I hate her. She ruined my life. And I'm not sorry. I'd do it all again if I could. I'd burn everything she has.'

Doctor Gilyard waited for me to stop and take a breath, then nodded. 'You'll talk about the bad things you've done, Emily. But you won't talk about the good things.'

I held my arms out. 'There's no good here.'

'You can talk about her because you hate her. But you can't talk about him because you love him.'

I glared at her and shook my head.

'And that's understandable; you're happy to get rid of your feelings for Juliet because they're a burden, but you hold on to your feelings for him because they're what make you human. What make you more than Emily Koll the gangster's daughter.'

I continued to shake my head as though if I did it enough, I'd shake her away.

'He makes you want to be a better person but you don't think you can be.'

I put my hands in my hair and pulled. 'Stop!'

'This is it, Emily,' she told me. 'This is the line. You have to follow me across it.'

'Will you just go!' I roared. 'Get out!'

I didn't think she would, but she stood up. Before she left, she reached into her bag and pulled out a piece of chalk. She held it up to me and I watched as she drew a line on the floor between my bed and the door.

'When you're ready,' she said, closing the door behind her.

I've been crying since Doctor Gilyard left.

I can't remember the last time I cried. I used to cry all the time – at films and those ads on the telly for animal shelters, the ones with the big-eyed, shivering dogs – but I didn't think I *could* cry now, yet, as soon as Doctor Gilyard walked out, something in me buckled and I cried until I couldn't breathe. Until I thought I was dying.

I don't think I would have stopped if Naomi and Lily hadn't tried to pull me out. I'd been crying for a day, a week, a year, I don't know. I just remember hearing footsteps, then someone lying on my bed next to me. I knew it was Lily because the mattress barely registered the weight of her. Then Naomi climbed on top of me, like Olivia used to when we were at St Jude's and she was trying to get me out of bed.

'Get off!' I barked.

Naomi buried her nose in my hair. 'Not until you come for a fag.'

'I don't want a fag.'

'Oh, my God. She's dying! Nurse!' She lifted her head and called out while Lily giggled next to me. 'Nurse! Call an ambulance!'

'Fuck off!'

'Ladies don't say fuck, they say pardon,' she gasped.

She rolled off me giggling and I don't know how the three of us fitted on my narrow bed, but we did. Good thing Lily takes up less space than my blanket.

'What's his name?' Naomi asked when I rolled on to my back with a surly sigh.

'Who's name?'

Lily sat up. 'Is it Sid?'

I stared at her. 'What?'

'Don't wind her up, Lil!' Naomi huffed. 'She hasn't had a cigarette for six hours.'

Lily gave me her best lost-little-girl look. 'I'm sorry. It's just that you said his name the other day while you were sleeping so I thought he was the he.'

'You been watching me sleep, Edward Cullen?'

'Of course not! It was when you fell asleep while we were watching that episode of *Murder She Wrote*—'

'Lily, stop talking,' Naomi interrupted, rolling her eyes.

'Yes, stop talking. Both of you. There's no he.'

'There's always a he,' Naomi told me with another sigh.

I scoffed. 'So every time a girl falls apart, it's because of a boy?'

Naomi raised an eyebrow at me and I huffed. 'I don't want to talk about it.'

'You still love him!' Lily gasped, all big eyes and hair.

'I don't.'

'You do!' they said in unison.

They're turning into quite the double act.

'I don't! It was nothing. We didn't even—'

I couldn't finish the sentence, but I didn't need to because Lily was already shaking her head. 'That's worse.'

'How?'

'Because you'll never get over it.'

I laughed, but Naomi poked me in the side with her finger. 'She's right. You'll never get over it because you won't get it out of your system. It's there for ever.'

I laughed again. 'For ever? Stop being so melodramatic.'

'I'm not! It's like a dream. You never remember a dream if you dream it out, you only remember it if you're interrupted, like if you wake up, or something. So if you let a relationship run its natural course, it will just fizzle out and die and you won't give a shit. But if something happens, like the timing's off or he's with someone else, then it's just on hold, like you've hit the pause button or something.'

'Don't be ridiculous.'

'It's true.' Lily nodded. 'We did this poem at school and it said that only one type of love lasts – unrequited love.'

I rolled my eyes. 'I love you, Lil. You don't know who Hello Kitty is, but you can quote Somerset Maugham.'

'Whatever.' Naomi waved her hand. 'If you ever want to get out of here, you need to talk about it. You can't avoid Doctor G for ever.'

'Says the girl who schizes out every time her boyfriend comes to visit.'

Naomi sat up. 'At least I let myself feel something. *That's* what you're scared of, Emily.' She pointed at me. 'What all of us in here are scared of, of being happy. We haven't felt it for so long, we wouldn't know what to do with it.'

When I looked at Lily she was nodding and my heart clenched like a fist. This always happens to me, I look away for a moment and everyone grows up without me.

Doctor Gilyard didn't look surprised when I asked to see her this morning.

'Are you ready, Emily?' she asked when I'd sat down.

'No,' I said, but she smiled and opened her notebook.

'Tell me about Sid.'

As soon as she said his name, my heart started ringing like a bell.

It rang just now, when I wrote it down.

'When did you meet him?'

I had to close my eyes for a second. Then I took a breath and brought my legs up and rested my chin on my knees. 'That morning in English Lit, the morning after I dyed my hair.'

'What happened?'

'Nothing. He just walked in.'

He walked in and everyone looked up, because when Sid King walks into a room, you look up. Sometimes I wonder if time has softened his edges, if nostalgia has made his eyes darker, his skin a warmer shade of brown. But then I remember how every girl softened, how the boys sat a little straighter, their shoulders back as he walked across the classroom.

He was older than the rest of them, I knew – my age, at least. You could tell by the way he walked, by the way he didn't care where he sat, he just headed for the first empty seat rather than looking around the classroom for someone he knew.

His hair was long then and that morning it fell in still-wet waves over his ears. 'Sid plays with his hair a lot,' I told Doctor Gilyard as I thought about how dark it was, how the too-white fluorescent lights hit it so I could see the threads of brown it would eventually dry to. 'That's kind of his thing. He plays with his hair. Juliet pulls the sleeves of her jumper over her hands because she's always cold and I tug on my ear lobe when I lie.'

'That's good to know,' she said with a smirk, writing it down.

'He ran his hand through his hair twice before he even got to where we were sitting.'

'What else did you notice?'

'His tattoos, on his wrists: *sink*' – I touched the inside of my right wrist with my finger, then my left one – 'and *swim*. And he was wearing this black Sonic Youth T-shirt—'

Doctor Gilyard interrupted. 'Why do you remember that?'

'Because Juliet was reading a book about No Wave.'

'New Wave?'

'No Wave, y'know, post-punk, anti-new wave,' I started to say but Doctor Gilyard looked bewildered so I gave up. 'Never mind. It was just kind of perfect, that's all.'

And it was. I don't believe in fate – I don't believe in much any more – but it's those little things that make me think all of this was meant to happen.

I remember turning to look at Juliet to find her watching him too, her lips parted as he dropped his ink-stained backpack on to the desk in front of ours. Of all the desks. And that's another of those things: would any of this have happened if he'd sat on the other side of the room? Maybe not. But he sat there, so close that I could smell the shampoo in his hair.

'So what did you do?' Doctor Gilyard asked and I smiled to myself.

'I asked Juliet about her summer.' She raised her eyebrow at me as if to say, *And?* 'I called her Nancy. I made her name sound about a minute long.'

'Were you trying to catch her off guard?'

I nodded. And it worked because Juliet shuddered like I'd just shaken her awake in the middle of the night.

'What did Juliet say?'

'That she'd moved in with her aunt and uncle.' I remember how she said it, stiffly, as though she'd been practising it. She probably had.

'What did you say then?' Doctor Gilyard pushed.

'I asked her why.'

'How did she react?'

I shrugged. 'She looked at me like I'd betrayed her. She hadn't asked me anything about myself, so I guess she didn't think I'd ask her anything.'

That's the thing with not wanting to answer questions, you have to stop asking them.

'What did she say?'

'She told me that her parents had died the month before.'

'How did she say it?'

'Quickly, like she was trying to run away from it.'

I remember how Juliet looked at me after she'd said it; it was a look that said, *Enough*. I think she thought that would be it, that I'd leave her alone.

'How did you react, Emily?'

'I didn't feign horror or offer her a useless condolence, I just asked her how.'

'What did she say?'

'That they were killed in a house fire. That's when Sid interrupted.'

'What did he say?'

I sniggered. 'Shit.'

'Did you know he was listening?'

'No.'

'So you weren't trying to embarrass her in front of him?'

I frowned. 'I was goading her, but it was nothing to do with him.'

'Okay,' Doctor Gilyard nodded, 'so what happened then?'

'He looked mortified – I don't think he realised he'd said it out loud.'

'Did he apologise?'

I sniggered again. 'Yeah. He said he was saying shit about something he heard the day before. Then he flashed us a smile that would make girls lose their balance.'

'Did you lose your balance, Emily?'

'No.'

'So you weren't attracted to him immediately?'

I shrugged. 'I thought he was good looking.'

'Just good looking?'

'Yeah. He's my type: tall, dark, artfully untidy.'

'So you were attracted to him?'

I got what she was poking at and sighed.

Doctor Gilyard took off her glasses and looked at me. 'What, Emily?'

'So I did all of this because I fancied a boy?'

'I didn't say that.'

'No, but that's what you're implying.'

'I'm not implying anything, Emily. I asked you a question: were you attracted to him when you first met him?'

'Why does that matter?'

'Why are you finding it so difficult to answer the question?'

'I know what you're doing,' I told her, shaking my head.

'What am I doing, Emily?'

'You're trying to work out what came first, the chicken or the egg: did I fancy him all along or did I fall for him after I used him to get back at Juliet.'

'Which is it?'

'I did it for Juliet!' I hissed, holding on to the arms of the chair and sitting forward. 'Everything I did was to fuck her over! That's why I was glad that day, when they met.'

'Why?'

'Because I knew she liked him. He made his joke then he smiled at her – just at her, this slow, secret smile – and that was it, I wasn't in the room any more.'

'How did that make you feel, Emily?'

'Happy,' I said, my nails digging on to the arms of the chair.

'Really? It was the first time since she stabbed your father that you could get near her and suddenly this boy was between you.'

I shook my head. 'Do you wanna know why I didn't kill her?' I asked with a smug smile. 'Why I didn't just stick a knife in her heart and be done with it?'

'Why, Emily?'

'Because she was already dead.'

The words seemed to bounce off every wall. I imagined them rolling under the door towards the TV Room like marbles.

She frowned. 'Dead? How so?'

'Her mother died of breast cancer when she was four and she'd survived that, but then she stabbed Dad and she lost everything. *Everything*. Her father, her house, her school, her friends. There was no joy in killing her. No release. She had nothing to fight for.'

'Then she did,' Doctor Gilyard said and my smile widened.

It happened so quietly, her and Sid. It wasn't one of those stories they'd tell their children. There was no rain, no chance encounter. Sid didn't pull her out of the way before she stumbled into the path of a bus. But I felt the classroom hum with it. The floor shivered. Pens rolled off desks. Books fluttered off shelves like broken birds.

'I knew then that she had a life,' I told Doctor Gilyard. 'A future.'

'And why was that important, Emily?'

I had to take a breath before I said it. 'Because I could make her beg for it.'

Naomi is with Doctor Gilyard so I'm in my room. Lily is asleep on my bed, her eyelashes fluttering. I wish I could sleep like that; she looks so content. I think she's used to it now – this place. I think she might even be enjoying it. She certainly seems to relish asking me question after question. She just asked me what it was like, being someone else. I didn't lie. I told her that I enjoyed it; the lies, the melodrama, the weeks of smiling at Juliet and feeding her sweet little lies while she looked at me with wide brown eyes, devouring every word.

I expected her to be more suspicious – of me, of Sid – but she wasn't at all. Our three lives knotted together the moment we met in that classroom. We went to classes together and had lunch together. In the evenings, we went to the cinema and, while it was still warm, we sat in the park, sharing bags of crisps and watching the sky change from pink to purple to black, like an old bruise. On Friday nights there was a pub in Camden that didn't check IDs and on Saturdays there was always a party; Sid always knew someone who was DJ'ing somewhere or a mate who was turning eighteen. It was like the summer before I met them, the summer before Juliet stabbed Dad and everything fell apart, back when we were young and free and unbreakable.

I even started having dinner at Juliet's house two, sometimes three, times a week. Her foster parents – Mike and Eve – ate up my grumbles about my parents' divorce and how my mother was never home, just like Juliet had, and as soon as they did, as soon as they started feeding me roast chicken and asking about college, I knew that was it . . . I'd been invited in.

I didn't tell Lily this, but the best thing about being Rose Glass was that I didn't have to be Emily Koll. And the best thing about not being Emily Koll was that I could start again. I could cross that year out, the year Dad was on remand, the year I was in Spain, and be sixteen again.

It's a terrible thing, I suppose, to be seventeen and to want to start again. It's not like before then – before Juliet – I was unhappy. I was popular at school. Okay, I wasn't one of the shiny-haired girls who looked at your bag before they looked at you and I wasn't as cool as the girls who drank coffee and read Murakami, but I had found a corner for myself – I played the cello. It wasn't the guitar and I wore black dresses instead of black nail varnish, but I was good, good enough to make Dad and Uncle Alex cry when they came to my recitals. And I had friends;

I swapped clothes with Catherine Bamford and held Alma Peet's hair every time we went to a party and Max Dalton fed her vodka shots until she puked. And when Olivia's grandmother died, I got everyone to sign a card and we made a donation to Cancer Research.

But that was before. So forget about that Emily; she went away the moment Juliet stabbed Dad. Now I'm Harry Koll's daughter. That's all I'll ever be, so forgive me if I wanted to be Rose Glass for a while.

I know it's moments like this when I sound utterly insane, but I learned a lot from being Rose. Before I had to be someone else I didn't think too much about who I was. I was who I was, if you know what I mean. I didn't think that could change. I thought my personality was as much a part of me as the colour of my hair. But then I dyed it red and I didn't look like me any more. I looked like Monday Fitzgerald.

Monday was in Year 11 when I started at St Jude's. She didn't have shiny hair or read Murakami, but every girl in my year was in awe of her. Where we were small with too much hair and not enough personality, Monday was tall and graceful with huge cardamom-coloured eyes and a smile that could stop a horse mid-gallop.

Every girl at St Jude's wanted to be Monday Fitzgerald. Not because she was popular or pretty or destined for greatness, but because in a school where everyone looked the same and dressed the same and went out with the same handful of boys, Monday Fitzgerald walked through the halls in her rolled-up tartan skirt and Doc Martens absolutely and unashamedly herself. And we loved her for it.

If we'd had any idea who we were, we would have done the same.

It's funny how it took becoming someone else to realise who I am. Who I *could* be. I thought the world was split into people like Monday and people like me. I didn't think I could walk into a room with a swing of the hips and a smile for everyone. I don't know why; I only had to do it once and then I would have done it. But I guess if someone tells you something enough, you start to believe it. All my life, all I'd ever heard was: Emily's so shy, Emily's so quiet, Emily's so clever. Thinking back on it now, I don't know if I ever was any of those things, or if I just became shy and quiet and clever because everyone said I was.

But when I was Rose, I didn't have to be. It was as though I could shuffle off Emily like she was a winter coat and it was too warm to wear it any more. Then I was free to say what I wanted, wear what I wanted. I listened to bands because they made me feel restless, not because someone said they were cool. In clothes shops, I began to stray towards the rails which previously I would just have gazed at, try on the clothes I thought didn't suit me. Maybe they still didn't suit me, but I didn't care, and that's the point: Rose was the girl I wanted to be but I was too scared that Dad wouldn't approve of or who my friends would think was weird. But the truth is: I am weird. I've always been weird. And when I was Rose, I could be. A mismatched, red-haired Kerouacian kind of weird perfectly fitting of a girl called Rose.

And I liked it.

Then I met Grace Humm.

Grace Humm was my personal tutor. It felt strange calling her that. Everyone at St Jude's was Miss or Sir. There were no first names. But at the College of North London we were adults, apparently, and could call teachers by their first name.

I met Grace the morning I started at the college and I spent the three weeks after that avoiding her. I'd ducked into classroom, locked myself in the toilet and once hid behind a bin in the canteen. But when I finally met her, I kind of wished I hadn't, because if Rose allowed me to be weird, then Grace showed me how to own it. How to wallow in it. She taught me to wear weird like a feather in my hair.

If I ever grow up, I want to be Grace Humm.

But I didn't know that back then. All I thought about was Juliet, so I didn't want to sit with a teacher and discuss how I was getting on with my classes and what universities I wanted to apply to. I wasn't going to university. I wasn't even going to be at college much longer. I thought another two – maybe three – weeks and it'd be done, I'd be gone and she wouldn't even notice. But that was my first mistake, thinking she wasn't paying attention.

'Rose,' she said, walking towards me one day as Juliet and I were standing by our lockers plotting how we could get Sid to try sushi. 'Are you avoiding me?'

Juliet and I exchanged a look and I contemplated making a run for it, but when I saw how busy the corridor was, I blew a bubble with my gum instead.

'Hello, Miss,' I said, tossing a book into my locker.

'Oh, Rose. I'm so glad this isn't awkward. I thought it would be awkward,' she said, her forehead pinched with mock concern. 'I was worried that I came on too strong after enrolment, calling and emailing like that. My ex-husband says I'm too needy. Was I being needy, Rose? Did I scare you off?'

I tried not to laugh as I closed my locker. 'It's not you, Miss, it's me.'

'Where are you going?' she asked, trotting after Juliet and me, her heels clicking on the parquet floor as we began to walk away. 'Don't leave me, Rose! Don't leave me like he did.'

'I have to get to sociology.'

She checked her watch. 'Not until eleven.'

'Yeah, but I have to do that thing first.'

She stopped in front of me so I couldn't get past. 'The thing in my office?'

'No.' I pointed over her shoulder. 'That thing at the thing.'

'Oh, *that* thing. The thing where you to talk to me now or I call your mother?'

I sighed and rolled my eyes at Juliet. 'Run. Save yourself.'

I didn't have to tell her twice and as soon as she had disappeared down the corridor, Grace turned to me with a smirk. 'Is she really going out with Sid King?' When I nodded, she laughed. 'Sid and Nancy. Too cute!'

'Yeah. *So* cute. Didn't he stab her?'

'Oh,' she said, drawing it out so it sounded about a week long.

I shouldn't have bitten, but I did. 'Oh, what?'

'You like Sid. *Awkward.*'

I chuckled. 'Yeah. Okay.'

She was the first one to call me on it. I hadn't considered it before then, but as soon as I did, the tops of my ears started burning.

'Awkward. Awkward. Awkward,' she said with each step.

I made myself look at her feet in case my cheeks looked as hot as they felt. She was wearing high heels, green suede high heels. I remember staring at them. The teachers at St Jude's didn't wear green suede high heels.

'Here we are! Come in,' she said when we got to her office, sweeping in with her arm out as though she were introducing me to an old friend. 'Welcome to Graceland. Get it? I'm Grace, and this is my, y'know, *land.*'

I raised an eyebrow at her. 'You're quite the wordsmith.'

When I stepped into the office, I had to stop.

'I know.' She nodded, walking over to the chair opposite her desk and picking up a handful of newspapers so that I could sit down. 'This is what the inside of my head looks like.'

I'd never seen anything like it. The teachers' offices at St Jude's had crooked stained-glass windows and oil paintings of sullen alumni glaring down from the wood-panelled walls. But the walls of Grace's office were covered with posters for giving up smoking and safe sex, and the light from the only window was filtered though the tired leaves of a spider plant that hung over the edge of the windowsill as though it was trying to summon the energy to throw itself into the bin beneath it.

When I sat on the chair opposite her desk, she had to slide a pile of paperwork out of the way so that she could see me. 'Peek-a-boo!' She grinned, then gasped, 'Oh!' and scribbled something illegible on to a pink heart-shaped Post-it note.

When she slapped it on the desk, I tried to read it. I think it said MILK, but I gave up and looked into the mug by her phone instead.

'Science project?' I asked, pulling a face.

'Don't worry about her, that's Penny,' she said, and I blinked at her.

'You named your mug?'

'Penny, penicillin, get it? She's gonna save the world one day, aren't you, Penny?' She tapped the rim of the mug with her pen. 'Yes, you are.'

Sometimes, when I'm sitting in Doctor Gilyard's tiny white office, I think of that moment, of Grace and her pink heart-shaped Post-it notes.

'Right, Rose. Rose Glass,' she said, sliding a file out of one of the precarious piles on her desk. The pile wobbled, but didn't fall. 'How are you doing? Tell me everything.'

I shrugged. 'Fine.'

'How are you finding the College of North London?'

'Fine.'

'And your classes?'

'Fine.'

'You're doing A levels, right?' She looked down at the file. 'English lit, sociology, history and art and design? That's a lot of reading. Are you keeping up?'

'Yeah, I suppose.'

'And I see you've made friends. Sid's in my drama class. He's brilliant, isn't he? So sweet.' She gave me a theatrical wink.

I noticed the framed *Spring Awakening* poster on the wall behind her desk and suddenly wished I was in her drama class. When Olivia had suggested doing *Spring Awakening* at St Jude's, Mr Carmichael almost had a stroke.

'And Nancy seems lovely, from what I've heard,' she said, and I remembered why I wasn't doing Drama. Why I was there.

'She's been through a lot,' she added and I looked at the poster again.

'You have too, Rose,' she said, her voice lowering. It made my stomach knot.

'I suppose.'

'How are things at home?'

I shrugged. 'Fine.'

'How's your mum?'

'Fine.'

'Your parents just got divorced, right? You're living with your mother now. How's that going?' She held her hand up. 'Don't say fine!'

'*Good.*'

'Good? That's two words! Now we're getting somewhere.' She

pointed at me over the desk. 'Let's make it three. Tell me about your dad, do you still see him?'

I knew she'd ask, but it still made the tops of my ears burn again so I lowered my chin until my hair fell over them, sure that if she saw how red they were, she'd know I was lying.

'No. He's a surgeon, so he works weird hours.'

'And your mum?'

'She's a medical rep so she's on the road a lot.'

'That must be hard.'

'I suppose.' I started to pick at my nail varnish. It was so quiet that I could hear a tutor in the corridor berating a student for not turning off his phone in class.

'How's your mum? All of this must have been really hard on her.'

'Fine.'

'Okay,' she said with a long sigh, pressing her fingers to her eyelids. If she wasn't a teacher, I think that's the point at which she would have picked me up and shaken me. I kind of want to introduce her to Doctor Gilyard, sometimes, but I'm sure that if you put the two of them in a room together, one of them would spontaneously combust.

'Okay, Rose,' she said, holding her hands up. 'Okay. I know things are all over the place right now and I'm the last person you want to talk to about it. I do. If I was seventeen, there'd be about forty-seven people I'd talk to before I talked to a teacher, including the bloke who used to stand outside Oxford Circus tube with a megaphone asking everyone if they're a sinner or a winner.' She smiled softly. 'All I'm saying is that I just got divorced. I know how horrible it is at home right now. I'm just grateful I don't have kids so that they don't have to see me sobbing and eating cheesecake straight from the freezer.'

'It isn't like that.' I sat back in the chair with my arms crossed. I don't know what she said to make me so defensive, if I'd agreed or pretended to cry about how miserable I was, like I did with Mike and Eve, she would have left me alone. But I glared across the desk at her. 'Mum's fine. Not all women are hysterical and eat their body weight in Ben and Jerry's because their husbands leave them.'

As soon as I had said it, I looked away, furious with myself. I don't know how, but she'd found a raw nerve and dug her five-inch heel in.

I expected her to swipe back, but her eyes lit up. 'Hello, Rose. There you are.'

She smiled but I couldn't look at her and stared at the Spice Girls alarm clock on top of her filing cabinet instead.

'Where've you been, Rose? This girl,' I could see her waving my file out of the corner of my eye, 'the girl who sits doodling in class and paints half-arsed bowls of fruit isn't the girl I've been told about. The girl with the bright red hair who reads Andrea Dworkin between lessons. What's going on, Rose?'

When I didn't respond, she carried on. 'Your English lit tutor says that you spend most of your time looking out of the window, but the moment he said something remotely negative about Daisy Buchanan you were all over him.'

I shrugged. 'That's what happens when you read too much Dworkin.'

'Hey,' she said, her gaze narrowing. 'Humour as a defence mechanism is *my* thing. Get your own thing.' She wagged her finger at me. 'And drunk on Dworkin or not, your English lit tutor said you were articulate and witty, if a little dismissive of the point he was trying to make. But then, you're sixteen, you're supposed to be dismissive. You know everything, right?'

I heard her chuckle and I think she was waiting for me to chuckle back. When I didn't, she sighed. 'Okay. Rose, I know how painful this is. I can feel it, believe me. I'd gladly have a bikini wax over this.' She sighed again, more melodramatically this time. 'But the reason I'm putting us both through this is because I think you need to talk to someone. You're obviously very bright but your tutors say that you're quiet and withdrawn in class and you've lost weight since I last saw you.'

That hit me like a slap. 'Hold on.' I glared at her over the cluttered desk. 'Let me get this straight, there are eight thousand students at this college. Eight *thousand*. Someone came into the canteen last week with a butcher's knife and you drag me in here because I've lost a couple of pounds?'

She rolled her eyes. 'I don't drag, Rose. I charm.'

'What do you want from me?' I snapped. And I shouldn't have, but I could feel the panic bristling across my scalp.

'I don't want anything from you, Rose. I just want you to be okay.'

'I am okay.'

The phone started ringing then. I waited for her to answer it, but she picked it up and put it back down again. 'Okay. If you say so. But I'm just saying: I know things are rubbish right now and it helps to have someone to talk to.'

'I do have people to talk to. Do you?'

She laughed at that, then looked at me with a small smile. 'Not really. My best friend had a miscarriage last week. She's been trying for years and it was her third so she's devastated,' she said, almost to herself. 'But I need to talk to her, about the divorce and selling the house and the twenty-minute row I had with my ex last week over a vase I threw against a wall so that neither of us could have it.'

She shook her head. 'But I can't talk to her because she's going through hell and she doesn't need to hear me ranting about a vase. But that happens sometimes, Rose, you want to talk about stuff but you can't because your friends are going through things – real things, painful things – and you can't talk to them because your stuff doesn't feel as important as theirs. So I'm just saying—'

'I know what you're saying,' I interrupted with a defeated sigh. 'You're not exactly being subtle about it. You think I can't talk to Nancy because my parents got divorced and hers died. I get it.' I sighed again. 'If I want to talk, I can talk to you.'

'Don't talk to me! I can't help you. Look at the state of me.' She pointed at her tangle of curls. 'I forgot to wash the conditioner out of my hair this morning.'

I couldn't help but laugh. Grace Humm is the only person

who has ever been able to make me go from livid to silly in less than thirty seconds.

'Of course you can talk to me, Rose. Or the qualified counsellor in Welfare who is less likely to use your parents' divorce as an excuse to whinge about her own.'

She winked at me and I smiled. 'Thanks, Miss.'

I stood up, but before I walked to the door, I turned to look at her again. 'Out of curiosity, how do you eat a cheesecake straight from the freezer without breaking your jaw?'

She stared at me like it was the most obvious thing in the world. 'Lick it like an ice lolly, of course.'

Of course.

I got a reprieve from talking about Sid today because Doctor Gilyard wanted to talk about Uncle Alex. I don't know why. Maybe she's trying to lull me into a false sense of security and I'll wake up tonight to find her standing over me with her notebook. *Tell me about Sid.*

I actually shuddered as I wrote that.

She started our session this week with: 'Your Uncle Alex was supposed to be looking after you while your father was in prison.'

It wasn't the best start. I wanted to punch her in the face.

'He *did* look after me,' I told her with a filthy look.

'But you were supposed to be in Spain with him and your grandmother?'

'Yeah. So?'

'You said that he was unhappy with your decision to go to London and befriend Juliet, so why didn't he stop you?'

'He couldn't.'

'Why not?' She took off her glasses to look at me. 'From what I've read, your uncle doesn't seem the type of man to be held to ransom by a seventeen-year-old girl.'

I tipped my head back and laughed. 'Have we met?'

'What does that mean?'

'Hello.' I waved at her. 'I'm Emily Koll, I'm a fucking nightmare.'

She chuckled at that and wrote something in her notebook. 'I know more than anyone how wilful you are, Emily. But your uncle was the grown-up in this instance, and you were the child. You said that you were relying on him for money, for the paperwork you needed to corroborate your fake identity, he didn't have to do any of that. He could just have said no and let you seethe impotently in Spain.'

'First of all,' I leaned forward, 'I'm not a child. Second of all, I was gonna do it, with or without him, and he knew that. At least if he was involved he could make sure I had what I needed so that I didn't use a shitty fake passport I bought off the Internet and get myself arrested.'

'But you did get arrested.'

I sat back again with sigh. I know Dad blames him for what happened, but I was gonna jump. All Uncle Alex did was try to break my fall.

'Did he ever try to stop you?'

'About once a week!' I chuckled to myself. 'He was always threatening to come to London and drag me back to Spain.'

'But he didn't?'

'He *couldn't*. The police were all over him. If he'd come to London, they would have been on him.'

'Why?'

'I was living down the road from Juliet. If Alex Koll showed up in Islington, they'd know why and arrest him before he got to my front door.'

'So you took advantage of that?'

'Of course! If Uncle Alex was in London, it would never have gone that far.'

She nodded. 'Okay. Tell me about the first time he tried to stop you.'

'I told you, he tried about once a week.'

'Did he ever risk a trip to London?'

'Once.' I sighed and crossed my arms. 'About a month after I started college, I came home to find him in my living room.'

'Why? What happened?'

'My personal tutor pulled me into her office and she must have called him afterwards,' I said with another long sigh. 'She had his number because I gave it to the college in case they ever needed to speak to my "Dad".'

'What did she tell him?'

'That she was concerned about my work. That I'd lost weight.'

'He must have been concerned, too, to risk being caught like that?'

'I guess.'

'What did he say?'

I sniggered. 'He didn't know I'd dyed my hair so that was his first concern.'

I remember the look he gave me, how his face went from bewildered to furious.

'Did he like it?' Doctor Gilyard asked and I sniggered again.

'Not really.'

'What did he say?'

'He said Dad would do a shit and die when he saw it.'

'What did you say to that?'

'I reminded him that Dad wouldn't let me visit him in prison so my hair would be grey by the time he got out.'

Doctor Gilyard nodded at that. 'What did he say?'

'Nothing.'

'What did you say?'

'Nothing.' I just looked out of the kitchen window as I filled up the kettle so I'd have something to do with my hands. You could see the council estate where I was born on the horizon – three tower blocks that didn't quite reach the clouds – and it made me think of Sid. I'd seen him scribble, *IS THIS IT?* into the corner of his notebook that afternoon in sociology and I'd been saying it to myself all day.

'Did you talk?'

'Sort of.' She waited for me to go on. 'He just told me that he'd had enough, that he didn't know what I was doing, wanting to be Juliet's friend. He said that it'd been two months and he didn't see the point so it was time to go home.'

'What did you say to that?'

'I told him that I didn't have a home, that I lived in a school.'

She wrote that down. 'What did he say then?'

I sighed. 'That he was stopping my credit cards and not paying for my flat.'

'How did you react?'

'I told him I'd get a job.'

'What did he say to that?'

'He laughed. He said that working in Starbucks wouldn't finance my sushi addiction let alone pay for my flat, so I might as well come home.'

'Did you agree?'

'I ignored him.'

I knew he hated it when I ignored him, but I was too angry. So I waited for the kettle to boil, then busied myself with making the tea, even though I knew I was out of milk and neither of us could drink it black. But I made it anyway, the china mug ringing as I stirred two sugars into his.

I handed it to him and he stared at it. 'I'm worried, Ems. Since Harry was arrested, you've changed, you've been drinking and I know you're smoking; I can smell it on you.'

'Do you really want to compare misdemeanours, Uncle Alex?'

He didn't bite. 'And you've lost weight.'

'My teacher tell you that?' I said, turning away from him to pick up my own mug from the kitchen counter.

'No. I have eyes. You're so thin, Ems.'

I ignored him, blowing at my tea. But he kept pushing and it was like he was poking me in the back with his questions. 'You look exhausted. Are you sleeping?'

I took a sip of tea. It was too hot and bitter. 'I'm fine.'

'No, you're not.' I heard him take a step towards me and my spine tightened like a guitar string. 'What are you doing, being her friend and going to her college? And now you're having dinner at her house, with her foster parents? Ems, come on. That ain't right. Why are you doing this to yourself? It must be killing you.'

I walked over to the sink and poured my tea down the drain. 'I don't expect you to understand, Uncle Alex.'

And I didn't, because, say what you like about Alex Koll, about the type of man he is, he didn't understand because he *couldn't*. He wasn't broken in the same way I am, in the same way Dad is too, I guess. He didn't get why I needed to do it. Why I needed to be her friend and go to her college. Why it hurt less to know she had to sleep with the light on.

Doctor Gilyard must have known what I was thinking because she asked me if Uncle Alex had ever asked me why I was doing it.

'Of course,' I told her with a small shrug. 'But I couldn't tell him.'

'Why not?'

'He wouldn't understand.' And he wouldn't. He wouldn't

114

understand how I wanted to bleed into every corner of Juliet's life.

'Did he offer to do it again, to –' she stopped for breath – 'to sort it out?'

I nodded.

'Why didn't you let him?'

I shrugged again. I knew that if I said it out loud, it wouldn't make sense. There's something about Doctor Gilyard, about this tiny white room, that distorts things. I say things to her sometimes, things that make sense, things that have always made sense, but when I hear myself say them, they sound weird. Cruel. Ugly. So I didn't tell her why, that I could just see Juliet, building this new life for herself, and I had to be in the middle of it, a red thread running through it. I had to be her friend. The one she split her Twix with. The one she called the first time Sid kissed her outside that curry house on Brick Lane.

'It made me feel better,' I said instead, lifting my eyelashes to look at her, 'to know that every good memory Juliet had from then on would involve me.'

'Why?'

'Because when the time came, she would question it all – me, Sid, her foster parents – just like I did when I found out about Dad. She would ask herself if any of it was real and *that*'s what I wanted, for her whole life to catch light and burn and burn and burn until all that was left was smoke. Then she would have nothing. Nothing.'

Doctor Gilyard waited for me to catch my breath, then said,

'Did you tell your uncle Alex that? Did he understand?'

I shook my head. He couldn't because he just wanted her dead. He'd never understand the satisfaction of picking her apart – slowly, slowly.

'Everything is black and white to Uncle Alex,' I told Doctor Gilyard. 'Left, right. Up, down. Love, hate. Right, wrong.'

'How are things with you, Emily?'

'I see everything in between. All those shades of grey and red and blue.'

She nodded at that and scribbled something in her notebook. 'What do you think would have happened, if you'd listened to him? If you'd gone back to Spain?'

I turned my face away. 'I don't know.'

'Should he have tried harder to stop you?'

'I don't know.'

'Would any of this have happened if he had?'

'I don't know.'

'Would you be happy, Emily?'

This is why I can't let her in, why I have to lock things in boxes and behind doors, because she makes me think about things. She makes me ask myself things like, *Would I be happy?* Thirteen hours later, I'm still sitting here asking myself, *Would I be happy? Would I be happy? Would I be happy? Would I be happy? Would I be happy? Would I be happy?*

These are the things that keep me up at night.

What I've lost.

The person I'll never be now.

I didn't tell Doctor Gilyard this, but as soon as Uncle Alex left that night, I ran to Juliet's house, resolve burning fresh and bright in my blood.

I was out of breath by the time I got there, my lungs throbbing as I went through the side gate and walked along the side of the house.

'Hey, Ro,' Mike said when he saw me. 'Where've you been? You missed dinner.'

'Sorry,' I said, stopping to snatch at a breath. 'My uncle popped round.'

It wasn't until I stopped that I realised how cold it was. September had come and gone like a fever. Branches had started to droop, leaves darken, and the nights began to creep closer, closer. I don't remember most of September, just coming out the other side of it that evening in October more Rose and less Emily.

'You okay?' Mike stepped away from the back door and when he turned to face me, his eyes looked inhumanly blue in the light spilling out from the kitchen.

'Yeah. 'Course. Mum just wanted us to have dinner. Sorry I didn't call.'

By then, the lies came more easily. I'd started to enjoy it, pretending to be sixteen again. Rose Glass felt more whole than Emily Koll sometimes. More of a person. I suppose it's because as Rose, I had to have an answer for everything. I never felt ready when I was Emily; I was always a few steps behind. I wasn't as pretty as the girls at St Jude's, as rich, as thin, as clever. They had boyfriends and were on the hockey team and had short stories published but still managed to get straight As while I struggled to read all the books on my reading lists. But Rose didn't need to pass any exams. She didn't need a boyfriend or a place at university. It was strangely liberating, not having to try to be someone.

The funny thing is, I think it might have made me someone.

'You're quiet tonight.' Mike frowned, obviously concerned when I didn't try to ponce a cigarette or ask if he'd saved me some dinner.

'Yeah. Sorry.' I shook my head, then smiled.

The back door was open and as I leaned against the frame, I looked in at the kitchen. It was empty. The dishes were done and drying on the drainer.

'What'd I miss?'

'Spag bol. Eve saved you some,' he said and I smiled again.

The kitchen still smelt of onions and garlic. It always smelled of something; burnt toast in the morning and on Sundays, when Eve's mother made gizzadas after church, it smelt of coconut. I'd never had a kitchen like that; Dad didn't cook and when I was at boarding school I was cooked for, so coming home to the smell of onions and garlic wasn't something I was used to. Maybe I found it comforting, that's why I was there so much. I don't know. All I know is that the first time Juliet invited me back to her house to have dinner with her 'aunt and uncle', I knew I was doing something right. That I was taking root.

It was a couple of weeks after we'd started college. I'd braced myself to endure dry pork chops and peas with a slightly overweight middle-aged couple, but when I walked into her kitchen, I found Mike and Eve already loose with red wine and singing along to Amy Winehouse as they chopped onions.

They seemed genuinely pleased to see me and before I could take my jacket off, Eve had me chopping green peppers next to her at the counter while Mike got me to sniff spices.

'Smell that,' he'd said, holding a jar of something that smelt of Starbucks under my nose. 'Nutmeg. Perfect with lamb.'

'Okay.' I'd nodded as he put some into the sizzling Dutch pot on the stove.

'Cinnamon,' he'd said, getting me to smell another jar.

'Smells like Christmas,' I'd told him and he'd grinned.

He wasn't the balding retired policeman I was expecting. He was a retired policeman, but he was in his mid-thirties, like Eve, with a shaved head and these enormous blue eyes, like the Johnson & Johnson baby all grown up. There was nothing remotely dad-like about him; he nudged me with his hip when he wanted to get my attention and let me have sips of his wine when Eve wasn't looking.

Not that she was paying much attention; she'd gone into the living room to find the book on René Magritte she'd been telling us about. She was an art teacher at a school in Islington and there was nothing remotely mum-like about her, either. She had short freeform dreads, a silver nose stud and a tattoo of three birds on her wrist.

When she found it, she came back into the kitchen saying, '*Ceci n'est pas une livre.*'

I had no idea what she was on about but I was impressed that she'd even found it. Nothing in the house seemed to be in any order so I don't know how on earth she saw the book on the bowing shelves in the living room. Maybe it wasn't there. Maybe it was in the pile by the battered leather chair next to fireplace, or on top of the fridge, or on the stairs, or on the windowsill in the downstairs toilet.

It could have been anywhere.

But that was the wonder of that house. It was nothing like mine. Dad liked things clean. Simple. The walls were white, the carpets cream. Everything had its place. Our housekeeper spent her days making sure his shirts were arranged neatly by colour in his wardrobe and all the calla lilies in the vase on the table in the foyer were the same height.

The flat I was living in then was a lot like my old house. Alex rented it furnished so the glossy floors, thick rugs and leather sofas weren't really me. But Mike and Eve's house bled personality, through the cracks in the walls and the holes in the floorboards. They were everywhere. In the mismatched mugs and painted sideboard. And there was stuff all over the place; pot plants and records and piles and piles of magazines – on every table and worktop. Even on the floor. Dad would have had a stroke. But I loved it.

I remember walking into the living room the first time I went there and seeing the framed God Save the Queen poster over the fireplace. I'd laughed and pointed at it saying, 'Sid and Nancy. How apt.'

That was the day after Juliet and Sid had kissed outside the curry house on Brick Lane so I expected her to laugh too, but she'd blushed and made me promise not to say anything. And I didn't; we were both raised by over-protective fathers so I understood her need to keep things to herself, but that's not why I didn't say anything. I kept it. Filed it away. Everything you say will be taken down and used in evidence against you, and all that.

'Ro?' Mike said, and when I looked up, he was leaning against the frame of the back door too. 'You sure you're alright?'

He turned his head to blow the smoke from his cigarette out across the garden. It was so dark that as soon as he did, it disappeared and it made me wonder how much of what surrounded us was smoke and how much was darkness.

'I'm fine. Weird day,' I told him, taking the can of Red Stripe out of his hand.

He watched as I took a long swig, then reached into the pocket of his jeans and pulled out his box of cigarettes. 'Here,' he said, opening it. 'Don't tell Eve.'

I plucked one out with a grin and he lit it for me with the neon-pink lighter he stole off me. Or I stole off him. I can't remember; I just remember it going back and forth a lot between us. I inhaled deeply and stepped back from the door so that I could tip my head and blow the smoke towards the sky. As I did, I could see Juliet upstairs in her bedroom. She was on the phone, obviously talking to Sid. She looked so happy. Content.

I took a swig of beer and looked at Mike. 'Who's Nance talking to? Sid?'

He frowned. 'Who's Sid?'

Lily's gone, back to the main wing. She's eating again and the livid cuts on her arms have faded to pink so a guard came to get her after breakfast. No fanfare. No card. No cake. I can't even remember the last thing I said to her.

I was sure Doctor Gilyard was going to ask me how I felt about it, but she just took off her glasses and asked if I'd ever tried to break Sid and Juliet up.

It was quite an opener.

'I told you already,' I said with a long sigh, inspecting my hair for split ends. 'It was nothing to do with Sid. Everything I did was to fuck Juliet over.'

'Okay.' She nodded. 'How did you use Sid to fuck Juliet over?'

(I got Doctor Gilyard to say fuck, I want that noted for the record before I continue.)

'I meddled.' I looked up with a mischievous smile.

'How did you meddle?'

'I told Mike that she was seeing him.'

'Didn't he know?'

I shook my head.

'Why?'

I rolled my eyes. 'She loves the drama.'

'And you don't?'

(I'm not sure I like the new sweary, sarcastic Doctor Gilyard, by the way.)

'How did he react?'

'He was fine,' I said with a shrug. 'She wasn't.'

'Was she upset?'

I chuckled to myself as I remembered how Juliet dragged me up to her bedroom after Mike and Eve confronted her and slammed the door. 'She was furious.'

'Why?'

'She'd told me not to tell them.'

'How did they react?'

'They were shocked and they weren't *thrilled* that he was eighteen, but they were cool.'

And they were. They were perfectly calm. Neither of them flipped their shit and threatened to lock her in her room until she was thirty like my father would have. If anything, they seemed happy for her and genuinely wanted to know all about Sid.

'That clearly wasn't the reaction you were hoping for, Emily.'

'I shouldn't have been surprised.' I laughed bitterly. 'It was the perfect reaction from her perfect foster parents to her perfect relationship with her perfect boyfriend.'

Doctor Gilyard wrote that down. 'How would your father have reacted?'

I didn't respond, but I know how he would have reacted: he would have demanded to see Sid like he did when he found out about Andre Alexander.

'I want to meet him, this Andre who thinks he can take my daughter to the cinema. Call him and tell him to come here now,' he'd said, pointing at me over the desk in his office. 'Call him or I'll get Alex to call him.'

I thought he was just being over-protective but I don't know any more and I hate that. I hate that now I look at every memory of my father from a slightly different angle so that even my fondest memories are dirty and dog eared.

'People say I'm spoilt,' I said, looking at the crack in the wall behind Doctor Gilyard's chair. 'But Juliet's a fucking *brat*. She had everything and she still wasn't happy.'

'In what way wasn't she happy, Emily?'

'Like that night, when I told Mike about her and Sid, she dragged me up to her bedroom and slammed the door like a twelve year old.' She's only a year younger than me, but sometimes it felt like ten.

'What did she say?'

'Nothing. She just threw herself on the bed.'

'What did you do?'

'Nothing.'

I distracted myself with the stuff on her chest of drawers before I slapped her and told her to grow up. I unscrewed a pot of hair wax and sniffed it, then picked up a pink and white tin of lip balm and dabbed some on to my bottom lip.

I did that a lot then. It was as though I had to touch everything that belonged to her, to hold it, smell it, turn it over in my hands. There was a pile of receipts and loose change next to her jewellery box and a cinema ticket for a film I wanted to see. She'd seen it with Sid and it made my heart hurt so much, I brought a hand up to my chest.

'When she got there, to Mike and Eve's house, she had nothing, just a suitcase of clothes that the Witness Protection team bought her,' I said. Doctor Gilyard stopped writing and her office was suddenly too quiet. 'She didn't have anything else – she had to leave it all behind.'

Doctor Gilyard took off her glasses. 'But you said that she had everything.'

'Yes she lost everything,' I snapped, suddenly out of breath. 'But what did she actually *lose*? Just stuff. Clothes and photos and books. Nothing she couldn't replace. And she got it all back, didn't she? She had a roomful of stuff while I had to question everything I had ever known. Everything. Every memory. Every present my father ever bought me. You even have me questioning my fucking cat!'

I was shaking as I said it. Just like I did that night in Juliet's room, when I wanted to rip the photos of her with Mike and Eve off the notice board and smash her bottles of perfume. But I had closed my eyes and sucked in a breath.

When I opened them again, I looked at the mirror over her chest of drawers.

'Who did this?' I'd asked, nodding at the picture of Maya Angelou taped to the frame of Juliet's mirror. Someone had written *Phenomenal woman, that's me* in lipstick across it.

'Guess?' she said with a small smile and I laughed.

'I need to introduce Eve to my mother. She has a picture of Audrey Hepburn on the door of our fridge with *What would Audrey eat?* written across it.'

She didn't, of course – I have no idea what my mother has on her fridge – but Olivia's mother did so it wasn't a lie. *Someone*'s mother has a picture of Audrey Hepburn on the door of their fridge with *What would Audrey eat?* written across it. I did that a lot then too, steal other people's memories and pass them off as my own. I still get them mixed up sometimes. I'll think of something – like that picture of Audrey Hepburn – and smile. Then I'll remember that it isn't my memory to smile about.

I looked at the picture of Maya Angelou and wondered what it would have been like to have a mum like Eve. It was Olivia's mother who taught me how to plait my hair and took me to buy my first bra and I wonder sometimes if things would have been different – if *I*'d be different – if I'd had a mum of my own to do those things with. If I'd strung pearls around my neck and shuffled around in too-big heels when I was little, like other girls.

'How come you only have photos of you with Mike and Eve?' I asked, making sure I had my back to her so that she couldn't see me smiling as I looked at her notice board. 'What about your mum and dad? Your mates?'

But she didn't miss a beat. 'They were destroyed in the fire.'

When I turned to face her again, she was on the bed, painting her toenails.

'Why are you doing your nails? It's October.'

I showed off my new patent Doc Martens to prove the point, but as soon as I did, my heart dropped into my stomach. Teenage girls only paint their toenails in October if they know they're going to be seen. I imagined her and Sid on her bed, his mouth on her neck and her toes curling in the sheets and turned to face her chest of drawers again, picking up an eye shadow and staring at it until the writing on it lost focus.

I wanted to take something. Something of hers. I did that a lot as well, take things. Nothing big. A pair of earrings. A lip-gloss. A picture she'd torn from a magazine. Nothing she'd miss straight away. Once I took a necklace I'd lent her and as I went home with it in the pocket of my jeans, I imagined her tearing through her room looking for it.

The next day she was almost in tears when she apologised for losing it and I saw it then, the doubt in her eyes. What had happened to them – the necklace, the earrings, the lip-gloss, that picture of that dress? Had she really lost *all* of them? I knew then – I saw it – she was beginning to wonder if she was losing her mind and the satisfaction was overwhelming. I was dizzy with it, drunk on it for the rest of the day. I was unpicking her – slowly, slowly.

I wanted to take the cinema ticket, but when I saw the charcoal drawing on her desk, I waited until she wasn't looking and knocked it off so that it fell between the desk and the wall.

'I always paint my toenails,' she said suddenly. I tensed, sure that she'd seen me do it, but she hadn't even looked up.

'I'm kind of paranoid about it,' she said, leaning down to blow on her nails. 'Ever since I watched one of those American crime scene investigation shows. They found this girl's body in an alleyway but couldn't identify it so they thought she was homeless. Then the detective saw that her toenails were painted and realised that she had to belong to someone, so he looked into it and found her family and they gave her a proper funeral.'

She looked so serious that I had to laugh. 'What?' Something in me relaxed as I realised what she was saying. 'You paint your nails in case you're murdered?'

She thought about it for a moment, then frowned. 'Yeah. I suppose.'

'Who thinks like that?' I laughed again, so hard that she laughed too. And when I looked at her, sitting on the bed with her red toenails, I wished Uncle Alex was there to see her. To see what Dad had done to her, how scared she was that he'd find her.

The next morning at college, I had to keep pressing my lips together to hide my smile as I watched her ripping through her locker trying to find the charcoal drawing.

'Did you leave it at home?' Sid asked, fanning through one of her textbooks.

'It was on my desk last night. I saw it,' she said, her head in her locker. 'But when I went to get it this morning it was gone. I checked everywhere.'

'Maybe Mike ate it,' I suggested, but they ignored me.

She slammed her locker shut and stepped back. 'I have to go home and check again.'

'Now?' Sid checked his watch. 'We have English lit. You'll be marked absent.'

She shrugged and took her bag from him. 'I know, but I have art straight after and it's part of my coursework.'

'I'll go with you.'

I had been leaning against the lockers, picking at my already chipped nail varnish and stood up then. I adored Sid, but I wanted to punch him in the face sometimes.

Thankfully, Juliet looked equally mortified at the suggestion. 'What? No, Sid! It's not your fault I can't find it. Why should you be marked absent too?'

'Nance—' he started to say, but she stopped him with a kiss on the mouth.

'Go,' she said, pushing him towards the classroom. 'I'll be as quick as I can.'

I watched as she ran towards the lifts, her bag bouncing

against her hip, and when I turned round again, Sid looked unimpressed.

'Why are you looking so pleased with yourself?' he asked as we walked to class.

That was the first time I missed a step.

Friday night. Fish for dinner. The nurses let us watch a film in the TV Room earlier. It was shockingly bad; some PG-13 shit about an awkward brunette who defeats the mean girls with witty banter to get the cutest boy at school.

I think it was supposed to be inspirational, but Naomi and I just talked through it.

'What would you be doing tonight if you weren't here?' I asked her during the makeover montage. I wished I lived in America; all you need to do to overcome your demons is to get contact lenses and a blow dry.

'Shagging Tom,' she said with a filthy laugh.

I rolled my eyes. 'You're *so* rock and roll.'

'Don't hate on me because the boy I love wants to shag me, not my friend.'

I kicked her so hard she fell off the sofa.

'Juliet isn't my friend,' I reminded her as she climbed back up, but she grinned.

'That's worse.'

Actually, it is.

'So what would you be doing, then? Trying to get your leg over with Sid?'

I ignored her. 'All sorts. We never stayed in on a Friday night.'

'What did you do?'

'We went to a lot of gigs. Juliet's a proper hipster – she only liked bands that played tiny venues. As soon as everyone at college started talking about them, she moved on.' I rolled my eyes. 'Me and Sid didn't care; we'd listen to anything—'

'Me and Sid,' Naomi sang.

I glared at her. 'Hands up who's not helping.' Reta put her hand up and I rolled my eyes. 'Put your hand down, Reets.' When she did, I crossed my arms. 'We went to this wedding once. It was Sid's cousin's cousin, or something. I don't remember. It was at this rugby club in West Ham.'

'Classy.'

I had to laugh. She was right. The last wedding I went to was at Claridge's so I'd never been to a wedding with paper plates and a balloon arch before. I should have been horrified, I suppose, but as the *Daily Mail* once said about me: you can take the girl out of the council estate, but you can't take the council estate out of the girl, so I loved it. What's not to love about sausage rolls and cheese and pineapple? Food of the gods, that.

By nine o'clock the father of the bride was shirtless and everyone was dancing to 'Come on, Eileen'. Sid had lost his black suit jacket and was twirling one of the bridesmaids. She was clearly besotted with him, ignoring another bridesmaid who was not so patiently waiting her turn. Three year olds don't fuck about, though, so after a few minutes, dresses were tugged and hair was pulled. I was horrified, but Sid was unfazed, and just picked them both up and danced with them at the same time, one on each hip.

I nudged Juliet, but she was fiddling with her phone. 'Let's dance.'

She wrinkled her nose and continued tapping away.

The DJ must have been on my side because he put 'The Way You Look Tonight' on.

I jumped to my feet. 'We have to dance to this!'

She wrinkled her nose again. 'What? This is old people's music.'

I stared at her, horrified. 'It's *Sinatra*.'

She ignored me and continued sending a text, but before I could slap some sense into her, someone took my hand.

I looked up as Sid tugged me towards the dance floor. 'I'll dance with you, Ro.'

'Okay,' I breathed, so bewildered, I almost tripped over my own feet.

We found a gap between a gaggle of cackling aunts and a group of thirteen-year-old girls who were swishing around in their dresses. They blushed in unison as Sid approached.

'Nice dress, Bex,' he said with a grin, sweeping a hand through his hair.

I knew immediately which one he was talking to because the poor girl looked ready to collapse. Not that I was much cooler; as soon as Sid pulled me to him and put his hand on the small of my back, my cheeks started to burn, too.

That was the first time he touched me. Not play-punched me or grabbed my sleeve at a gig when he was trying to get my attention over the roar of the band, but really *touched* me. I could feel the heat of his hand through the silk of my dress and when he lifted his other to reach for mine, his fingers were rougher than I expected. I remember the shock I felt when the calluses on the tips of his fingers brushed against my own. Until then, all I could hear were the aunts cackling and the swish swish swish of petticoats and taffeta as the girls spun around next to us, but then I couldn't hear a thing my heart was beating so hard.

He must have felt the shock as well, because he smiled. 'You play the guitar, too.'

'What?'

'The guitar,' he said, running his thumb over the callus on my right index finger.

I had to gulp down a breath before I could speak. 'The cello.'

'The cello?'

'I'm no Rostropovich, but I almost played at the Royal Albert Hall once.'

'Really?' His eyes went from brown to black. 'Why didn't you?'

I thought about Dad, the trial, the newspapers and realised what I'd said.

'I—' started to say, as a voice in my head screamed at me to pull my hand away so he couldn't feel it shaking, but I couldn't let go. 'Something came up.'

When I turned my face away, he held my hand a little tighter, but he didn't push it.

We didn't speak again for the rest of the song. When 'Mack the Knife' came on, I waited for him to take a step back, but he didn't, he twirled me and I giggled. I giggled again as one of the page boys skidded past us on his knees. Sid laughed, too, and I'll never forget how it felt, how his whole body trembled. It made my heart throw itself against my ribs like a rubber ball. He must have felt it.

'Why the cello?' he asked, pulling me closer, so close that I could feel the chill of his belt buckle through my dress. He said it with a whisper, his breath warm against my ear, and it was enough to make one of the locks in me buckle and fall apart.

'My dad,' I whispered back. I lifted my eyelashes to look at him again. His eyes were still black. 'I wanted to learn how to play the guitar but he's kind of old fashioned. He left school at fourteen so he's obsessed with me getting a *good education*.'

'What's that, then?'

'Proper A levels like physics and economics.'

'Not art.' Sid grinned.

I shook my head with a small smile. 'Not art.'

'And no guitar.'

'When I told him I wanted to learn how to play the guitar, he bought me a cello.'

'But you're doing art now,' he whispered, looking at me like he was waiting for me to tell him about the epic battle I'd had with my dad, how I'd gone against him and won.

I looked over at Juliet. She was still fiddling with her phone. 'Yeah.'

'Hello,' a voice said, and I turned my head to find a woman about Eve's age – maybe a little younger – smiling at me.

'I thought I'd better introduce myself,' she said, shooting Sid a filthy look. 'Well, you're not going to do it, are you?'

He took a step back. 'Not now,' he said, lowering his voice.

But she didn't listen and put her hand on my shoulder. Her fingers were cold. 'Hello,' she said, stopping to kiss me on both cheeks. She smelt of cigarettes and hairspray. 'I'm Gina, Sid's mum.'

'Oh,' I gasped, blushing a little. 'Hello, Mrs King. It's a pleasure to meet you.'

She held up her glass of white wine. 'Lovely to meet you too, sweetheart.' She winked at me and, in that moment, she looked just like Sid. They had the same dark hair and eyes, the same honey-coloured skin. You could tell that, when she was my age, she was stunning. I imagined her at seventeen, her eyes thick with eyeliner, curls tumbling over her shoulders. I bet she could have broken a boy's heart with a wink.

But that day at the wedding she looked exhausted, the skin under her eyes dark with some misery that wasn't letting her sleep. Her make-up was smudged, her leopard-print dress too tight. She had a tattoo of a Chinese symbol on her left arm and it made me think of Olivia's sister. She'd got a similar tattoo on her hip while she was travelling through Asia. She thought it meant lady but later found out it meant whore and was thrilled. 'How apt!' she'd howled when she told Olivia and me, tipping her head back and slapping the table with her hand so hard that the salt and pepper shakers shivered.

'Are you having a good time? Decent spread,' Sid's mum said, nodding at the buffet table that had been all but picked clean. She looked unsteady on her heels as she lifted the glass of wine to her mouth. When I felt Sid tense next to me, I realised that she was drunk and I felt as if I should look away; he wouldn't want me to see her like this.

'He doesn't shut up about you,' she said after a long gulp. There was an edge to her voice. It wasn't a compliment.

'Mum—' Sid tried to interrupt, but she carried on with a wave of her hand.

'Nancy this and Nancy that.'

Nancy.

'I'm Rose,' I said, my voice shaking as I dug my heel into the dance floor hoping that a hole would open up and snatch me.

She looked confused. 'What?'

'Mum, come on,' Sid said tightly, reaching for her arm, but she pulled away.

'I'm not, Nancy, Mrs King. I'm Rose.'

She stared at me for a moment. 'Who?' She had to shout as

the DJ put 'Don't Stop Me Now' on and everyone on the dance floor cheered, doubling my humiliation.

'Rose,' I repeated, a little desperately. 'Rose Glass.'

I watched for a flicker of recognition, but there was nothing.

'Rose,' she said as though she was tasting it, rolling it around on her tongue. Then she sneered and swallowed another mouthful of wine. 'He's never mentioned you,' she said with a sharp smile, then waited, like a magician holding up a white rabbit, waiting for a reaction. But I didn't give her one; I just lifted my chin and smiled back.

I didn't realise until that moment that Sid was still holding my hand, but he squeezed it and I began shaking for another reason.

'I saw you dancing with Sid and assumed,' she continued, finishing her glass of wine with one last gulp. 'Which one is Nancy, then? The half-caste one?'

'Mum!' Sid barked.

'What?' she sneered. 'Am I not supposed to say that?'

Sid glared at her and she rolled her eyes. 'What? People call us Guidos.'

'When has *anyone* called you a Guido?'

She lifted her chin. 'I'm just saying: they're so sensitive.'

'Mum—'

'Alright, alright. I'm going.' She held her hands up. 'I'll stop embarrassing you.'

Sid and I watched her stumble over to the bar with her empty wine glass and when she was out of sight, he turned to me.

'I'm sorry about that,' he started to say, but I stopped him.

'It's okay.' I shook my head.

'Yeah, but she isn't always—'

'I know.'

'I wish you'd met her when—'

'Don't, Sid. Please don't apologise.'

I squeezed his hand again and he squeezed it back and you know what? I don't care. Say what you like at me. Yes, I'm mad. Yes, what I did was awful, but I made him feel better that day. I know I did. Because I was the only person in the room who knew how he felt. Who knew what it was like to be ashamed of someone you love.

Doctor Gilyard thinks I didn't do anything to Juliet, that I *couldn't* do anything, but that isn't true. I *wanted* to do stuff. I wanted to ruin everything she had, to carve my name across it all, but I had to be careful. I couldn't do anything to scare her, anything she'd tell Mike and Eve about, because the Witness Protection team would move her and I might never find her again.

That's why I followed her when I first found her. I got to know her routine, what books she liked, what films she'd seen. It was those little things that made her trust me, that made us friends. Like the first time we went to the canteen at college and I ordered a green tea because I knew she'd get one, too. If I hadn't done that, we would never have been friends and if we weren't friends, she wouldn't have invited be back to her house and as soon as she did that, I could do other stuff. Nothing big. I took things. Moved things. Tore pages out of her notebook.

I suppose you think that's nothing. After what you've read in the papers, you were expecting something awful, blood even, a few broken bones. But that would have been too easy. It was the little things, I knew, that would unpick her – slowly, slowly. Like when she bought that book from the stall under Waterloo Bridge. When she put it on the shelf in her bedroom, I waited for her to go downstairs and I took it. She asked me if I'd seen it a couple of days later, if she'd left it in one of my bags.

I'd frowned. 'You didn't go to that stall with me. Sure it wasn't with Sid?'

She'd wavered then, her forehead creasing. I wonder if she'd asked herself if someone had been in her room, if Mike had rearranged her CDs or Eve had borrowed her yellow scarf.

She must have thought she was going mad.

I called her Juliet once. I remember the thrill of it – even now, as I'm writing this – how it made my heart flutter. We were at a pub in Camden. Sid and I were playing darts and he was apologising to everyone standing within ten feet of the board when I threw a dart clear across the pub. It almost hit an old boy who was sitting at the bar reading a copy of the *Mirror*. He looked unamused, so Sid offered to retrieve it. Juliet was in the loo at the time so when she returned to find him gone, she looked bewildered.

'Oh, Juliet,' I said with a sigh, letting the name hang in the air between us for too long before I tilted my head. 'Missing your Romeo?'

She tried to smile, but I saw.

I saw.

The next day I sent her flowers – a bunch of pink roses. It was her birthday; not Nancy's birthday, Juliet's birthday. 2 October. She told me once that her parents used to buy her a bunch every year for her birthday, I knew she meant her father did, so you should have seen her face when Mike walked into her room with them. I'd asked her what was wrong as she tore through the bouquet looking for a card, spilling pink petals across her bed.

'Nothing,' she'd said, out of breath. 'Nothing.'

Doctor Gilyard asked me once if I got any pleasure out of being Rose Glass. How could I not enjoy that? Enjoy asking Juliet question after question; if she missed her parents, how she was related to Eve, why she didn't see the friends from her old school any more. I'd ask and ask and ask until she began fidgeting and changed the subject with a brave smile.

But the first time I saw her cry wasn't as satisfying as I thought it would be.

I suppose if I wanted to play the villain here – be the gangster's daughter – I wouldn't admit that. I'd say that I'd enjoyed seeing her cry, that it had renewed my conviction. But it didn't.

It was a Sunday. I always had lunch at her house on a Sunday, but when Mike answered the door, he looked surprised to see me. When he let me in, the kitchen didn't smell of anything, either. There was nothing in the oven, no smell of coconut. Eve's mother wasn't there, fussing over the roast potatoes and adding more salt to the gravy. Eve was sitting at the table, staring at a mug of tea she obviously had no intention of drinking. When she looked up at me, I could see that she'd been crying.

'What's wrong?' I asked, my heart dropping to my feet.

For a moment, I thought that was it, the blade had dropped and they knew. I half expected Mike to grab me by the arm and shake me, tell me that he knew who I was.

But he just sighed. 'It's nothing.'

'It's not nothing,' Eve snapped.

My cheeks burned, even though it wasn't aimed at me. When her gaze found mine across the kitchen, I had to tell myself not to run.

'Mike and I had a row this morning,' she told me. My shoulders fell.

'If your mother hadn't—' he interrupted.

She glared at him, her hands clenching into fists on the table. 'Can we not?'

He glared back at her and it seemed to go on for ever before he huffed and marched over to the kettle. Eve sighed to herself and rubbed her forehead with her hand as he began banging around, getting a mug out of the cupboard and slamming it down so hard on the counter, I don't know how it didn't break.

Then she looked up at me again. She looked exhausted. If Juliet had been there, she'd have known what to do. She would've leaned down and hugged her, told her that everything was going to be okay. But I just looked at her as I tugged on a loose button on my jacket.

'We had a row.' Eve sighed again. 'Nancy overheard. She got

upset and ran off. We don't know where she is and she won't answer her phone.'

I looked over at Mike. He still had his back to us and my nerves felt as tight as ropes as I watched him make me a cup of tea I didn't even want. I'd never seen him like that before – I'd never seen either of them anything other than sparklingly happy – so I could see why Juliet was so freaked out. I was freaked out, too.

I should have been thrilled, I suppose, that Juliet was upset, that there was a crack in her perfect little life. But then I thought about her, sobbing into Sid's chest while he stroked her hair, and something in me hardened.

'I'll find her,' I said with a sigh.

Eve's face brightened. 'You will? Oh, thank you, Rose.'

When I looked at Mike, I saw the muscles in his back relax through his T-shirt.

'Thanks, Ro,' he said, turning to face me again.

'Don't worry,' I told them both with a small smile, heading out of the kitchen.

As soon as I got outside, I called Juliet. She answered, which I wasn't expecting.

'You alright, Nance?'

'Have you been to the house?' she asked. She always called it the house, never home.

'Yeah. What happened?'

I heard her sniff. 'They had an argument. It was awful, Rose.'

'What about?'

147

'I don't know. I was upstairs and I heard Mike screaming. Literally screaming, Rose.' She stopped to suck in a shaky breath. It sounded like something in her was broken. 'I had no idea he had such a filthy temper. I thought he was going to hit her.'

Something in me tightened and I laughed. 'He wouldn't.'

'You should have heard him, Rose.'

'Where are you? Are you with Sid?'

'No. I'm on my own.'

I wasn't expecting that, either. 'What? Why didn't you call him?'

'I'm a mess,' she said with another sniff. 'I don't want him to see me like this.'

I should have respected her for that, for not running to him sobbing, begging to be rescued, like most girls would have. But really, it made me hate her more, because she had him but she didn't think she needed him.

'Where are you?'

'At the bookshop.'

When I got there, I found her sitting on the floor of the poetry section. A friend would have brought her a green tea, but I just sat next to her.

'Hey,' she said when she saw me. She seemed relieved and I tensed, half expecting her to start slobbering all over me. I don't do well with slobber. Mercifully, she didn't move.

I nodded at the book she was holding. 'What you reading?'

She closed it and showed me the cover. *To Kill a Mockingbird*.

'Atticus is about to shoot the dog,' she said. The *so maybe everything will be okay* floated unsaid between us.

We sat there for a minute or two, her staring at the red cartoon bird on the cover and me staring at her staring at the red cartoon bird on the cover.

Some girls are good at this. Juliet is. If we're out, at a gig or in the pub, and she goes missing, Sid sends me to the toilets to look for her. She's almost always there, sitting on the edge of the sink consoling a hysterical girl whose boyfriend has just got off with someone else. It's sort of amazing, how she can talk to anyone. I don't know how she does it, but she always knows what to say, knows the right way to stroke someone's hair so it isn't creepy. When to speak, when to listen. The truth is, Juliet is actually really sweet. So sweet that I wanted to break her open sometimes, find that bad bone.

I know she has one.

'You alright?' I said eventually.

She shook her head and sniffed. 'Not really.'

I began tugging on the loose button on my jacket again. 'Was it that bad?'

She looked up at me then. The skin under her eyes was bruised with mascara but she didn't look ugly, she looked vulnerable. Even when she was broken, she was beautiful.

'You know when you think everything is perfect,' she said, lowering her voice as though she was telling me a secret, 'then you find out it's not?'

I thought about Dad and I almost laughed. I used to want things, you know, before then, before her. I wanted to live in

Paris and play my cello on street corners for spare change and applause. I can't imagine doing any of that now.

I tried to smile. I wonder if she could see it – the bitterness – haemorrhaging out of me, bleeding through my pores. 'Yeah.'

'It kind of breaks your heart, doesn't it?'

I nodded and tugged on the loose button so hard, the last thread gave way. 'Life is never what you think it is, Nancy. What you need it to be.'

I suppose I could have said something more comforting, but I wasn't trying to comfort her.

She looked at me and I was sure she was about to start crying again, but she just smiled. 'Thank you.'

I frowned at her. 'For what?'

'For never lying to me.'

I nodded and it was one of those perfect, perfect moments. I had to look down at the button in my hand in case she saw my eyes light up. 'Everybody lies, Nance.'

'At least you tell the right ones, Rose.'

I know I said I had to be careful, that I couldn't go too far, but I did once. I didn't think I was ashamed of anything I did to her, but I guess I'm ashamed of that because I didn't write it down earlier. Some part of me mustn't want it to committed to paper forever, but you should know, in case you think I lost my nerve, that I had my head turned by a pretty boy.

You should know what I am capable of.

Juliet had a photograph. She didn't show it to me, I found it, between the pages of a book I'd taken from her room. I'd had the book for weeks. My intentions only strayed as far as taking it, I had no purpose for it after that, so it had languished at the bottom of my bag until a particularly restless night when I went in search of something to read. I can't even remember what book it was now, I just remember how my heart stopped, then restarted at double speed as the photograph fell out and landed on the floor by my feet.

I picked it up, turned it over and there they were: Juliet, her mother and father. I didn't know what to do; I felt like an old lady on *Antiques Roadshow* who'd found a priceless brooch at the bottom of her jewellery box. So I just stared at it.

Juliet was tiny in it – three, maybe four – with the same big eyes and wild curls. It was her birthday, I guess, she was wearing a green dress not unlike one I had when I was that age, except that mine had a ribbon around the waist and a pink silk rose. She was laughing – dancing, I think – and her mum and dad were clapping. Her dad looked younger, but just as I remember him. I'd never seen her mum before, though. She was thin, too thin, the veins in her hands as thick as ropes. Her head was wrapped in a brightly coloured scarf and I realised that it must have been the last photograph of the three of them.

I don't know how Juliet had it. Maybe she had it that night – the night she stabbed Dad. Maybe she carried it everywhere with her, tucked into some secret pocket in her purse. Or maybe she begged one of the Witness Protection team to go back to the house and get it.

Either way, it had survived, and I had it.

The shock dissolved and I reached into my bag, my fingers fumbling through the empty fag packets and balled-up tissues for my neon-pink lighter. As soon as the flame touched the corner of the photo, it caught and began to curl. The flame was orange,

I remember, bright orange, and I was rapt as I watched it devour the photo in one hot gulp.

When the flames reached my fingers, I ran into the bathroom and dropped it into the sink. Of all the things that come back at me at night, it's the image of that burnt photograph in the sink. If I closed my eyes right now, I'd see it. I wonder sometimes, when I think of her, of what I did, if that's what my heart looks like, if it's thin and burnt and black.

Val's back. I walked into the TV Room after breakfast, and there she was, staring at the telly like she never left.

'How come she's back?' I asked Doctor Gilyard when she asked me how I was.

'Valerie was readmitted this morning.'

'Why? I thought she got a suspended sentence?'

'She did.'

'So how come she's back? Her bloody chair's still warm.'

Doctor Gilyard opened her notebook. 'Why is it upsetting you, Emily?'

'I'm not upset,' I said, but it sounded much harder than I intended, like a door slamming shut. 'I thought she was better, that's why they let her go home.'

'What do you mean by better?'

'Better. You know, *better*. Un-mad. I thought you'd fixed her.'

'Is that what you think I do, Emily, fix people?'

I couldn't sit still. My skin was itching, my blood fizzing. 'What do you do, then?' I asked, pulling at the loose thread under my chair. 'Why aren't you trying to help her?'

'I am, Emily.'

'You're not! She's still here, staring at the television!' I sat forward and pointed at the door to her office. 'Do something. Give her something.'

Doctor Gilyard thought about it for a moment, then took off her glasses. 'This is a prison, Emily, not a hospital.'

I felt it like a punch.

When I looked away, she carried on. 'Do you need to be fixed, Emily?'

I got up and walked over to the window. It was raining so I couldn't see anything. Not that there was much to see; just walls and fences topped with razor wire. But if you tilt your head, you can see the sky. Just a piece. A strip. It's usually the only blue thing you can see but today it was grey. Everything was grey; the sky, the walls, the razor wire. Grey, grey, grey.

'Naomi says Val's mum died when she was little.' I knew Doctor Gilyard wouldn't respond, but I still felt a small sag of disappointment when she didn't. 'That was ages ago. Shouldn't she be over it by now?'

'Grief is tenacious, Emily.'

'Naomi says she shoplifted something to get back in here.' I traced the edge of the window frame with my finger. 'Why would anyone want to do that? Why would you want to come back here?'

'Why do you think someone would want to do that, Emily?'

I stared at the rain for a moment or two, watching the fat drops chase one another down the other side of the window.

'Her life must be pretty shit if she'd rather be here.'

Doctor Gilyard was quiet for a long time, then she said: 'When people are here for a long time, Emily, they find it hard to adjust to living in the outside world again. They get home and realise that home isn't what it was before they left, that home isn't *where* it was before they left.'

My chest felt so tight then that I crossed my arms as though that would relieve it. It didn't and the more I thought about Val, the more it hurt. She's seventeen, her life is supposed to stretch out in front of her like a red carpet. It shouldn't be a chair, here, surrounded by girls who don't even realise she's there. This can't be it; there has to be somewhere else, some other place where she's missed, where someone is waiting for her.

'They say home isn't where you live,' I said, 'but where you're understood.'

I heard Doctor Gilyard shift in her chair, heard the scrape of her heel on the lino as she crossed her legs, and I held my breath.

'Perhaps she needs to find somewhere she'll be understood, Emily.'

I hate this. This is why I don't tell Doctor Gilyard things. It's three in the morning and I'm sitting in the bath writing this because I'm not allowed to have the light on in my room. I lied and told the nurse I couldn't sleep because I had to write something for Doctor Gilyard – which is sort of true – so she said that I could sit here as long as I don't lock the door.

I'm so tired that I can't read my own handwriting. I'll probably read this back tomorrow and it'll be gibberish, but right now it makes perfect sense.

Today, in my session with Doctor Gilyard, after we talked about Val, she returned a book to me.

'Where did you find this? I thought I'd lost it,' I asked with a frown.

'In the TV Room.'

'I must have left it in there yesterday.'

'Do you do that a lot?'

'Do what?' I asked, running a finger over the cover.

'Lose things?'

I chuckled to myself. I lose something about once a week. Even here; I'll put a mug of tea down somewhere or leave my shoes under a chair.

'Uncle Alex says I'm scatty.'

'Does it bother you? Losing things?'

'I'm always losing stuff. It's never bothered me, even when I was little.'

'Why not?'

I thought about that time I left Henry Bear on the tube. His fur was worn away and the red ribbon around his neck was frayed, so Dad was bewildered when I sobbed and sobbed.

'Don't be silly, little one,' he'd said, picking me up and kissing me between the eyebrows. 'It's just a teddy.'

The next day he came home with a bigger one.

'It was no loss, I suppose,' I told Doctor Gilyard with a shrug.

She nodded and wrote that down. 'Do you think he was overcompensating?'

'For what?'

'For your mother? For what he did for a living?'

My stomach turned inside out and I looked away. 'I'm not spoilt,' I told her.

But I am. Whatever I asked for, I got. Especially when I went to St Jude's; he wanted so much for me to fit in that he made sure I had everything the other girls had. If Olivia got a new laptop, I got a better one. If she got a Mulberry satchel, I got one in every colour.

'I didn't say that you were spoilt, Emily.'

'I've never thrown a tantrum in my life.'

'You haven't needed to.'

I turned to look at her again. 'What's that supposed to mean?'

'It means that your father would have done *anything* to make you happy.'

I laughed at her, but I've been thinking about it all day. I can't stop thinking about. That's why I'm sitting here now, shivering in this stainless-steel bathtub. Dad didn't care how he earned his money and he passed that on to me, didn't he? I was raised with no concept of money, of the value of anything. Why else would I have a hundred quid in my purse and nick a nail varnish from Boots because I couldn't be arsed to queue up and pay for it?

As I'm writing this, I'm thinking about a night in October when I couldn't find my purse. I was more concerned about not having milk for a cup of tea when I got home as I stood in the petrol station, rooting through my bag. I thought it was because I was tired, but, thanks to Doctor Gilyard, now I'm not so sure.

'It's here,' I told the bored-looking bloke behind the till as I tipped the contents of my bag on to the counter. My keys clattered hysterically and my tube of lip-gloss rolled towards him.

He caught it before it rolled off the counter. 'I bought a round earlier so I must have it.'

He looked at me as if to say, *Okay, love.* I couldn't blame him; I must have looked a right state in the harsh light of the petrol station with my tangled red hair and ruined make-up. I'd just been to a gig with Sid and Juliet so I was a sweaty mess. I could feel my T-shirt sticking to my back. He probably thought I was a drug addict.

Who else buys a pile of chocolate bars and a pint of milk at midnight?

'I got it,' I heard someone say.

I looked up as Mike handed the bloke his credit card. 'That better not be your dinner, young lady,' he added with mock disdain, nodding at all the chocolate.

I smiled sweetly. 'I was studying so hard that I didn't have time for dinner.'

'You mean the crisps you had at the pub before the gig weren't enough?'

I giggled and he shook his head with a tut.

'Anything else?' the bloke behind the counter asked flatly. The look he gave us said, *Please go away now.*

Mike nodded out the window towards his car. 'Pump number four.' Then he turned to me again. 'What are you doing, hanging around petrol stations at midnight?'

'I needed milk. And cigarettes.' I fluttered my eyelashes at him.

He rolled his eyes. 'And twenty Marlboro Lights, mate.'

When I grinned at Mike, I imagined saying something like that to Dad and couldn't. He'd have an aneurysm.

'So how were The Ruby Bullets?' he asked as he took back his card.

I laughed. 'What do you know about The Ruby Bullets?'

'I'm still with it.'

'People who're with it don't say they're with it,' I told him, as I put everything back in my bag and followed him out of the petrol station.

'Nance's been playing their album all week. They're alright.' He nudged me with his hip and I nudged him back with a girly giggle. 'The riff from that song about the girl from Shoreditch totally rips off "I Fought the Law", though.'

I gasped. 'That's what I said. But Nance thinks they're *so original*.'

'What do you know about The Clash?'

'I'm with it.'

'People who're with it don't say they're with it, Ro.'

He nudged me with his hip but before I could nudge him back, I stopped to stare as a police car pulled on to the forecourt. My lungs seemed to seize up as I watched the officer get out. She stopped to nod at Mike and there was an endless moment where I was sure he was going to talk to her, but, mercifully, he just nodded back.

'Come on. I'll give you a lift,' he said, but I shook my head. I never let anyone near my flat. As comfortable as I felt as Rose Glass, possessions don't lie – what if the bedroom I was saying was my mum's didn't look slept in, or someone noticed that there were no photos on the walls? Juliet asked all the time, but I always had an excuse; Mum had a migraine or there was no food in so we might as well go out to eat.

'It's alright. I only live down the road,' I told Mike, but he ignored me and opened the passenger door to his car.

'I'm not letting you walk down Upper Street by yourself at midnight.'

It wasn't a discussion so I got in. As soon as I did, I inhaled the fake smell of vanilla and realised that I reeked of cigarettes and beer. It wasn't pleasant; I smelt like a pub carpet. I wanted to take the freshener hanging from the rear-view mirror and rub it all over me.

'Seat belt,' he muttered, climbing in next to me.

I rolled my eyes. 'Yes, Dad.'

'Jesus,' he groaned. 'Don't call me that!'

'Do you miss it?' I asked as I watched the police officer at the till, paying for a can of Red Bull. I don't know why. I didn't think. Looking back on it now, I must have enjoyed it, the thrill, the farce. If I told Doctor Gilyard, she'd ask me if I wanted to get caught.

'Miss what? The police?' Mike thought about it for a moment, then nodded.

'So why'd you leave?'

'After I got shot, Eve said she couldn't do it any more.'

I turned to blink at him. 'You were shot?'

'Yeah. Didn't you know?'

'No! When?'

'About three years ago. Here.' He took my hand and put it under the neck of his jumper. The muscles in my arm tensed as my fingers brushed over his warm skin, but I didn't pull my hand away. I should have, but I didn't, I let him move my hand to his right shoulder.

'Oh!' I gasped, yanking my hand away as I felt a sudden pucker in his skin.

He laughed as I stared at him, my fingers still trembling.

'Did it hurt?'

He nodded. 'I was in hospital for *weeks*. But when I was discharged, I promised Eve I wouldn't put her through that again.' He smiled when he said it, but I remember it now, the trace of regret in his voice, just for a second.

'So is that why you work with young offenders now?'

He nodded.

'Do you enjoy it?'

'Ask me again tomorrow,' he sighed, starting the car.

As soon as he did, I heard the hum of a cello and my heart fluttered. 'Bach.'

'The Clash? Bach?' He winked. 'You're a girl after my own heart, Rose Glass.'

I giggled as we pulled on to Upper Street. 'Why are you listening to Bach?'

'After the day I've had, I need a bit of Bach.'

'Why? What happened?'

'I've been at the police station most of today.'

For an awful moment, I thought I was going to throw up. *He knows*, a voice in my head began to scream. *He knows who you are. That's why he insisted on giving you a lift, why he showed up from nowhere.* He didn't, of course. But that happened a lot then; someone would say something, however benign, and I was sure they knew.

It was like this blade, swinging over my head. It had to fall eventually.

'How come?' I asked carefully.

'One of the kids I'm working with got in a fight.'

My lungs finally relaxed. 'Why?'

He was quiet for a moment too long as he stared out at the road. I'd never seen him look so sad and I suppose most people would have tried to console him, would have told him it'd be alright, but what did I know?

'I dunno,' he said, finally. 'I mean, I get it. I get that this other kid was chatting shit, trying to wind him up, and he lost his temper, but I don't *understand* it. I work with kids like that all the time, kids who've had horrible upbringings and don't know up from down, let alone right from wrong, but,' he stopped to shake his head, 'I'll never understand how you can stick a knife in someone. Never.'

Back then I didn't, either.

I thought of Dad and turned to look out the window at the shuttered-up shops on Upper Street. I wanted to tell Mike to ask Juliet; she knew.

'What's going to happen to him? Will he go to prison?'

He shrugged. 'He's only fifteen and it's his first offence. He'll probably get a supervision order for wounding with intent.'

Like Juliet.

'What about his parents?' I asked when we stopped at the traffic lights.

'He doesn't know who his dad is and I'm trying to find his mum.'

'Can you do that if you don't work for the police any more?' I asked, and I don't know how I said it; I couldn't breathe.

'You can find almost anyone if you know where to look for them.'

'What do you mean?'

'It isn't like it used to be, Ro. The Internet has changed everything. Google is a powerful thing if you know what to do with it.'

'So, that's all you need to do, look on the Internet?'

When he nodded, I thought about Mum and my heart started to throb.

In another life, I might have asked him to help me find her.

'You alright?' he asked as we pulled up outside my mansion block. I didn't think he knew where I lived, but I didn't dare ask; I just wanted to get out of the car.

'Yeah. I'm just knackered. I'd better go.'

When I turned to open the car door, he put his hand on my knee to stop me. My whole body tensed. It just tensed again as I thought about it. I can still feel the weight of his hand, the heat of it through my jeans.

This is what I hate. All these pieces. I didn't think they meant anything, but Doctor Gilyard is putting them together. She sees something I didn't.

I must look exhausted because no one lectured me about not eating my breakfast this morning. Even Naomi ate in silence as I opened packet after packet of sugar and poured them onto the table in front of us.

Doctor Gilyard, however, took this as a sign of weakness and went straight for the jugular. 'Let's talk about your mother.'

'Jesus fucking Christ,' I muttered, rubbing my eyelids with my fingers. 'You're like one of those games at the fairground where that rat pops up—'

'Mole,' she corrected.

'Yeah, that mole, rat, whatever. And you have to whack it with the sledgehammer.'

'Are you saying I'm a rat?'

'I'm saying I need a sledgehammer.'

I heard her writing. 'Why don't you want to talk about your mother?'

'I don't want to talk about anything,' I said with a long yawn. 'I think it's time to move on to the interpretive dance portion of these sessions.'

She ignored me. 'You haven't mentioned her once.'

I got up and walked over to the window. There was a pigeon on the windowsill strutting back and forth as if to say, LOOK AT ME. LOOK AT ME. I'M FREE.

'Free?' I wanted to tell it. 'You can go anywhere in the world and you came here. Idiot.' But I didn't, because if I start talking to pigeons, Doctor G will full on McMurphy me. So I just slapped the glass and smiled as it jumped, then flew away.

'Why don't we start with something small? What's your first memory of her?'

'I don't have any memories of her,' I said, pressing my finger against the glass and watching the fingerprint appear then disappear like a ghost.

'Why not?'

'I don't remember her.'

'You don't remember anything?'

It's true, I don't remember anything. I was tiny when she left and when she did, Dad got rid of every trace of her. There were no photos, no mementos. He wouldn't even say her name. It was like she never existed. All I remember is her being there, then she wasn't. There were no raised voices, no slammed doors. There was no *incident* before she left; she didn't forget me at the supermarket one day or lock herself in the bathroom.

But there are pieces, tiny pieces. The colour of hair, the same as mine, yellow as a freshly baked cake. Her laugh, loud and bright. Her gold rings, one on every finger. Her bracelets that I used to tug when I wanted her attention. And she would sing this song, every time it came on the radio, something about a train, leaving on a train. It was years before I realised it was 'Midnight Train to Georgia'. The first time I heard it on the radio I cried for hours. *I got to go. I got to go. I got to go.* I cried so much Dad kept coming into my room to ask me what was wrong. I had to tell him that I'd had a row with Olivia.

'Emily,' Doctor Gilyard said, but I didn't turn around, I just stared out the window and thought about the jumper I'd found, the one in Dad's wardrobe.

I used to look through his wardrobes a lot when I was little, hunting for some clue about where Mum was, some sign that she might come back.

One summer, I was so determined to find something that I looked every day. Dad was always at work so I did it while the housekeeper was downstairs because she couldn't hear me rooting around over the wheeze of the vacuum cleaner. I had to be careful because Dad's wardrobes were so neat. Even at twelve, I knew to line the coat hangers up and smooth down his ties if I disturbed them. I eventually learned what went where so I could put everything back. I made sure that the toes of his shoes were facing out and his heavy bottles of cologne were in a straight line on the bathroom counter.

But I found nothing.

That's the trouble with being neat, you can see *everything*. Dad's bedroom, much like Doctor Gilyard's office, was stripped clean. Everything he owned was immaculate; his bed linen looked new, the soap by the sink in his bathroom untouched. There was a wardrobe for everything; one for shirts, one for suits, one for what he wore at the weekend. Everything had its place. There was nowhere to hide anything. Or so I thought; I guess I should have known then just how adept he was at hiding things, the moment I saw the shirt box.

It was on the top shelf of one of his wardrobes so I probably wouldn't have noticed it if I wasn't so desperate to find something. But there it was, the one white box in a neat row of grey ones. And I knew. As soon as I saw it, I knew.

I was so excited that I didn't care if the housekeeper heard me drag Dad's favourite Eames chair across the bedroom. It was far too expensive to stand on, but I didn't care about that, either, I just had to look in that box.

I opened it and tore past the tissue paper with Christmas morning impatience and there it was: the jumper. It was Mum's, I knew it was before I even touched it, before I even pressed my nose to it and inhaled the smell of her: washing powder and white musk.

At last, something of hers, some evidence that she existed. Every day after that, I went into Dad's room and smelt it. I memorised the weave of it, learned the colour. (Pink. The colour of the strawberry Quality Streets no one ever eats.) But each time I opened the box, a bit more of her scent escaped until, eventually, it was all gone. I had taken it all, drained it. Then it smelt of nothing, just wool, and it broke my heart.

That's why I have to be careful now, why I hold on to everything, in case that happens again. I guess that's why Dad tucked that jumper into that shirt box and put it on that out-of-reach shelf. I understand now. So when I told Doctor Gilyard that I didn't remember anything, what I meant was, *of course I do, but you can't have it.*

I'm on nicotine smack down again.

It's not my fault, it's this place, it's ridiculous. It's a young offender's institution, but they had us decorating cupcakes in art therapy this morning like we're children. Aren't we supposed to be shanking one another and touching each other inappropriately in the shower? I'm eighteen. I don't *decorate cupcakes*. I smoke cigarettes and drink vodka and kiss boys without knowing their names. So I decorated mine with a variety of swear words, which isn't the most mature response, I know, but I almost wet myself laughing when the nurse changed one of them to DOCTOR GILYARD LOVES DICKENS.

Naomi took pity on me and let me share her cigarette after dinner in exchange for another story about Rose. I knew she just wanted to mock me mercilessly about Sid, but I didn't care; I needed a cigarette. So I told her about last Halloween.

The girls at St Jude's seemed to stumble from one Martini melodrama to the next, so when it comes to mid-party break-ups, I've seen it all. Girls slapping girls. Boys slapping boys. I even watched someone go at a vintage Aston Martin with a cricket bat once.

Dad would have cried.

I honestly thought it was just them, that as soon as you mixed all of that privilege with lashings of Veuve Clicquot and a handful of hormones, they lost their minds. But the parties in London were no different. Yeah, the houses were smaller and we drank warm cans of cider instead of shots of Patron, but when it comes to drama, we're all created equal.

'Give me that,' I heard someone shout at Simone Campbell's Halloween party. I was dancing with Juliet at the time and looked up as a boy barged the DJ out of the way.

'Listen up, yeah!' he shouted.

The music stopped so abruptly that everyone in the living room turned to look at him. It was a strange scene; Simone hadn't insisted that any of us dress up, so the crowd was an odd mix of boys in their Saturday Best dancing with girls dressed as sexy witches.

'You heard of the Whore of Babylon, yeah?' he asked, and we all looked at each other, completely bewildered. Conversations stopped mid-sentence. Marilyn Monroe and Elvis stopped kissing. I shrugged at Juliet. She shrugged back.

When he didn't get a response, he grabbed the mic from the DJ and asked us again.

'Yeah?' I heard someone shout back.

The boy nodded slowly and raised his hand as though he was preaching. 'Yeah? Well, Ashley Hensman is the Whore of Basildon!'

I had no idea who Ashley Hensman was, but I gasped. So did Juliet. We gasped again when we saw a flutter of movement in the corner of the living room. A girl appeared from nowhere, rising above the cluster of heads as though she was floating. She was dressed as an angel, which made the scene even more surreal.

'You're a prick, Jason!' she shouted, pointing at him across the cluttered living room.

'And you're a whore!' he reiterated, in case he was being too subtle with the Whore of Basildon thing.

There were more gasps as everyone charged into the living room to find out what was going on. A girl in a purple wig almost knocked me off my feet as she pushed past Juliet and me to get a better look. I shouted after her, but I was interrupted by Ashley who began to tell us – in full, *breathtaking* detail – just how inept Jason was in bed. (I won't repeat what she said because Jason has been humiliated enough, but let's just say that it was enough to make me spill my drink over my shoes.)

Everyone in the house seemed to hold their breath as we waited for Jason to retaliate, but when he dropped the mic and stormed out, there was a collective groan.

'We're disappointed now, but if he's gone to get a gun,' I said with a sigh, then looked down at my wet shoes, 'I need another drink.'

Juliet leaned closer as the music started again. 'Can you get me one too, please?'

'What do you want?'

'Anything.'

Thanks to the drama, the living room was full so it was an effort just to get to the door. I stepped on people's toes and knocked a row of beer cans off the sideboard as I slid past Marilyn and Elvis who had started kissing again with such abandon that I had to look away.

In my haste to avoid them, I walked straight into someone wearing a Scream mask. He raised his arms and I jumped back into a group of girls from my art class who cheered when he pretended to kiss me.

When he let me go I staggered into the hallway giggling, only to be confronted by a guy in a Ghostbusters uniform who charged towards me holding a water gun.

'Who you gonna call?' he asked with a filthy smirk.

I nodded at the water gun. 'You're the one who's going to need to call someone if you spray me with that.'

'It's got vodka in it. Open up, darling!'

'Vodka?' a girl in a red dress said, turning away from her conversation to eye the water gun with a wide smile. 'What flavour?'

'Roofie, probably,' I muttered. But she ignored me and I retreated down the hallway in disgust as she tipped her head back and opened her mouth.

The hallway was just as busy as the living room and the music was louder, somehow. I could feel the bass line everywhere; in my bones, in my teeth. I even felt it when I reached out for the radiator to steady myself as I almost stepped on an empty sambuca bottle, this *buzz*, deep, deep in the metal, as though the radiator was alive. That's how the whole house felt – alive. The curtains fluttered and the framed photos of Simone and her brothers rattled against the walls. Even the floorboards shuddered beneath my feet as I stumbled towards the kitchen door, spilling what was left of my cider as I did.

When I finally got there, I half walked, half fell in to find Sid on the other side of the kitchen, sitting on the worktop, talking to a group of lads. I didn't know he was there, so my heart started to beat too hard. He smiled when he saw me and I smiled back, but when he went back to his conversation, I suddenly felt very alone. I didn't know why; I could have gone into the living room and danced with Juliet until the booze ran out or the neighbours called the police, whichever came first. And in that moment it hit me – it *came at me*, actually, like a rabid dog – why I was there. It wasn't to dance with Juliet or to be friends with Sid. So I staggered back, the can of cider falling from my hand. I didn't hear it hit the floor as I pushed my way back out of the kitchen. I don't even remember hearing the music, just this voice in my head saying, *What are you doing? What are you doing?*

I needed to get out, but a crowd had gathered by the front door as Jason returned, not with a gun, fortunately, but he'd found his second wind and was roaring at Ashley, so I went upstairs. All the doors were locked expect for a tiny room next to the bathroom. It was more of a cupboard than a room, but compared to the rest of the house, it smelt so fresh, so *clean*, like freshly washed towels and baby powder. Apart from the futon tucked into the corner, the room was cluttered with boxes. They weren't sealed so I peered into one. They seemed to be full of the things Simone didn't want broken; gold-edged plates and hastily wrapped figurines. I realised that there had to be a decent bottle of booze in one of them and after a few minutes of rummaging around, I found a bottle of red wine.

'You found the good stuff,' someone said as I pulled it out of the box.

I looked up as a boy with dirty blond hair swept into the room and closed the door behind him. I recognised him, but I didn't know his name. Danny something, I think. We had sociology together. He sat in front of Sid.

He took the bottle of wine from me and inspected the label. 'Rioja,' he said with a frown. Except he pronounced it Ri-oh-ja.

'Ri-ock-a,' I corrected, taking it back. 'You can't have it if you can't pronounce it.'

I unscrewed the lid and swigged some. It was awful – *cheap* – but just what I needed.

'Please?' he said with a laugh as I winced, and when he did, I noticed that he had the same colour eyes as Mike, that impossible *blue* blue. Swimming-pool blue. It didn't do anything for me, but if Olivia had been there, she would have licked his face. I don't even know why I thought of her then. I shouldn't have. Say what you like about me, but as soon as Dad was arrested she walked away from me without so much as a glance over her shoulder.

Even with my black heart and rotten bones, I could never do that to someone.

I held the bottle to my chest for a moment, then handed it to him. 'Okay.'

'So,' he said, stopping to swallow a mouthful. 'Why are you hiding up here?'

'Not hiding.'

'If you want to be alone, I'll go,' he said, making no move to.

'Do what you like,' I told him, taking the bottle back.

'We have sociology together,' he said, watching me drink.

'I know.'

'I really fancy you.'

'Oh,' I said with a gasp, almost dropping the bottle. And that's all I could say. No one has ever just come out and said something like that to me before. It usually takes weeks of hair pulling and flirting to get a boy to admit something like that.

I must have been staring at him, because he laughed. 'Sorry. I can't believe I just told you that.' He stopped to take the bottle from me again. 'Bloody Rioja.'

He said it wrong again, but it made me giggle. He looked down at me with this soft, loose smile and when I smiled back, he leaned down and pressed his mouth against mine. With hindsight, I should have seen it coming, but at the time, it seemed to come from nowhere so the shock of it made me take a step back.

'Sorry,' he breathed, but he didn't look sorry at all.

'No. It's okay. I just—'

'I know,' he interrupted with a nod.

'I wasn't expecting it.'

'I didn't mean to pounce on you.'

'That's okay.' It wasn't, but I didn't know what else to say.

I think he took that as my blessing, because he reached for the bottle of wine and put it on top of one of the cardboard boxes. I wanted to take it back because I felt like I needed to do something with my hands, but he stepped closer before I could.

'I really like you, Rose,' he said, his voice lower. Warmer.

'Okay.'

'Really, *really* like you,' he said with a wicked grin.

'Okay.'

I waited for something to happen, for my hands to shake or my heart to flutter in that way it did whenever the sleeve of Sid's shirt brushed against my bare arm. But there was nothing. Then he pressed a finger to the heart-shaped locket Dad bought me for my thirteenth birthday and it made me shiver. Not in a good way, but it wasn't bad, either. It was kind of between the two.

When he lifted his hand and tucked my hair behind my ear, I knew what was coming and held my breath as he dipped his head towards mine again. My instinct was to put my hands up, but as soon as I felt the nearness of him – the *heat* of him – I suddenly couldn't move. My fingers brushed against the cotton of his T-shirt for just a moment and I lifted my eyelashes to look at him as I pressed my palms against his chest. I immediately felt the steady throb of his heart and when his lips touched mine, his heartbeat got quicker and quicker and quicker. I did that to him, I realised, as I felt his chest heave. I did that to him.

I hadn't kissed a boy for such a long time and it felt strange. There was no choir of angels, no butterflies in my stomach, and the only movement I felt beneath my feet was the vibrations from the party below. But it was nice. Easy. And after feeling so alone a few minutes before, it was a relief not to be.

So I closed my eyes and kissed him back, not because I fancied him or because what he said was particularly charming, but because I wanted to feel something that wasn't the loss or pain or anger that had made the edges of my heart hard. The wine hadn't helped. Finding Juliet hadn't. For a moment, I thought he might. And even if he couldn't, it was a relief to feel normal again, to be at a party, dizzy on wine and kissing a boy.

His cheek was rough and when it grazed against mine, his stubble sent little shocks along the line of my jaw. It made my eyelashes flutter and he must have felt it, because he ran his tongue along my bottom lip. I hesitated for a second, but when I opened my mouth, there was a moment when our tongues touched when I almost felt something. Almost. But then I heard someone laughing on the other side of the door and my nerves jumped.

'Give us a minute, will you?' he snapped at the couple who stumbled in.

'No. It's alright,' I told them, wiping my mouth with my fingers.

He said something, but I wasn't listening as I grabbed the

bottle of wine and slid out of the room. He called after me, but I didn't stop and almost knocked someone down the stairs as I rushed towards the front door. Jason and Ashley were gone so I ran out, closing the door behind me before staggering down the garden path towards the street. I know my lungs can't speak, but if they could, at that moment, they would have been gasping, AIR, AIR, AIR.

'Only you'd find red wine at a party like this,' I heard someone say.

I turned to find Sid sitting on the low wall outside the house.

'Hey,' I said, and it sounded like I'd just run up a flight of stairs. Or down them.

'Hey,' he said with a slow smile.

When he looked at me, I felt it, what I'd been waiting to feel in that tiny room. Angels and butterflies and rainbows and fireworks and all those other things that are so clichéd when you write them down, but aren't clichéd at all when someone actually looks at you like that. But I did write it down and I shouldn't have, because I've ruined it now. Reading it back, it sounds so cheesy. But it wasn't.

It wasn't.

Last night I had a dream about Sid. We were here. I was standing outside my room, smoking a cigarette, and he was walking up the stairs. When he saw me, he smiled. Not just any smile, not the smile that makes most girls lose their balance, but the smile that always makes me reach out for something solid because it feels like the earth is about to fall off its axis. A floor-shifting, wall-wobbling, breath-snatching smile.

The way he used to smile at Juliet.

'Only you,' he said, nodding at the No Smoking sign over my head.

He took the cigarette from me and when our fingers touched – just the tips, just for a second – I woke up gasping, the sheets sticking to my skin.

You know how, sometimes, something can hurt so bad that

185

after a while it starts to feel kind of nice? Like pressing a bruise with your finger. This was the opposite; this felt so good it hurt.

It hurt so much I thought I was dying.

I don't know why I've started dreaming about him again. I haven't dreamt about him since I got here. I guess I was thinking about him, about the party. Something happened, that night, something I haven't told anyone, but I can't stop thinking about it.

I have to write it down.

When we got off at Angel, Sid and Juliet offered to walk me back to my flat. They didn't mean it, of course, they'd been fidgeting with excitement since we'd left the party; she'd had her hand in the back pocket of his jeans as we'd stood on the tube and he couldn't stop touching her, adjusting her curls and straightening her necklace each time her swallow-shaped pendant got caught in her scarf. They obviously wanted to be alone so I reminded them that I lived in the opposite direction and said I'd be fine to walk by myself.

I shouldn't have, but halfway down the road, I looked over my shoulder at them just as Sid picked her up. Juliet screamed, her hair everywhere as he spun her. When he put her down again, they laughed – loud and bright – and I don't think I've ever felt so alone. I waited for them turn onto Juliet's road, then I started to cry.

That happened to me a lot then; one moment I'd be fine and the next I'd be sobbing so much I couldn't breathe. It was another of those emotions I tried to keep on a leash and couldn't. So I wandered back to my flat with a cigarette between my fingers, waiting for it to pass. But it didn't and by the time I got to my front door, I was crying so much I blindly scratched the lock with my key for a few minutes before I managed to open it. As soon as the door closed behind me and I knew no one could see me, I started to cry more. Louder. More desperately. I wandered from room to room peeling off clothes and leaving them behind like a trail of breadcrumbs – my jacket in the hallway, my shoes in the bedroom, my bag on the counter in the kitchen. It was as if I thought I could walk it off, but it was there.

There.

Always there.

When I sat on the sofa, I realised there was no one I could talk to. That's a terrible thing, to be seventeen and have no one. People say it all the time, don't they? *I'm lonely*. But they're not. Not really. They have friends. Family. They don't want to talk to them, there's a difference. They're not lonely, they're stubborn or embarrassed or scared.

I thought about that for a moment and realised how full of shit I was.

I don't remember dialling the number – I think I had it saved on my phone – but I remember having to endure several automated menus before I got through to a human being. It was only a call centre – I heard the murmur of voices before the operator said hello – but it was enough, hearing that one voice.

'This is Emily Victoria Koll. I would like to speak to my father.'

187

The man on the other end should have hung up, but he didn't. 'You know I can't do that, darling.' His Scottish brogue was so soft that I wanted to curl up and go to sleep in it.

'Yes, I know,' I told him. 'But I need to speak to him. It's very important.'

'Is it an emergency?'

'He's my father. I have a right to speak to him.'

'Of course you do, darling, but not at one in the morning.'

'What's your name?' I asked in my best St Jude's voice.

'You can call me Bean.'

'Bean? As in baked?'

He chuckled. 'Yes, as in baked.'

'Okay, Bean. I need you to pass on a message to my father. His name is Harry Koll. Do you know him?' When he said he did, I laughed. 'Of course you do! Everyone's knows Dad. There's the Devil, then Hitler and Dad's somewhere between cancer and famine.'

I laughed. 'Anyway, I need you to tell him something from me. I need you to tell him that he ruined my life. Will you go into his cell tomorrow morning and tell him that for me, Bean? Say, *Hey, Harry, your daughter has nothing because of you. She can't go home, she can't go back to school, her friends won't answer the phone to her and she has no idea whether her mother is dead or alive.* Will you tell him that for me, Bean?'

I pointed at the phone even though he couldn't see me. 'Go on. Write it down, in case you forget. Write it on a Post-it note and stick it on the bars of his cell. *You ruined your daughter's life.*

Make sure you use one of those big Post-it notes or it won't fit.'

The line was quiet for a moment or two and I thought he'd hung up. But then I heard him sigh. 'I don't think you should be on your own right now, Emily.'

'Who else is there?' I laughed, even though it wasn't funny.

'Emily,' he started to say, but I shook my head.

'I have to go now, Bean,' I told him before I started to cry again. 'You're a very nice man. If you could pass on my message, that'd be great. Okay. Thanks. Bye.'

I only remember pieces of what happened next. I don't remember hanging up the phone, just waking up on the sofa. I don't know how long I was asleep. It didn't feel long, but I remember being absolutely desperate for a cup of tea, but having no milk.

I guess that's how I ended up on Upper Street.

Everything was shut, so I headed for the petrol station. It was weird; the lights in the shops were off and the shutters were pulled down to expose graffiti I never knew was there, like secret messages you could only read at night. It was kind of strange, not seeing tables and chairs outside the cafés and walking past shop windows with immaculately dressed mannequins standing stiffly in the dark. It was like being in one of those zombie films, like I'd woken up to find I was the only person left on earth.

I wondered what that would be like as I passed the piles of bin bags and the empty bus stops. What it would be like to survive, rather than be left behind. It made me think of that tree near our cottage in Brighton, of sitting up there claiming everything I saw. I imagined that something had happened while I was asleep and London was mine. I could live where I wanted, eat where I wanted. I started to claim things as I passed them; the post box at the top of the road, the champagne bottle painted on the wall above the off-licence, the stickers stuck to the lampposts. It was all mine. The shops, the houses, the cars. All of it.

But then a night bus rolled past and I became aware of small signs of life; a dog barking, an empty pint glass left on a wall, the distant call of a police siren. Then I heard a car – slowing, slowing – and I turned my head as it began to drive alongside me.

There are very few moments that I remember with absolute clarity, but I remember that one. I remember the car; silver, dirty, with a string of rosary beads hanging from the rear-view mirror. I remember him, how he opened the window and smiled at me, his eyes black. And I remember the dread deep, deep in my bones as I looked away.

'Need a lift, sweetheart?' he asked. I could almost feel the heat in his voice – the *hunger* – and I wanted to be alone again, just me and London.

So I crossed my arms, lifted my chin and kept walking.

'Pretty girl like you shouldn't be wandering around by yourself this late,' he told me when I didn't respond. There was another half of that sentence, I knew, but when he didn't finish it, it was worse somehow, because I had to let myself think it. I had to let it in.

'I'm only going down the road,' I said, nodding towards to petrol station.

'I'm going that way. Get in.'

He had an accent – Eastern European, I think – I remember telling myself to make a note of it. Not that I was likely to forget. I'd only glanced at him quickly, but I saw that he was wearing a black leather jacket. There was a tear in it. There are girls I went to school with, teachers who taught me for years, and I can't even remember their names, but I'll never forget that tear. Never. It's like that tear is in my brain now.

'It's alright. I'm nearly there.'

'Come on, sweetheart. We'll be there in a minute.'

I was relieved to see the yellow light of the petrol station further down the street – I would have made it if I had run – but I wished I wasn't on a main road. He was too close. At least if I was walking down one of the thinner residential streets there would have been a row of parked cars between us.

'I told you, I'm alright,' I said, trying to sound firm. But I still couldn't look at him.

'What's your problem? I'm just being nice. Why you got to be like that?'

I heard the snap in his voice – the shift – and slipped my hands into the pockets of my jeans hoping to find my phone or something to defend myself with; a key, a pen, anything. But my pockets were empty. I hadn't even remembered to bring my purse.

'Thanks, but I'd rather walk. I need to clear my head,' I said, deciding to be polite this time. I don't know what difference I thought it would make, but I could feel my heart – thumping, thumping – and didn't want to provoke him.

It seemed to work, because he softened, his voice nothing but pink frosting and sprinkles again. 'Come on, sweetheart. It's freezing and you're not even wearing a jacket.'

'It's okay. I'm alright.'

I heard him sigh then and the car stopped. When I turned to look at him, he was getting out and I took a step back. 'Just get in the car,' he said, and I swear – I swear – my heart threw itself at my ribs so hard, I thought they were going to break.

'Oi!' I heard someone shout, and when I looked up, Mike was jumping out of a black cab. I don't know where he had come from, but as soon as I saw him, I went weak with relief. If I didn't think my legs would betray me, I would have run to him.

The man shot me a look over the roof of the car before he got in and drove off. I just stood there, watching his tail-lights as they disappeared down the street, the horror of what had almost happened echoing through me.

'Ro,' Mike breathed when he got to me. 'Are you alright?'

I looked up at him, my lips parted and my heart thumping on and on. I don't think I responded, because he took my face in his hands and asked me again. His fingers were cold, like Sid's mum's were that day at the wedding. I remember thinking, cold hands, warm heart.

'Yeah,' I said with a small nod.

'Are you sure?'

My brain recovered from the shock then, and I blinked at him as though I'd just woken up. 'What are you doing here?'

He looked relieved and tucked my hair behind my ears. 'Eve and I are on our way home from a midnight showing of *Nosferatu*.'

'That's a great film,' I muttered and he chuckled to himself.

'What are *you* doing here?' he asked, but before I could respond, Eve was next to me.

'Oh, Rose,' she gasped, her eyes wide.

Mike looked furious. 'I told you to stay in the cab.'

She ignored him and pulled me into a hug. 'Are you okay? What happened?'

I'd never been hugged like that before. It was a proper hug – a mum hug – and it made my heart hurt so much that I couldn't breathe for a second. I closed my eyes and pressed my cheek to the wool of her coat. She smelled like Eve, of Palmer's cocoa butter, and there was a smudge of green paint on her scarf.

'Oh darling girl,' she said, kissing the top of my head. 'Are you okay?'

'I'm fine,' I murmured. I could have gone to sleep right there and then.

'You're freezing!' She rubbed my arms with her hands. 'Come on. Get in the cab before you catch pneumonia. Where's your jacket?'

I shook my head. 'I don't know.'

Mike followed us into the back of the cab. He apologised to the driver, then turned to look at me, the skin between his eyebrows pinched. 'Are you drunk, Rose?'

I shook my head again. 'No.' I wasn't, but I was, drunk on the attention. I hadn't been made such a fuss of since I was fourteen and had that kidney infection. I fainted in class and Mr Lyndon, my oh-so-delicious English lit teacher, insisted on carrying me to the nurse's office. The girls in my class worshipped me for a week.

'Why are you on your own?' Eve asked, her forehead creased too. 'I thought you were at that Halloween party with Nancy?'

'I was.'

Mike looked confused. 'Where is she now?'

'At home, I suppose.'

'You suppose?' Eve blinked. 'Didn't you go home together?'

'Yeah, but when we got off the tube, she went home.'

I saw Mike and Eve exchange a glance. Eve thought about it for a moment, then asked, 'So Nancy walked home on her own too?'

The old cab creaked as it turned a corner. I slid along the back seat and when I nudged into Eve, I giggled. 'No, she was with Sid.'

They exchanged another glance, then Eve looked murderous. 'Wait. She left you to walk home alone at two-thirty in the morning while she walked home with Sid?'

'Yep.'

It was such a pretty little lie, almost true, but not quite. It was hard not to smile because, oh it was *delicious*. I remember the taste of it, the thrill, how the air in the cab tensed as Mike looked at Eve and Eve looked at Mike, then they looked at poor little me.

'Hang on, it's two-thirty in the morning?' I added. 'We got the last tube so we must have got off at Angel at about half twelve.'

Eve gasped. 'What've you been doing since then?'

'I dunno.' I shrugged, swaying a little for effect.

I saw Mike shake his head, but he didn't say a word and as soon as the cab pulled up outside their house, he jumped out. Eve paid the driver and as she led me up the path, her arm across my shoulders, Mike was already opening the front door and roaring, 'Nancy!'

Eve took me to the kitchen and sat me at the table. I immediately started rearranging the fruit in the bowl and when I heard Mike yell, 'Are you kidding me?' from upstairs, I dropped a plum and looked up at the ceiling.

A moment later, he paced into the kitchen and glared at Eve, who was holding the kettle, looking bewildered. I waited for him to tell her what was wrong, but when I realised he *couldn't*, my hands froze. Juliet had said Mike had a filthy temper, but I hadn't believed her. He's the most laid-back bloke I've met. I didn't think he could get angry, but he was *furious*.

'What, babe? Is everything alright?' Eve asked, her voice shaking a little.

But then Juliet walked into the kitchen, her head down and her curls ruined. For a moment, I thought Mike had woken her up, but when Sid followed her in, my heart.

My heart.

Eve stared at them for a moment, then looked at Mike. 'Were they?'

He nodded and she slammed the kettle down on the counter. 'Oh, no,' she said, shaking her head, her dreads flying in all directions. 'No. No. No. No. No.'

It was a perfect, perfect moment. Everything I'd been plotting for weeks. I should have been thrilled; at last, a not-so-perfect response from Juliet's oh-so-perfect foster parents. It was working. I was unpicking everything – slowly, slowly – but I wanted to cry my heart out. I know people say that, but I'm sure that if I'd started crying then, my heart would have dissolved so my tears would have been pink for hours.

'This isn't how I hoped it would happen, but it's a pleasure to meet you, Mr Brewer.' Sid held out his hand but Mike just looked at it.

'I've just seen your bare arse. I think we can dispense with the pleasantries, Sid.'

Sid looked at me. I looked away.

Mike pointed at Juliet. 'First things first,' he said, and Eve came to stand beside him with her arms crossed. 'Nancy, I know you're sixteen and there's nothing much I can do to stop you, but you do not do *that* in this house. Do you understand?'

'We weren't—' Juliet started to say, but Mike killed the protest with a look.

'Enough,' he snapped. 'That's the end of it. This isn't a discussion.'

Her gaze dipped to her red toenails. She'd never looked so small.

'Do I make myself clear?' he asked, looking between them. 'If

I ever come home to find you doing something like that again—'

Eve put a hand on his arm and he stopped.

'Moving on,' he said, putting his hands on his hips. 'Why did Eve and I just stop Rose from being pulled into the back of a man's car?'

Sid and Juliet gasped in unison, then looked at me.

'What? What happened?' Sid asked. He looked so concerned that I almost felt sorry for him. Almost.

'What happened,' Mike said, crossing his arms, 'is that you two left Rose at the tube and two hours later, she was almost raped on Upper Street.'

There was a long silence after he said it. I hadn't thought about it until that moment, but as soon as I did, I had to wipe a tear from under my eyes. I glanced up to find Sid looking at me and turned my face away again.

'What happened?' Eve asked, finally breaking the silence.

Juliet lifted her head to look up at her. 'What do you mean?'

'I mean,' Eve explained, clearly unamused about having to do so, 'how could you leave Rose to walk home on her own?'

Juliet opened her mouth to say something, but Sid immediately leapt to her defence. 'We asked her if she wanted us to walk her home, I swear, but she said she was fine.'

'First of all, it's Rose, not *she*,' Mike said tightly. He was the same height as Sid, but he suddenly looked ten feet taller. 'And let me tell you a little something about chivalry, Sid. Chivalry is doing, not asking. It was gone midnight and Rose was on her own. You should've walked her home, or at least put her in a cab if you couldn't be arsed.'

Mike may as well have punched Sid in the face because he looked crushed and when he looked at me, his forehead creased, I won't lie, it made my heart flutter just a little. I know how cruel that sounds, but Sid's undivided attention was finally divided.

'You're right, Mr Brewer,' he said with a nod.

Mike turned to Juliet. 'What were you thinking? This is Rose.' He nodded at me. 'The girl who eats dinner with us almost every night. The girl you leaned on when you started college. You told me that you would never have got through moving in with us without her. So, what? Now you're all settled you don't need her any more?'

Juliet crossed her arms. 'Of course not.'

'Then, regardless of what she said, you should have made sure she got home okay.'

'She walks home by herself all the time.'

'She shouldn't!' Eve interrupted. 'Do you?' Juliet shook her head. 'Of course you don't, because you have Sid. Rose probably doesn't want to intrude when you're with him.'

Eve stopped as if she was waiting for it to sink in, through Juliet's pores, into her bones. Then she delivered that final, *beautiful* blow. 'Don't be that girl, Nancy. Don't be that girl who dumps her friends as soon as she gets a boyfriend.'

When I looked at Juliet, she had tears in her eyes and I knew then that I'd finally done it.

I'd left a crack.

Naomi's trial started this morning. It was strange seeing her in a suit, her face scrubbed pink and her hair tied back. She looked tiny as the guard led her away. No one wished her luck. Not even me. I didn't hug her, I just pressed the emergency cigarette I've been hiding on top of my wardrobe into the palm of her hand as she left.

Doctor Gilyard went with her to court. I was grateful for the reprieve, until we had to do art therapy instead. It's Easter so they wanted us to paint boiled eggs.

I walked out, and fell asleep in the TV Room. I was woken up an hour later by a burst of canned laughter and when I peeled my eyes open, Val was sitting in the chair next to mine, gaping at the screen.

'Hey,' I said, but she didn't flinch.

We sat like that for a while, her staring, me waiting, waiting for what I don't know. A smile, maybe, a chuckle at one of Dick Van Dyke's jokes. But she didn't make a sound.

It was nice at first. Quiet. But after a while, the silence started to make me itch. I began to fidget in my chair, drawing my knees up to my chest, then putting my feet on the floor again. I tapped my foot, my fingers, my chin, in time to the cheesy eighties music, then twirled my hair around my finger so tightly it made my scalp sting.

After five minutes – five hours, days, weeks – I looked at Val.

'Why don't you want to leave?'

Silence.

'Don't you want to get better?'

Silence.

'Isn't there anyone out there waiting for you?'

Silence.

'Aren't you lonely? I'm so lonely.'

I looked back at the screen.

I don't know what I expected. If this was a television show, Val would have reached for my hand and said something profound to help me find my way back. But she didn't. How could she? She's out there with me.

Doctor Gilyard's didn't have to go to court with Naomi today.

'What was the tipping point?' she asked me this morning.

I didn't know where this was leading so I hesitated. 'The what?'

'Every relationship has a tipping point, Emily, the point where it tips from one phase into another. What was the tipping point with you and Sid?'

I crossed my arms and sat back in the chair. 'What do you mean?'

'When did you know that you had feelings for him?'

'Feelings,' I scoffed, looking away.

I pressed my lips together. I didn't want to tell her; it felt like one of those things I had to hold on to. But holding it in isn't helping. You know how you think of some people and you feel butterflies in your stomach? When I think about Sid now, after everything I've done, I feel moths chewing at my insides.

'Juliet saw her counsellor on Wednesday afternoons,' I said, literally spitting it out before I could stop myself.

Doctor Gilyard sat a little straighter, pencil poised.

'I didn't know what to do with myself,' I admitted. I waited for her to interrupt. She didn't. 'I usually sat in the park and read a book, but by November it was too cold. So one Wednesday I sat on the bus sketching.'

'Sketching?'

'Yeah. I'd never done art before and I had to, because Juliet was doing it. I was struggling. People were using spray paint and computers and I didn't even know to wash the oil paint off my brushes with turps. My tutor was horrified when she caught me rinsing them under the tap.' I blushed at the memory. 'I didn't know why she was being so impatient, but I found out later that I needed a portfolio to get on the course. Turns out Uncle Alex bought one off a student at Central Saint Martins.'

When I looked at Doctor Gilyard again, she was nodding.

'So I was sitting on the bus practising. I was still shit, but working in pencil was a bit easier because I could rub it out if I did it wrong.'

Doctor Gilyard smiled at that as she scribbled something in her notebook. I wonder if that's why she writes in pencil, too.

'What were you sketching?'

'Things people left behind; jackets on the tube, umbrellas on park benches. Rubbish, I suppose.' I shrugged again. 'But things that would be missed. Like, that afternoon, I was sketching the book on the seat in front of mine on the bus. It was nothing, really, just a cheap novel, but someone will always wonder how that books ends.'

Before I could finish the sketch, someone sat on the seat and picked up the book. I guess I should have been annoyed, but when they started reading it, I couldn't be mad so I closed my sketchbook and looked up at the gaggle of girls in black-and-white school uniforms who were sitting a few rows in front of me. They kept looking towards the back of the bus, whispering breathlessly about a girl called Amy. Curiosity got the better of me and I turned to find a boy and girl kissing like the world was about to end.

I rolled my eyes and when I turned back, the bus pulled into the next stop. Someone at the front stood up and I don't think I would have noticed much more than that if the girls hadn't stopped whispering to watch, utterly rapt, as he walked towards the stairs.

'Alright, sexy,' the boldest one said, sitting up and grinning. 'Where you going?'

I saw the briefest flash of a smile through his dark hair, before he disappeared down the stairs, then I was out of my seat and following him down them.

When I got to the bottom, he was helping a lady with a buggy off the bus.

'Sid,' I breathed, and he looked up.

I hadn't seen him since that night in Juliet's kitchen so I wasn't sure how he'd react, but his face lit up when he saw me. 'Hey, Ro. You alright?'

I nodded.

'What you doing 'round here?'

I held up my sketchbook with a small smile. 'You?'

'I was just saying hello to my dad.' He nodded over his shoulder.

I hadn't realised, but we were standing in front of a cemetery. I was so surprised that I dropped my sketchbook. It landed on the pavement with a loud SLAP. 'Oh I'm sorry. I—'

'It's okay,' he said, with a warm chuckle, bending down to pick it up. As he did, his hair fell forward over his face, so that when he straightened, he pulled it back with his hand and I could see his eyes. I'd never really looked at him before. I mean, I had, of course, but not for more than a few seconds, and not like that, not him looking at me and me looking at him.

'That was the tipping point, I guess,' I told Doctor Gilyard. 'When he asked me if I wanted to meet his dad. He said he wasn't as mouthy as his mum.'

She raised an eyebrow. 'His father is dead?'

I nodded.

'Did you know before that day?'

I shook my head.

She began scribbling furiously.

'Did Juliet know?'

'No.' I said it like I was proud, held it up as though it

204

was proof that I'd meant something to him, that it wasn't all in my head.

'How did he die?'

'Breaking up a fight outside a pub. Smacked his head on the pavement.'

'That's very noble.'

I scoffed. 'Seems like a waste to me.'

'Why?'

'Dying like that, in the street, bleeding into the cracks of the pavement while your wife and kid are waiting for you to get home. And for what? To stop a couple of idiots kicking the shit out of each other? He should have left them to it. It's natural selection.'

Doctor Gilyard nodded. 'Do you think that's why Sid did it?'

'Did what?'

'Tried to save you.'

I had to look away because I know that's why he did it. That's why Sid is the way he is. Something like that would make most people hard. Cold. Not Sid King. His eyes remained wide, his heart restless. If anything, his father dying like that made him see the good in people. I don't know how, but where most of us would kick and spit at the injustice of it, the way Sid saw it, his father died trying and it made him want to try, too.

When I didn't respond, Doctor Gilyard moved on. 'So what happened?'

I'd never been in a cemetery before. I've never needed to, which is a good thing, I suppose. Gramps died when I was eight, but Dad wouldn't let me go to the cemetery because he said I was too young. I went to the funeral, though. I don't remember much, just climbing into a big car and umbrellas, everyone had an umbrella. And I remember that the church smelt of furniture polish and blown-out birthday candles.

When Sid led me through the cemetery gates, I held my breath. It was bigger than I had expected; wide and flat and green with a road that cut down the middle. Sid and I didn't speak as we walked down it, just looked out at the headstones studded across the grass. Most of them were simple; rectangles of moss-softened stone or Celtic crosses that were chewed around the edges. But every now and then we passed an angel standing over a grave, its wings spread, or a plump cherub sitting with its legs crossed.

I didn't think too much about those graves; they were old and worn with ivy climbing up the sides as though they weren't there. Maybe in a few years they wouldn't be, they'd be swallowed completely. Earth to earth, and all that. I thought of Mum then, wondered whether she was lying somewhere under a tangle of brambles. It made my hands shake so much that I rolled up my sketchbook in case Sid saw.

The headstones towards the end of the road were newer, the flowers on them fresher. I passed one shaped like a teddy bear and when I read the dates on it, I had to look away before my brain could do the calculation. I ended up looking at a grave edged with plants instead. An old lady in a heavy wool coat was on her knees next to it, plucking away the dead heads and kneading the soil in each terracotta pot with her knuckles. She looked up and smiled at Sid and me as we passed and I must have stepped closer to him, because my hip knocked into his. The shock of it made me miss a step.

He asked me if I was alright and when I found my balance again, I nodded, I think. I don't remember. I just remember staring at a grave with a single red rose on it. Not all of them had flowers on them, but those were the graves I couldn't look at; the ones no one visited. They looked so empty next to the graves cluttered with wreaths and balloons and those coloured pinwheels you get on Brighton beach. You could tell who was missed. Those graves wailed, *come back.*

It was almost too much, seeing people's grief like that. It made me wonder what my grave would look like. It wasn't an unusual thing to think, I suppose, but I realised mine would be one of the empty ones. I decided then to be cremated, that way someone can climb the tree near our cottage in Brighton, throw me in the air and I can fly off on the wings of the seagulls.

I think Sid knew I was freaking out, because he kept turning his head to look at me as he led me towards the back of the cemetery, near the railway tracks. It's a stupid thing to think, but as we walked past them, I hoped his dad wasn't near there because it wasn't a very peaceful place to spend eternity. But Sid stopped under a tree with crooked branches and a fat trunk. It was almost stripped bare, its leaves scattered across the grave like brown confetti. But they were the only things on it. There were no wreaths, no candles, just those leaves and a bunch of dead roses, their petals dried up and curling.

'Sorry,' he muttered when he saw them, reaching down and snatching them out of the vase as though I'd shown up at his flat unexpectedly and he hadn't done the dishes.

'It's okay,' I started to say, but when I looked at him standing there, the dead flowers dripping on to his trainers, my throat hurt so much that I couldn't say any more.

Thankfully, I didn't need to as a woman not much older than Dad approached us with a carrier bag. 'Here you go, darling,' she said, smiling at Sid as he put the flowers into it. Some of the petals dropped off as he did and they fell on top of the dead leaves already on the grave. It was actually kind of pretty.

We stood there for a moment, the three of us, me with my sketchbook, Sid with his hands in the pockets of his hoodie and her with a bag of dead roses hanging from her finger.

'My dad,' he said eventually, nodding at the grave.

Her face brightened. 'You Gina's boy?' Sid smiled, but she frowned. 'She alright? I ain't seen in her weeks. She not well?'

'She'll be alright.' He shrugged and looked down at the grave.

'This your girlfriend?' she asked, smiling at me.

Sid grinned. 'This is Rose.'

'Pleasure to meet you,' I told her with a small wave.

'Rose! What a pretty name.'

When I looked at Sid, he was still grinning and as soon as the woman looked down to tie up the plastic bag, he pulled my hair. I swatted his hand away so he did it again and we both giggled. But when I realised that she was watching us, I blushed.

'It's alright, sweetheart,' she said, waving her hand at us. 'Don't worry. My son was your age so it's nice to be around teenagers again.'

Was. The word dropped to the grass between us like a cannonball. I was sure I felt the ground shudder beneath my feet and the headstones rattle.

'This is him,' she said, nodding at the grave opposite.

She took Sid by the elbow and led him over to it with a wide smile, as though she couldn't wait to introduce us to him. The grave was one of the ones that wailed, *come back*. There were teddy bears and roses and a red-and-white scarf tied around one of the vases.

I couldn't look at it.

'My Jamie,' she said, squeezing Sid's arm. 'A right Jack the lad. Always had people around him. The weekend he died, he'd just come back from Ayia Napa. Seventeen of them went, all boys. I dread to think what they got up to!'

She smiled at Sid and he smiled back, smiled like he meant it, and I don't know how; it felt like someone had punched me in the chest.

'He didn't wear enough sunscreen,' she told him. 'He came back bright red! His nose was starting to peel.' She laughed and touched her own as she looked down at the grave. 'Seems such a shame to leave him here by himself. He hated being on his own.'

She stopped laughing, then it was so quiet I could hear the faint rumble of a train rattling past the cemetery. I looked at Sid and we exchanged a pained look.

'Dad was an Arsenal fan, too,' he said, nodding at the scarf as though he was trying to distract a toddler from having a tantrum. 'I haven't been back to the Emirates since he died. I can't even watch the games on the telly.'

I wanted to step forward then, tell them that I was an Arsenal fan, too, that I couldn't go back to the Emirates without Dad, either. But the moment wasn't about me.

We stood there, looking at Jamie's grave, then she leaned down and scooped a handful of roses from one of the vases. I wasn't sure what she was doing, but when she walked over and put them in the empty vase on Sid's dad's grave, my chest felt so tight, I couldn't breathe. It made me think of Bean. I'd forgotten people could be so nice.

'That was it,' I told Doctor Gilyard, lifting my chin defiantly. 'That was the day everything changed.'

'How do you know?'

'Because I reached for his hand and held it, just for a second.'

'What did he do?'

'When I let go, he reached for my hand again and squeezed.'

'Why do you think he did that, Emily?'

I have to stop now before I say too much.

This is another of those things I need to hold on to. Before I got here, I strung each of my memories together – the good ones, the ones about Mum and Sid and the dad I knew, the dad who put me on his shoulders at Arsenal games and read me *Goodnight Moon* when I couldn't sleep and came to all my cello recitals – and at night I would thumb through them like rosary beads.

I can't do that any more. Now I have to lock them away where no one will find them so they can't take them away from me. That's it, isn't it? It's not that Doctor Gilyard can't have them, it's that I'm terrified she'll say *I* can't have them.

That I don't deserve to keep them after everything I've done.

I'm in the bathroom again. I don't know what time it is, but my brain is spinning. Tumbling, actually, like a ball down a hill. Why am I writing this? I should stop. I should close this notebook and never write another word, but here I am, in this bathtub – my toes curling, I'm shivering so much.

I've never told anyone my story before. I've never had to; everyone knows it. I thought that's what this is – my side of the story. But the blackness that began to creep into the corners of my life after Juliet stabbed Dad is getting closer. I can feel it. Everything is greyer now. Memories that used to be as clean as glass are smudged. I think that's why I'm writing it all down, in case the blackness wins. I can feel it sometimes, chewing at the edges of my brain. If it ever devours the rest of me, these are the things I'll want to remember.

So I'd better keep going.

As soon as we left the cemetery, Sid announced that he was hungry. I think he was trying to ease the awkwardness of the moment, or he was hungry, which is equally likely. Whatever his reasons, we ended up getting chips and eating them in the park.

It was only 4 o'clock, but the day had started to dim. Winter was coming. A chill nipped at the tops of my ears and steam rose, thick and fast, from the bag of chips I was cupping in my hand. The heat of them warmed the bones in my fingers and the air smelt of salt and onion vinegar. I haven't eaten chips since then, but even now, thinking of that smell reminds me of that afternoon, of how Sid and I just walked and walked.

'Is that why you took a year out? Because of your dad?' I asked, staring at my chips, too scared to look up in case I'd crossed a line he hadn't invited me across.

'A year out is a polite way of putting it. I fucked about,' he told me with a laugh, and I thought about his tattoos. Sink. Swim.

'Was it sudden?'

He nodded. That's when he told me what happened, about his dad, about the fight. He called him a hero. He was looking at the benches that lined the path as he said it. Each one had a brass plate – *In Loving Memory of Edna* or *For Albert Chapperton*. *His favourite walk*, stuff like that. He said he wanted to do something like that for his dad. A bench or a tree. Something permanent. Something everyone would see.

'What would you want?' he asked me between mouthfuls of chips.

'When I die?'

He nodded. 'Do you want to be remembered?'

'Of course. I want people to know I'm gone, to look up at the sky and think of me.'

'You want someone to name a star after you or something?'

I shook my head. 'When I go, I want to punch a hole in the sky.'

He stopped and looked at me. I think that was the first time he saw me, saw me as someone other than Juliet's mate, the girl with the too-red hair and dirty laugh.

He nodded again and we carried on walking in silence for a while.

As we approached the bandstand, he frowned. 'You only eat chips in twos.'

I forgot that I still had my sketchbook tucked under my arm and almost dropped it as I turned to blink at him. 'What?'

'You only eat chips two at a time.'

I stopped and looked at my hand. Sure enough, I was holding two chips and I dropped them as though they'd burned me. 'I had no idea,' I muttered.

There was a bin next to the bench we were walking past, so I dropped the white paper bag into it. When I turned to look at him again, he looked mortified.

'Sorry,' he said, throwing his chips in the bin, too. 'I didn't mean to embarrass you.'

I blinked at him again. 'Embarrass me?'

'That's the most I've seen you eat since we met. I—'

'I eat!' I interrupted. I didn't think I was being defensive, but I said it so loudly that a man walking his dog looked up as he passed us.

Sid smiled. 'Sushi isn't food, Ro.'

'Yes it is!'

He shook his head. 'No, it isn't. Nance made me go to one of those restaurants last night, the ones with the conveyor belt where you have to pick the plates off as they go past and I can confirm that a bit of rice with a slice of salmon on top isn't food.'

He laughed, but I didn't. I crossed my arms and turned away. We – Juliet, Sid and me we, not Sid and Juliet we – were supposed to have gone to that restaurant together. I shouldn't have cared, but knowing that Juliet either forgot or wanted to be alone with him made me feel tiny.

'Here,' he said. When I glanced over at him he was tugging at one of the bushes.

'What are you doing?' I murmured, but when he turned to me again, I felt a rush of blood flood my cheeks as he held out a rose. It was well past its best, its red petals bruised and weeping on our shoes as he handed it to me, but it was still the prettiest flower I'd ever seen.

He grinned when I took it. 'Cheesy as fuck, right?' he said, sweeping the hair out of his eyes with his hand. 'I bet every boy you meet gives you one.'

I frowned. 'Why?'

'A rose for Rose.'

I brought it to my nose and smelt it with a slow smile. 'You're the first.'

'Yeah, right. I bet—' he started to say, but stopped as a boy on a BMX rode between us. The shock of it made me jump and I jumped again when the boy turned around and rode back towards us.

'Safe, Sid,' he said with a sniff, stopping at our feet.

Sid nodded at him. 'Alright, Owen?'

'Yeah. Yeah. Who's this?'

I waved. 'I'm Rose.'

Owen didn't look at me. 'What happened to that fit one?'

There was an awkward silence after he said it and I felt tiny again.

Sid kicked the wheel of his bike. 'Where'd you get this?'

'Borrowed it, innit.'

Sid rolled his eyes. 'How's school?'

He sniffed again and wiped his nose with his sleeve. 'Shit.'

'How's your mum?'

'Alright.'

'How's Patrick?'

'Alright.'

My gaze flicked between them. I think it was a conversation. I've had conversations with the bloke at the Chinese takeaway that were more involved.

'You'd better get home, O,' Sid told him, 'your mum'll be waiting for you.'

217

'Alright,' he said, putting his foot back on the pedal of the bike. 'Later.'

They nodded at each other again, but before Owen started to ride away, Sid grabbed something from the back pocket of his jeans.

Owen stopped and gasped. 'Oi! What you doing?'

'What are *you* doing, O?' Sid held up a box of cigarettes. 'You're twelve.'

Owen lifted his little chin defiantly. 'They ain't mine, they're Patrick's.'

'Well, tell him to come and get them off me, then.'

'Ah, come on, Sid,' he whined, trying to take them back.

Sid ignored him and slipped the thin gold box into the pocket of his hoodie. '*Come on, Sid* nothing. Don't you know they'll kill you? Someone's got to save you from your stupid.' He nodded towards the gates. 'Now piss off home. Don't keep your mum waiting.'

Owen huffed and said something I won't repeat before riding off again.

'Little shit,' Sid muttered, pulling the box back out of the pocket of his hoodie and opening it. He lit one and I watched as he inhaled then exhaled with a long, contented sigh.

'I didn't know you smoked,' I gasped. We'd known each other for three months, *how* did I not know that?

'I gave up, but I started again recently.' He winked at me. 'Don't tell Nance, she'll do her nut. She hates smoking; her aunt died of breast cancer.'

Her mum, I wanted to correct, but I eyed the box instead. 'Give me one.'

There were only four cigarettes in the box, but we smoked them all – two each – under the bandstand, sitting side by side on the ledge with my sketchbook and the rose between us. It was our first secret, those cigarettes. If I really wanted to hurt Juliet, I could have told her – should have told her, I suppose. That was another tipping point, I know now, the moment I realised I wanted to keep it for myself more than I wanted to hurt her.

'Let's do something,' he said, when he finished his last one, his left leg bouncing.

I checked the clock on my phone. 'Nance should be done with Sahil by now.'

'Nah.' He shook his head. 'She's going to that thing at the National Theatre with Eve. I meant let's you and me do something.'

'Like what?'

He jumped down from the ledge. 'I dunno. I just feel like –' He threw his arms out, then turned to look at me again. 'Do the muscles in your legs ever shake sometimes like they're restless? Like you just want to run?'

'You want to go for a run?' I frowned and flicked my spent cigarette into the bushes.

'No.' He started to pace back and forth over the worn boards. 'You know how in the olden days they thought that if you sailed a ship too far it'd fall off the edge of the earth?' I nodded warily. 'Well, that's what I want to do, I want to run until I find the edge.'

He walked over to where I was sitting. 'Come on, Ro,' he said, looking at me from under his dark eyelashes. It made my heart throb. 'Let's do something.'

'Like what?'

'I dunno.' He looked over my shoulder. 'I mean, look at these people.'

I turned to see who he was looking at. It was almost dark so the park wasn't busy. There were a few commuters cutting through on their way home from the station and a man in red shorts had been running laps since we got there, a heart-shaped patch of sweat in the middle of his grey T-shirt.

'They're all going somewhere, doing something. I want to do something.' He looked at me again. 'Do you ever feel like that, Ro? Like stuff is going on and you're missing it?'

I thought about him and Juliet at that sushi restaurant, giggling as they tried to grab plates from the conveyor belt. 'All the time.'

'Let's do something, then.'

'Like what?'

'Anything. Anything that isn't sitting around waiting for Nancy.'

'Okay,' I said with a small smile, jumping down from the ledge. 'I have an idea.'

His eyes lit up. 'What?'

'Just stay here, okay? Don't move. I'll be back.'

I all but ran to the shop opposite the park and back.

He was waiting for me under the bandstand, right where I had told him to. He smiled when he saw the blue plastic bag in my hand. 'What's that?'

I grinned. 'You'll see. Come on.'

I led him to the biggest tree in the park. When we stopped under it, he looked up, clearly bewildered as I put the rose and my sketchbook into the bag. 'What's this?'

'It's a tree, Sid.'

He rolled his eyes. 'I know that. What are we meant to do with it?'

'We're gonna climb it.'

The crease between his eyebrows deepened. 'Do what?'

'Come on.'

I took a step towards the base of the tree as he crossed his arms. 'When I said that I wanted to do something, Rose, I meant drink something. Perhaps do something illegal.'

I ignored him as I tried to find my footing. I hadn't climbed a tree since I was at St Jude's, so it took a couple of attempts. But, eventually, I got high enough to reach for a branch then another and another. The blue plastic bag rustled hysterically each time I raised my arm; it sounded like applause.

'I'm not doing that,' he called out as he watched me. 'I can't climb trees.'

''Course you can,' I shouted back, my nails digging into the rough trunk.

'I'm a London boy born and bred, Ro. They only have parks

here so we know what trees look like. If you were asking me to climb a McDonald's, maybe.'

'Get up here, London boy,' I told him as I tested the weight of one of the thicker branches. Content that it was sturdy enough to support my weight, I clambered on to it. I laughed when I did it, a breathless gasp of a laugh. My hands were cut, my nails ruined, but it felt so good to be up there, sitting on that branch with the whole of London at my feet.

When I caught my breath, I reached into the bag and pulled out a can of beer. I waved it at him with a grin and as soon as he saw it, he launched himself at the tree. My heart leapt into my mouth when he lost his footing once, then twice, but he got to me eventually and the fact he did was a testament to what a teenage boy will do for a can of Stella.

'You're nuts, Rose Glass,' he said, completely out of breath as he pulled himself on to the branch. He wobbled around for a moment or two, but when he found his balance, he leaned back into the curve of the tree and reached his hand out. 'I almost broke my neck getting up here, so give me my beer. I've earned it.'

I handed it to him with a proud smile. 'Here you go, Tarzan.'

He turned away from me to open it, but as he brought the can up to his mouth, he stopped and stared out at the horizon, his eyes wide.

'I know,' I said smugly, getting a can for myself out of the bag. I thought about the first time I climbed that tree in Brighton, how I'd looked out and seen things I'd never seen before. Secret things only I knew about. Me and the seagulls.

'You can see for miles!'

'I know.'

'You can see the gherkin.'

'I know,' I said with a giggle, opening the can and leaning back against the tree.

He looked at me, his cheeks pink. 'Why have I never climbed a tree before?'

I shrugged and took a sip of beer. 'I dunno. It's better in summer, when there are leaves and stuff, because you can hide,' I told him, but it was still amazing up there. It smelt so clean, of wet leaves and earth and old wood.

'I can't believe it.' Sid shook his head. 'It's like seeing London for the first time.'

It was, I suppose, from a different angle, anyway, which is why I took him up there. It's good to see things the wrong way around sometimes, to see the bits you're not supposed to see, like the tops of vans and people's underwear hanging on washing lines.

The sky was a different colour up there, too. It was this deep, deep red – cough-syrup red. I wanted to reach up and lick it. I think that's why I liked climbing trees, because I felt closer to it, like if I stretched a little further, I could touch it and it would be mine. I think Sid got that because he was looking up at the sky as though he was claiming a piece of it, too.

I heard someone walking along the path beneath us and looked down as a man walked under the tree. He was on his phone and kept saying, 'Yeah, I told him.'

Sid and I watched him pass and when he was out of sight, Sid looked across at me. 'He doesn't know we're here.'

I raised an eyebrow and smiled. 'I know.'

'This is amazing, Rose.'

He shook his head again and finally took a mouthful of beer. I'd already finished my can and was opening another when he turned to his left and gasped, pointing at the three tower blocks on the horizon, the ones that didn't quite touch the clouds.

'You can see where I live from up here!'

I turned to look at them too. 'Which one do you live in?'

'The middle one.'

'I used to live in the one on the left.'

I shouldn't have told him, I know, but up there I felt safe. Protected.

He stared at me, open mouthed. 'You lived on the Scarbrook Estate?'

'Yeah.'

'I thought you were born 'round here? Don't you live in Islington?'

'Yeah, now. I was born on the Scarbrook Estate. *Literally*, the lift was broken so my mum gave birth in the stairwell. I couldn't wait to get out, apparently.'

I chuckled to myself, but he kept staring at me, his forehead creased. 'You're winding me up. You don't talk like you're from the Scarbrook Estate.'

'Well, I am.'

'What floor?'

'Twelfth. Penthouse, baby.'

'Why didn't you say?'

'I dunno.' I shrugged and looked away. 'I heard you telling Nancy that you were from the Scarbrook Estate, but you weren't really talking to me.'

As soon as I said it, the air between us tightened. I don't know why I said it. I didn't mean to. I guess it was true, but I didn't know that it had upset me until I heard myself say it.

'It's okay. You weren't even looking at me,' I added with a small laugh, trying to sound nonchalant. 'I don't think you knew I was there.'

He didn't say anything to that, just looked at me for a long moment.

I shrugged at him. It wasn't his fault; it was just this thing, this force, that brought him and Juliet together the moment they met. He looked at her sometimes like he didn't know how to stop. Walls fell, the ceiling peeled off, furniture blew away like dead leaves until all that was left was her, and he'd look at her like she was the only thing he could see for miles.

No one will ever look at me like that now.

I would look at him, looking at her, and I'd want to tell him that I understood, that I knew what it was like to have Juliet Shaw punch a hole right through your life. Yeah, Sid and I had entirely different motives, but the need was the same, the focus. If anyone knew what it was like to think of nothing but Juliet Shaw, it was me.

The silence curled around us like smoke and when I saw him look down at the can of beer in his hand, I laughed, trying to soften the moment.

'It's alright, Sid,' I said with a shrug, then took another long sip of beer. 'I'm not having a go. I'm just saying. I know if it wasn't for Nancy, we wouldn't be friends.'

I watched his cheeks go from pink to red and when he turned his face away, it hurt. Not because he didn't insist that we were great mates, but because I didn't know until that moment how deeply Sid felt things. Say something like that to him and it hooks in, takes root.

'So where did you move to?' he asked suddenly, turning to look at me again.

The shock of it almost made me say Godalming, but I managed to catch my breath and remember Rose's back-story. I thought of all those afternoons in the park, all those gigs singing along until we'd lost our voices and I couldn't believe we'd never talked about it.

'Barnsbury.'

He nodded. 'Very nice.'

'We don't live there any more. When Mum and Dad got divorced, they had to sell the house. Mum and I live in the flat near Angel tube now.'

'Still, much nicer than the Scarbrook Estate. How'd you get out?'

I paused to swallow a mouthful of beer. I didn't look at him again, I stared at the can. When I didn't respond, I heard him say, 'You don't have to tell me if you don't want to.'

'It's not that,' I told him with a shrug, stopping to trace the letters on the side of the beer can with my finger. 'I was just thinking about how long we've known each other.'

He finished my thought. 'And we've never talked about this stuff?'

I smiled to myself and took another swig of beer.

'I don't even know what your dad does, Ro.'

He's a surgeon. I'd said it so many times – to Juliet, to Mike and Eve, to Grace. It should have been on the tip of my tongue, but I said, 'He's a mechanic.'

As soon as I'd said it, I pressed my lips together, but it was too late.

It was out.

'A mechanic?'

I began tracing the letters on the side of the beer can with my finger again. 'Yeah. He and my uncle used to own a garage. It was doing well, but then Mum got pregnant with me. Dad says I was a surprise, but he was being nice, I was an accident.' It wasn't funny. I don't know why I laughed. 'They weren't ready. They weren't even nineteen. Dad wanted to be living in a house when they started a family, not in a one-bed flat on the Scarbrook Estate.'

I finished the beer and threw the empty can into the plastic bag. 'So Dad started working his arse off to make some money,' I continued. It was only then that I realised what I was doing, that I was telling him about Emily, not Rose. After months of being so careful, I don't know why. I should have stopped, but he was looking at me, waiting for me to go on, and I thought – just for a second – that if I said it in the right way, he would understand.

'He started working on account,' I said, my voice not as steady, as I opened another can of beer, 'fixing cars for cab firms and stuff. Then the accounts got bigger and when he landed one with the police we moved off the estate.'

Sid looked impressed, but I had to stop. I don't know what happened next. I mean, I've read stuff in the newspapers; I know Dad wasn't just fixing cars. But I don't know what happened to Mum, why she didn't come with us. When I was old enough to ask, Dad told me she was too young, that she couldn't cope with being a mother. I don't know what he did to her. Maybe he didn't do anything. Maybe she couldn't cope. Wouldn't it be funny if she was in a place like this, writing in a notebook of her own about all the things she's done?

'So your dad did it all for you?' Sid said then.

I remember how the beer can crumpled under my fingers. 'Did what?'

'All of it; built up his business, moved off the Scarbrook Estate, bought a house in Barnsbury. He did it all because he wanted you to have a better life.'

He smiled at me as though it was a good thing, but I wanted to be sick. I'd always blamed myself for my parents breaking up. After all, if I'd arrived five years later, would they have been stronger? Would Mum have coped? But the rest of it? Did he do that for me? That's all he ever said to me, I want you to have everything, little one. Everything. You can have it all. Whatever you want. Just ask. But he meant take, didn't he? That's what he did.

What did he do?

'You okay?' Sid asked, and I caught myself, remembering to smile.

'Just drunk, I think.'

He stared at me and when I looked at him again, he asked me if I was sure. But when I told him I was, he went from un-convinced to frustrated.

'You always do this, Ro,' he said, shaking his head.

'Do what?'

'Talk. You talk, talk, talk, about everything. About books you're reading and films you want to see and that mad bloke who hangs around outside the police station wearing a bin bag as a cape. But you never *say* anything. It's like there's this line.' He drew one between us with his finger. 'You get so far, then you stop.'

'I do not.'

'Yes, you do. Like just now; I obviously upset you with what I said about your dad, but when I ask if you're okay, you lie about being drunk.' He ran a hand through his hair. 'Nance does the same thing. She gets to a point and won't go any further. She won't let me in.'

I didn't know what to say to that. I couldn't find the words quickly enough. I was scrambling around trying to grab them but

I couldn't. It was like I had greasy fingers. So I resorted to stroppiness. 'My parents just got divorced. It's hard to talk about it, okay?'

He pointed at me. 'It's more than that, Ro. I know it is. There's something else.'

'There isn't!'

'There *is* and you don't have to tell me what it is, but I know there's something because I do the same thing when I have to talk about my mum.'

'Don't talk about her, then.' I reached for another beer, but there were none left.

'I think she's an alcoholic,' he said in a rush.

I almost fell out of the tree. I mean, I knew, I *thought*, but I didn't think he'd tell me.

'What?'

'I've been finding bottles around the flat.'

'Where?'

'At the back of wardrobes. In the cupboard under the kitchen sink.'

'What sort of bottles?'

'Wine, at first. Now vodka.' He shook the can he was holding. I could hear the beer swilling around inside of it. 'You know that really cheap vodka you get in supermarkets? A litre bottle for a tenner?'

'How long has she been doing it?'

He shrugged. 'She's always liked a drink. Her and my Aunt Bridget used to sit in the kitchen on Friday nights, howling and drinking Southern Comfort and lemonade. But it's got worse since Dad died. She does it on her own now. I don't know what to do.'

'What does Nancy think?'

He looked at me, then licked his lips. 'I ain't told her.'

My heart started to throb again. 'Why not?'

'I can't.' He shook his head. 'Things are so good between us. Easy. I just need to have that one good thing, you know?' He frowned. 'Does that make me a total dick?'

I thought about it for a moment, then looked at him. 'My cousin Ian had a drinking problem.' I hesitated. It was another Emily thing, but it was only a tiny piece and he really needed it, so I went on. 'His wife stuck with him through the whole thing. Through the years of him starting arguments just so that he could leave the house, and nicking money from her purse. But as soon as he was better, he left her.'

'What? Why?'

'Because he'd moved on. He wanted to put all of those things behind him but he said that he couldn't because she remembered all of it. She remembered things he couldn't. So he said that he'd always be an alcoholic to her.'

Sid looked at me for a moment or two, then nodded.

'So you keep your one good thing, Sid,' I told him with a smile. 'But if you need someone to talk to, or climb a tree with, tell me. I have an awful memory.'

A group of schoolgirls passed under the tree then. They started to hold on to one another and laugh wildly as a Jack

Russell nipped at their heels. The owner tried to tug him away, but not before one girl screamed – Janet Leigh screamed – and ran away. It was so melodramatic that it made me giggle and when I looked up again, Sid was watching me.

'Here,' I said, reaching into the plastic bag. 'Hold out your hand.'

'Why?'

'You know what we need?' I pulled out a tube of Smarties and shook them at him. He grinned, offering me the palm of his hand. I tipped them out and picked one off the top of the pile. 'I only eat the orange ones so you can have the rest.'

He frowned as he watched me push them around with my finger trying to find another orange one. 'What? Why?'

' 'Cos they're the odd ones out.'

'How? They're all the same.'

I shook my head. 'No, they're not. The orange ones aren't like the rest.'

'Are they fuck.'

I knew I was about to expose him to some of my crazy, but he needed to know.

'They are! Here, I'll show you.' I picked out a pink one and held it up. 'The pink ones are the mum. The blue ones are the dad. The purple ones are the kid—'

'Why are the purple ones the kid?'

'Because pink and blue make purple.'

'No, red and blue make purple.'

'No, Smarties pink and Smarties blue make Smarties purple.'

'Sorry. I didn't realise there was actual logic behind this.'

I raised an eyebrow at him. 'There is.'

'Okay. So what are the red ones?'

'The dog.'

His gaze narrowed. 'Why are the red ones the dog?'

'Because when I was little we had a dog called Red.'

'Of course. So what are the brown ones?'

'The house.'

'Naturally. And the green ones?'

'The earth.'

He thought about it for a moment. 'So are the yellow ones the sun?'

'Yes! See, I told you.' I tapped my temple with my finger. 'Logic.'

'I'm not sure logic is the right word, Rose.'

'So that just leaves the orange ones.' I popped one in my mouth. 'They don't belong. Plus, they taste different. They're orange chocolate.'

'Lies!' he said, pointing his beer can at me. 'That's a total urban myth.'

'Yeah. Okay. If by urban myth you mean fact.'

'No.' He shook his head, 'I mean urban myth. That's why I said *urban myth*.'

'I'll prove it to you. Close your eyes.'

He groaned but closed his eyes anyway and when he did, I picked out a blue one. He giggled when I touched his bottom lip with it, then let me feed it to him. He chewed on it for a second then opened his eyes again, grinning smugly. 'Told you. Doesn't taste of orange.'

I feigned annoyance. 'Fine. Let's try it one more time.' I fed him a brown one this time. He did the same thing.

'Okay, okay,' I said. 'Best of three?'

This time I actually gave him an orange one. As soon as he tasted it, his eyelids flew open and he looked at me, horrified. 'It's orange chocolate!'

I slapped my leg with my hand. 'I told you!'

'Give me another one.'

'No,' I whined. 'There's only one left. You can have all the other colours.'

'I climbed a tree for you, Rose Glass. Give me one.'

'You climbed a tree for beer!'

'Please.' He fluttered his eyelashes and I gave in. He looked suitably smug.

'Happy now?' I pouted. 'No more Smarties for me.'

'Here,' he said, holding up a pink one.

I almost fell out of the tree recoiling from it. 'No!'

'Come on, Ro. For me?'

'No. I can't eat the mum!'

'I climbed a tree for you, Rose Glass!'

I pointed at him. 'You only get to use that once!'

He chuckled to himself then picked out a blue one. 'Okay,' he said, holding them up. 'If you have the pink one and I have the blue one we'll be friends. Proper friends. Not just friends with Nancy, okay?'

'Fine.' I closed my eyes and when I felt his thumb touch my bottom lip I pretended to wince, but my heart sang. Sang like a bird in a cage.

It became a regular thing after that. Every Wednesday afternoon we'd go to the cemetery, get chips, then do something together. We'd bicker about books or fight over band T-shirts in the charity shop. Once we even went into a bookies on the high street and put a bet on the 3.55 at Wetherby. My horse won and I was insufferable for the rest of the day. I think Sid would have gone home and left me if I hadn't bought us a curry with my winnings.

One Wednesday he turned to me as we were coming out of the chip shop with the most wicked grin. 'I know what we can do. Come on.'

I frowned at him. 'What?'

'There's someone I want you to meet.'

We got the tube to Camden and he led me down one of the narrow roads near Camden Lock market to a small shop. I didn't even get a chance to see what kind of shop it was before he pulled me in by the sleeve of my coat.

As soon as I stepped inside, I smelt it – wood and old paper – and my heart was hysterical, as though I'd just bumped into an old boyfriend.

A music shop.

I stopped and stared at it for a moment. It was nothing like the shop in Soho Dad took me to, to buy my cello, the one with the white walls where the cellos and violins were wooden works of art you had to be invited to touch. The shop Sid took me to was tiny and filled with instruments. Guitars lined the walls and violins hung in rows from the ceiling like bunting.

Sid charged on ahead of me, stopping to slap a pair of bongos before disappearing behind a cherry-red drum kit.

'Here she is,' he said with a proud sigh when I found him at the back of the shop.

My heart pounded then slowed as I looked down to find a guitar at his feet. He sat down on an amp and lifted it into his lap as though he was lifting a newborn baby.

'This is Nancy,' he said with a sly smile. 'The original Nancy. Say hello.'

I rolled my eyes. 'What is it?'

'Not it,' he hissed. 'She, Rose. She.'

'Fine. What is she?'

'A Martin D-one-eight-E acoustic.'

'She's very pretty.'

'She's more than pretty.'

'Special, is she?'

'My first love.'

'I see.' I raised an eyebrow at him. 'What makes her so special?'

He began strumming and it took me a second, but when I realised what he was playing, I pointed at him. ' "The Man who Sold the World"! It's Kurt Cobain's guitar.'

A tiny woman with white-blond hair and bright red lips appeared from behind a double bass. She was scowling, but when she saw Sid, her face softened.

'You can't have it until you learn how to play the rest of it,' she told him, crossing her arms. Her skin was laced with tattoos – flowers and feathers – and when she turned towards me, I saw that she had a naked pin-up girl with big eyes and victory rolls on her right arm.

'I'm Deb. Are you Nancy?' she asked with a wide smile.

I should have been used to it, but I still felt a stab of humiliation.

'This is Rose,' Sid said without looking up from the guitar.

Her face lit up. 'Oh, Rose! The cellist, right?'

Heat rushed through me. My cheeks must have been blood red. 'Yeah.'

'I like your hair.'

I reached a hand up to touch it. 'It used to be red. I haven't had time to dye it.'

'Pink's cool, too.'

'Thanks.'

'Come with me,' she said, turning and disappearing behind the double bass again.

Sid got up too and when we followed her into the corner of the shop, I stopped and took a step back. Sid yelped as I stepped on his toe.

'No,' I said, shaking my head when I saw the cello.

Sid held my elbows so I couldn't take another step back. It made my heart beat even harder. 'Come on, Rose. I want to hear you play.'

'No. No. I can't.'

'Don't be embarrassed.'

'I'm not,' I told him, pulling away and crossing my arms. 'I just can't.'

'Please, Rose,' Deb said, nodding at the cello. 'This has been here almost a year. We don't get many cellists in here.'

I looked at the cello, then at Sid. 'I haven't played for ages.'

'It's like riding a bike, Ro.'

'Yeah, but I'm so rusty. It'll sound rubbish.'

'I know the opening riff of "The Man Who Sold the World" and a bit of "Wonderwall". Who am I to judge?'

I raised an eyebrow at him. 'And that gave you calluses?'

'I'm a bit slow,' he said with a smile that was enough to make me surrender and shuffle over to the cello.

The muscles in my legs twitched as I sat on the orange plastic chair Deb put in the centre of the small space. I was excited, I realised, my heart trilling as she handed me the cello. I didn't know what to do with it at first, then I remembered to part my knees and stand it on the floor between my legs. The endpin sunk into the Persian rug and when I cupped the neck in my left hand, it felt strange; heavy and hollow, all at once.

I could tell by the colour of it – the weight, the tangle of scratches on the back – that it wasn't as valuable as the cello Dad had bought me, but when I drew the bow across the strings, it still made the most beautiful sound. I had to stop and take a breath.

When I looked up, Sid was staring at me, his lips parted. It made my heart beat so hard I had to look at the cello. As soon as my fingers pressed against the strings, the calluses on my fingers and the stiffness in my joints made sense again and when I drew the bow across them again, I felt the vibration from my wrist right up to my elbow. I did it again and again, adjusting the tuning pegs each time until the cello began to speak, deep then high, higher until I reached that first, perfect note and I began to play. It wasn't great – at moments, the cello screeched rather than sang – but I dipped my head and closed my eyes and, just for a moment, I let go of that invisible edge I'd been clinging on to and fell.

Eventually, my fingers found the right spot on each string and the music began to rise and fall around me. I didn't realise what I was playing until I heard it, and as soon as I did, I was back at St Jude's, in the music room, practising and practising and practising for the prom at the Royal Albert Hall. I never got to be that Emily, the Emily who was a cellist for the National Youth Orchestra of Great Britain, but for a few minutes that day I did.

When I stopped, I looked up and Sid was still staring at me, his lips parted.

Then he smiled and when I smiled back, I don't think I've ever felt so happy. It was the cleanest, most pure thing I'd felt in *months*. I had to look away, I was smiling so much. I was sure that if I tried, I would fly, that if I jumped and thrust my arm up I'd soar into the sky and feel the clouds against my cheeks.

I know what people say about me, about what I did. I've said it myself, that I used Sid to fuck Juliet over, but I didn't. Not really. Maybe if I had, I wouldn't be here now, in this tiny room with bars on the windows and a smudged line of white chalk on the floor. Because that's how he made me feel, like I could fly, like I could do anything. That's all love is, you know, wanting to be the best person you can be for someone. Sometimes I think all of this would go away – I would be cured – if I could just be that girl all of the time.

The girl I was when I was with him.

'Did you ever consider just being Rose?' Doctor Gilyard asked me this morning.

I looked up at her, my heart suddenly in my throat. 'What do you mean?'

'Did you ever consider leaving Emily behind, like Juliet did, and becoming Rose?'

I stared at her, incredulous. 'Rose wasn't a person, she was a disguise.'

'Was she?'

I closed my eyes and sighed. 'Stop it.'

'Stop what, Emily?'

'This.' I waved my hand at her. 'This, whatever you're doing.'

'What am I doing, Emily?'

'Can you just say something?'

'Say what, Emily?'

'Anything. Just say something that isn't a question.'

We looked at each other for a moment too long, then she nodded.

'Why didn't you kill Juliet?'

I flew out of my chair with a roar. A cry. 'Why won't you listen to me?'

She just looked at me, so I kicked my chair over. It landed on its side on the lino with a loud CRACK that brought one of the male nurses sweeping into the room. Doctor Gilyard didn't take her eyes off me, just held her hand up until he went away.

'Did you like her, Emily? Is that why you didn't do anything?'

'No, I hated her!' I spat out, my fists clenched.

'Do you think you could have been friends, if this hadn't happened?'

'Stop! Please, just stop!'

My heart was beating so hard I felt dizzy. I snatched at a breath, then another and another until I realised that there was nothing I could do. So I gave into it, let it rip through me, and it was such a relief that I smiled. I love it, you know, the anger. I love it when it's like that; wild and deep and unreachable. Because when I'm angry, it isn't me reacting, it's my body. I can't stop it. I have to let it run its course, like a fever.

'You obviously have a lot in common, Emily,' Doctor Gilyard said then and my hands started to twitch. I needed something to knock over, to kick, to break. But there was nothing; no pot of pens on her desk to tip over, no framed wedding photo to hurl across the room. So I went over to the bookcase and began pulling off the textbooks. They landed on the floor at my feet with a succession of loud slaps.

When the last one hit the top of the pile and slid off, it was over. Passed. I stopped and stood there panting and it felt like I was dying, like I was choking on my own breath. I had to reach out for one of the empty shelves to steady myself.

After a minute or two, I closed my eyes and slumped against the bookcase. 'You enjoy this, don't you?'

'Enjoy what, Emily?'

'Pulling and pulling,' I said, still panting. 'Until I unravel.'

She didn't say anything for a long time, so I turned to look at her, my heart still throbbing as though someone had kicked it. 'What's your name?'

I'd hoped it would throw her, but I guess patients ask her that all the time, because she didn't flinch. 'You know my name, Emily.'

'Doctor Gilyard isn't a name.'

'It's what I'd like you to call me, Emily.'

'This isn't fair.' I shook my head. 'I have to tell you everything. Things I don't want to tell anyone, things I don't want to say out loud and you won't even tell me your name.'

She nodded, but she didn't say anything. There was no apology. No explanation. Then it was so quiet that I could hear the television murmuring in the TV Room and it made my heart twitch. It's never that quiet in here; someone is always shouting.

Laughing. Crying. Keys jangle against hips. Doors open, then close again. And there are footsteps, always footsteps, back and forth, back and forth.

'You don't wear a wedding ring,' I told her, as if she didn't know.

She shook her head. I could hear an advert then. Washing powder. Washing liquid, maybe. Something that got 99 per cent of household stains out in a jiffy.

I tilted my head and looked at her from under my eyelashes. 'Is that because you're single, or because you don't want us to know that you're married?'

She nodded, then looked at me. 'We're building an intimate relationship here, Emily. There are certain expectations, levels of trust. It's perfectly natural to want to know—'

'I didn't ask if it was *perfectly natural*. I asked why you don't wear a wedding ring,' I hissed, crossing my arms. If I was closer to her, I think I might have slapped her.

'Let's move on, Emily,' she said tightly.

How does it feel? I wanted to roar. *How does it feel?*

'Have you ever been in love?' I pushed.

She took off her glasses and looked at me, her eyebrows knotted. 'I hear you're not eating much, Emily. And you look worn out; when was the last time you slept?'

'When was the last time you answered a question?'

'Would you like me to prescribe you something to help you sleep?'

'No. I'd like you to answer my question.' I felt like a toddler in the sweet aisle at the supermarket screaming for a Mars bar and being ignored. 'Have you ever been in love?'

'Have you, Emily?'

I turned my face away. 'No.'

'I thought that you love Sid.'

I sank to floor, next to the pile of textbooks. 'That isn't love,' I told her, leaning back. The edge of the bookcase dug into my shoulder blades. 'Loving someone who doesn't love you back is like throwing a ball against a wall.'

She didn't say anything to that and I was surprised. I thought she'd push back, tug on the other end of the rope for a little longer.

I turned to look at her again. 'You wear a crucifix.'

She nodded.

'Why?'

She pressed her finger to it. 'Why not, Emily?'

'Because you're a doctor.'

'Not all doctors are atheists.'

'How does that work? If you can't save them, pray for them.' I raised an eyebrow at her. 'The best of both worlds, I suppose.'

She nodded, then put her glasses back on. 'Einstein said that science without religion is lame and religion without science is blind.'

'Einstein?' I scoffed. 'What did he know?'

She smiled at that.

'Do you pray for me?' I asked. My voice sounded tiny, like when I was little and I had to tell Dad that I'd broken something.

The time I broke the Chinese vase in the dining room, I said it so quietly I had to repeat myself.

When she didn't respond, I sat forward. 'When you go to church on a Sunday and you sing your hymns and light your candles, do you pray for me? For poor, mad Emily Koll?'

'No,' she said, without missing a beat.

I had to turn away because it hurt, deep, deep in my chest. I wanted to run out of her office, to throw myself on my bed and weep. But I couldn't move and the longer I sat there, next to that pile of textbooks, I began to think that maybe she doesn't pray for me because she knows she can fix me, because she meant what she said when she came to my room and drew the line on the floor – I am not beyond repair.

As soon as I thought it, I felt it, hot and bright in my blood. Hope. Wild, useless, *unshakeable* hope.

So I looked at her. 'Sid won these tickets.'

'Tickets to what?'

'The Beastie Boys. We love them.'

'We?'

'Sid, Juliet and me. We were so excited.'

I sucked in a breath. My lungs rattled. 'I told them that the last time I saw the Beastie Boys was at Glastonbury and Juliet grabbed my arm. She'd seen them at Glastonbury, too, and lost her phone during Sabotage. She said –' I stopped for breath again – 'she said that I could have been standing right next to her.'

I heard Doctor Gilyard write that down. 'You could have been.'

It had never occurred to me until that afternoon by our lockers that Juliet and I might have been friends if none of this had happened, if we'd just bumped into each other at a gig and I told her that I liked her shoes and she told me that she liked my hair. But as soon as I considered it, I felt that wall between us tremble, like a sheet on a washing line. It did that sometimes, when we were in the canteen and she'd buy me a chocolate croissant for no reason, or when she'd laugh at something I'd said so hard that it made me laugh too.

Maybe we would have been friends, if she really knew me. Not the Emily who wanted to pick her apart, bone by bone. The Emily who went to Glastonbury and wore her wristband until it fell off. She'd never know that Emily, though, and I'd never know the Juliet who went to Glastonbury and lost her phone jumping up and down to Sabotage.

The Juliet who didn't stab my father.

Maybe there's another world somewhere, another plain, where she and I are friends. Where we're happy and whole and not the product of our fathers' decisions. Where we can be ourselves, not these made-up people with made-up names and made-up memories.

'Sid only won two tickets,' I told Doctor Gilyard, tracing the edge of one of the textbooks with my finger. 'I thought I couldn't go, but Juliet wasn't having any of it. She said I had to go because she'd had no music when she moved to Islington, and I bought her "Licensed to Ill". She said she'd rather go without Sid than without me.'

'So what happened?'

'She had a plan, but she said that if it didn't work and I couldn't get in, we'd sell the tickets and go get drunk.'

'She was pretty determined, then?'

She was adamant and I should have been beside myself; my plan was working, I was her friend, I was part of her life, but it made something in me curdle.

'How did it make you feel, Emily?' Doctor Gilyard asked, reading my mind.

'I hated her more in that moment, than I ever have,' I told her, my voice shaking.

'Why?'

Doctor Gilyard was right, Juliet and I do have a lot in common. She lost her mother, I lost my mother. She lost her father, I lost my father. She had to start again, I had to start again. She had to pretend to be someone else, I had to pretend to be someone else. But where she was better for it, I was worse. Where she used what happened to her to be stronger, I held on to it. I let it distil into something filthy and black. And I hated her for that.

Hated her.

'Why do you hate her, Emily?'

'For reminding me that I did this to myself.'

Monday. Tuesday. Wednesday. I don't even know any more. I just know that I seem to be talking to Doctor Gilyard more. I don't mean to, it just slips out, like I'm talking in my sleep.

'It's Reta's birthday today,' I told her this week.

'Yes, it is.'

'She's eighteen.'

'Yes, she is.'

'It must be strange, having a birthday in here,' I said. I thought Christmas Day in here was tragic, having to eat turkey and Brussels sprouts with a plastic knife and fork, but celebrating your birthday in here must be miserable.

'How did you spend your last birthday, Emily?'

I looked at her again, my nerves thrumming. I don't know how she does it, how she always knows what I'm thinking. It's moments like that when I think that I don't hide it very well. I must want to tell her these things, to understand. But then I think: what's to understand? I'm my father's daughter. I am who I am. It's in my DNA.

'I went to a gig with Sid and Juliet.'

She looked down at her notebook. 'The gig you mentioned last time?'

When I didn't respond, she lifted her chin to look at me. 'Are you thinking about Sid? Is that why you're so fidgety this morning?'

I crossed my legs and curled my fingers into fists. 'Is fidgety even a word?'

'Have you been sleeping?'

'Not really,' I told her with sigh, looking over her shoulder at the crack in the wall.

This time she didn't respond, so I sighed again. 'I've been thinking about Dad.'

She sat a little straighter. 'Have you?'

'Yeah.'

'Do you miss him, Emily?'

It was so brutal, I couldn't look at her. I couldn't even be near her in case she saw my chin trembling, so I got up and walked over to her desk. I was going to take a cigarette, but when I saw her swivel chair, I sat in it. I've never sat there before, I don't know why.

'Emily,' Doctor Gilyard said as I began spinning in it, around and around.

When I was dizzy I stopped, my palms flat on her desk. I heard myself laugh as my eyes swam back into focus, and it sounded strange, like it was coming from the next room.

'Do you miss him, Emily?' she asked again.

I ignored her, picking up a pen and doodling on her blotter. I don't know what I drew; hearts and flowers and butterflies and all that other crap girls draw.

When I stopped, I looked down at the tangle of blue Biro.

'I miss him today,' I told her.

That sounded like it was coming from the next room, too.

'Because of the gig?'

I nodded.

'Why?'

'I wanted to go so bad. I don't think I've ever wanted something so much in my life.' I started doodling again. 'I knew we only had two tickets so I was trying not to get too excited, but then, when we were on our way there, this group of lads got on to our carriage on the tube wearing white T-shirts with NO SLEEP TILL BRIXTON written across them in black felt tip.' I smiled at the memory. 'We spent the rest of the journey throwing shapes in the aisles while the commuters scowled at us over their copies of the *Metro*.'

I looked up at Doctor Gilyard and she was writing something in her notebook. 'When we got to Brixton, we ran up the escalators. I hadn't run like that since I was a kid. My heart was beating so hard I was dizzy. But it was that good dizzy, excited dizzy, y'know?'

She nodded.

'When we got through the ticket barriers, the touts were waiting, pacing back and forth hollering "BUY OR SELL BEASTIE BOYS TICKETS" as though they were flogging apples at Chapel Market. And there was this buzz – this charge – in the air. I could feel it crackling off my bare arms. By the time we got to the Academy, I was almost in tears at the thought of not getting in.'

I looked up then. 'Have you ever been there?' When she didn't respond, I carried on. 'It's nothing special. There's no tree-lined road, like at Wembley, no blocks or stands or tiers. You probably wouldn't even notice it unless you were looking right at it.'

Or the Beastie Boys were doing a gig there.

Chaos is the only word I can think to describe it. Traffic was backed up and the pavement outside was a mess of people either waiting to get in, or trying to. Juliet, Sid and I stood across the road, watching them all. Everyone seemed to be shouting; bus drivers leaned out of their cabs to swear at people who stepped off the kerb to take photos of the red letters under the dome – BEASTIE BOYS SOLD OUT – while men in neon yellow vests shouted at everyone in the queue to stay behind the barriers.

I don't know how long the queue was, but it was long; there was a BBC truck parked in the narrow street next to the stage door and the queue went past it. It was too dark to see how far it stretched, but men in thick hooded coats with fur-lined collars walked up and down the length of it, handing out brightly coloured flyers for bands and club nights in Dalston.

I overheard the group of girls standing near us say that people had been queuing all day. I don't know how; it was so cold. We were only across the road for a few minutes before I started shaking. Apparently, the bloke in the Check Your Head T-shirt at the front of the queue had been there since dawn. He'd come all the way from Berlin and tried to sleep outside the Academy overnight, but a police officer had warned him that he'd either be pissed on or arrested, so he went back to his hotel and got the first tube back.

Sid, Juliet and I had only travelled from Angel, which was no effort in comparison, but I was devoured by hysteria. I had to get in.

'I missed Dad then,' I told Doctor Gilyard.

'Why, Emily?'

'If he was around, we wouldn't have had to do any of that; I would have just phoned him, told him that I needed tickets and he would have asked me how many.'

'So what was the plan? How did three of you get in on two tickets?'

'Sid didn't get tickets, he got passes, so he and Juliet went in, then he took Juliet's pass, came back out and got me.'

'That's quite clever, actually.' She sounded impressed.

I guess. But the wait was excruciating. I stood across the street and watched as Sid and Juliet joined the end of the queue. Watched as they waited. Watched them walk up the steps.

Watched them go in. Five minutes turned into ten, then into fifteen.

I waited, waited and waited. By then, I was so cold I couldn't stand still. Wearing a coat would have helped, of course, but wearing a coat meant carrying a coat, or worse, paying to check it into the cloakroom. So, fortified by the quarter-bottle of vodka I'd shared with Sid and Juliet while we'd walked to the tube, I thought I'd be okay.

'There was this bus,' I told Doctor Gilyard, 'waiting in the traffic outside the Academy, so I couldn't see the doors any more. There was an ad on the side for this cheesy Christmas film. Something about a lost elf or penguin, I can't remember. I just remember lighting a cigarette and staring at it.'

'Then what happened?'

'It rolled out of the way and there was Sid.'

I smiled then. I don't often smile in Doctor Gilyard's office, but as soon as I thought of that moment, of Sid, on the other side of the road, grinning at me, some invisible lock at the corners of my mouth gave way and I smiled.

It felt like an unbearable amount of time before there was a break in the traffic and Sid ran towards me. As soon as he did, I flew at him, wrapping my arms around his neck and sprinkling cigarette ash down the back of his T-shirt. He laughed and staggered back, his hands on my waist and his cheek against mine. His skin was warm and he smelt of, well, *him*. I love that smell. I still don't know what it is, but whatever it is, that night, I pressed my nose into the curve of his neck and breathed him in.

'Here,' he said, when he put me back on my feet. He pressed a sticky guest pass with Sid King + 1 written on it to my chest. I grinned when I saw it. Then he took the cigarette out of my hand. 'Give me that,' he said with a loose smile. 'I told Security I was coming out for a fag, so I'd better have one.'

I couldn't stop looking down at the pass. It was the most beautiful thing I'd ever seen. I smoothed it down with my hand then looked up at him with a grin. 'You did it!'

He slung his arm across my shoulders and pulled me to him, kissing me on the top of the head. 'Told you I would.'

He handed me back the cigarette and the tip was wet. Ordinarily, I would have been appalled, but when I took a drag and handed it back to him, I made sure our fingers touched.

I felt the shock run right down to my elbow.

'Come on,' he said with a grin, taking my hand and leading me across the road.

We were almost hit by a bus, but when we got to the steps of the Academy, he took one last drag on the cigarette, then made a point of flicking it near the feet of the security guard. 'We're on the guest list,' he told him. 'We just went out for a fag.'

The security guard nodded, but as we were about to go through the doors, he turned to us and my heart screeched to a cartoon halt. Sid squeezed my hand and I squeezed it back.

'It's murder tonight,' he told us with a bored sigh. 'Once the warm-up gets on, only people with crew passes and triple As will be readmitted.'

I had no idea what a triple A was, but I assumed we didn't have one.

'Oh, alright,' Sid said, running a hand through his hair. 'No worries.'

The security guard turned away again and as soon as he did, Sid literally *pulled* me through the circular entrance. We had to be patted down by more security guards, then we were in and when we got through the second set of doors, we started jumping up and down.

Mid-jump, he hugged me again. I felt the BANGBANGBANG of his heart next to mine and my heart BANGBANGBANG-ed back as though it was responding, as though his heart and my heart were talking to one another. When he put me down, I heard the crowd roar as the warm-up took to the stage and we smiled at each other.

'Let's find Nance,' he said, grabbing my hand.

It wasn't easy. The narrow lobby was cluttered with people who were in no hurry to get inside. They seemed quite content to hang around talking and drinking plastic cups of beer as we bumped, tripped and giggled our way through them.

By the time we reached the merchandise stand, the back of my T-shirt was soaked. I could feel the cotton sticking to my skin and beer seeping through the canvas of my Chucks. I must have *reeked*, but I didn't care, because as we approached the doors to the stalls, the warm-up band got louder and louder until I could feel the air rippling.

I squeezed Sid's hand and he looked at me over his shoulder.

'It's heaving in there, so don't let go, okay?'

I held my breath while a security guard checked our passes, then she opened the doors and we were greeted by a punch of heat and sound that almost knocked me off my feet.

'Jesus, Sid,' I gasped, but when the doors closed behind us, he wouldn't have been able to hear me as we began working our way through the crowd towards the stage.

It was so loud that everything was blurry. The floor turned to sponge, the walls to water, then all I could feel was his hand in mine, the lines of his palm, his calluses. As the crowd responded to the call of the band, everyone rose then fell like a wave that Sid and I were pulled along with, and I held on tighter, so tight that I could feel the bones in his fingers.

The air had this tang of sweat and beer, which sounds disgusting, but I couldn't stop smiling. I love it, I always have. The heat of a crowd, the buzz of a bassline. For a moment I was back at Glastonbury with my back-combed hair and too much eyeliner, shoving my way to the front of the Pyramid Stage with Olivia. So when Sid turned his head to look at me, I wanted him to stop so that we could stand there for ever, him and me, right there in the dark.

I smiled at him and he smiled back and it was this perfect, perfect moment. But then my hand slipped from his as a blonde girl barged past us on her way to the bar. I turned to swear at her, but before I could finish the threat, Sid grabbed my hand again and yanked me away so suddenly, I thought he was going to pull my arm out of its socket.

'This way!' I heard him shout, as he led me to the side, where it wasn't as busy.

As we got deeper into the crowd, it got darker and the air felt thicker. It stuck to my skin as I stumbled behind him, stepping on people's shoes. The closer we got to the stage, the more reluctant people were to move as they tried to hold on to their spots before the Beastie Boys came on. I could hear Sid apologising as we slid past them, and I don't know whether it was because he was polite, or twice the size of most of them, but they shifted grudgingly. Not an inch more than they had to, though, so I felt damp T-shirts against my bare arms and at one point, I felt a girl's hair drag across my cheek.

I didn't think we'd ever find Juliet, but finally – *finally* – there was a break in the crowd and there she was, waiting for us by the column to the left of the stage.

When she saw me, she jumped on me. She'd never hugged me before and I was so surprised that I laughed and hugged her back. She smelt of daisies.

'We did it!' she said, stepping back with a grin.

'I know!' I shouted over the din, holding out my right hand. 'My hands are shaking!'

Sid smiled smugly. 'I told you!'

'Great spot! It's so close to the stage. I usually stand on the other side.'

'This side is better.' Juliet pointed at the plinth at the bottom of the column. 'We can take it in turns standing on this, otherwise we won't see a thing!'

'Who are LM and DM, do you reckon?' Sid asked, reaching up and running his hand over the initials scratched into the column. 'Do you think they're still together?'

Juliet pretended to gasp. 'What if they've broken up?'

'I bet they have!' I said, already hoarse from shouting over the band. 'I bet she can't stand here any more because it hurts too much so she has to stand on the other side. I probably stood next to her the last time I was here.'

Sid tipped his head back and laughed. 'Your brain, Ro.'

He pulled my hair and I grinned. 'I very much need a drink! Beer?'

They both nodded and I turned back towards the crowd.

I remember thinking, once more unto the fray, as I started to make my way through it again. But then I realised that I hadn't asked Sid and Juliet which beer they wanted and turned back. There were only a few people between us, and as they stepped out of the way to let me back through, I saw Sid smile at Juliet, then dip his head. His hair fell across his face, and when their mouths met, my heart caught in my throat.

'Emily,' Doctor Gilyard said then.

I looked down at her desk and realised I'd been writing my name – EmilyEmilyEmilyEmilyEmilyEmily – over and over. The blotter was covered.

'I saw them kiss,' I whispered, like it was a secret.

'Why did that upset you, Emily?'

'I'd never seen them kiss.'

Doctor Gilyard sounded surprised. 'You'd never seen them kiss?'

I had, of course, but not like *that*. It was always quick – a peck between classes or when she bought him a can of Coke at the canteen. I don't know why. I guess the three of us were together so much they didn't want to make me feel uncomfortable. I'd never thought of them as the type of couple who spent hours kissing, but as I watched them, his hands on her face and hers cupping his elbows, I saw that they were, they just didn't do it in front of me.

'How did it make you feel, Emily? Were you jealous?'

I shook my head and stared at the blotter. 'I was embarrassed.'

'Why were you embarrassed?'

I looked up. 'They were waiting for me to walk away so that they could kiss, weren't they?' That's why it took Sid so long to come out and get me. He wasn't waiting for the right time; he was prolonging it for as long as he could. I imagined Juliet telling him to go, while he kissed her again and said, *one more minute.*

I wondered how often they looked at me when we were together and thought, *I wish she'd take the hint and leave us alone.* How many times they'd lied to me about not being about to go out because they were tired or had too much reading so that they could snatch an evening alone to go to the cinema or eat sushi.

The thought made my skin burn. I stared at them as they kissed, but when they stopped to giggle and Sid wound one of her curls around his finger, I had to turn away.

'Make up your mind, love,' a bloke muttered as I headed back to the bar. But I didn't apologise. I didn't apologise to anyone, just pushed my way through until I got there.

As I waited behind a girl with a tattoo of a barcode on the back of her neck, I looked at the doors to the lobby and I wanted to run for them, to run and keep running until my legs gave way. I didn't want to be there any more. I didn't want to stand next to Sid and Juliet, pretending that I didn't see them holding hands and snatching kisses when they thought I wasn't looking. But when the girl stepped out of the way and the guy behind the bar asked me what I wanted, I didn't want to run, I wanted beer.

I ordered four and downed one at the bar, before I turned to face the crowd again. I tried to go a different way this time so I wouldn't spill the beer, but it meant going through a knot of blokes who cheered when they saw me.

'Alright, Pink Lady?' One of them said, reaching down to pinch my arse.

I hissed at him, but with three beers in my hands, I couldn't do much else. So he pinched it again and I pulled away, stomping back to Sid and Juliet, seething impotently.

They were still kissing and Juliet giggled when she saw me. 'Sorry!' she said, taking one of the beers, and I had to resist the urge to throw the other two in her face.

As soon as I gave Sid his, I started to slide back into the crowd, but he grabbed me by the elbow. 'Hey. Where you going?' he asked with a frown.

'Sorry!' I said, peeling off the pass and handing it back to him.

I tried to slide away again, but he wouldn't let go of my elbow. 'I don't mean that!' The band was so loud that he had to lean towards me, his mouth against the shell of my ear. The heat of his breath felt so nice, I wanted to cry. 'What's wrong, Ro?'

'Nothing!' I leaned in to tell him, but there's no way of *shouting* that without sounding like something's wrong.

'Sorry if we embarrassed you! We don't want you to feel left out!'

We. We. We. I hate that word. Never has a word made me feel so lonely.

I could hear Juliet asking what was wrong, and I pulled away. 'I don't!'

'Where are you going, then?' he asked when I started to walk away.

'I'm getting another beer! I'm not going back to the bar once they get on!'

Except I didn't go back to the bar, I downed my beer and headed straight for the doors to the lobby. I made a point of passing through the knot of blokes and they cheered again when they saw me. This time I had my hands free, so I put them on the shoulders of the one who had pinched me on the arse and kneed him right in the bollocks.

When he folded to the floor, I kept walking. I walked and walked until I was in the lobby, then on the pavement, then on the tube.

'What did you do, Emily, when you saw them kissing?' I heard Doctor Gilyard ask, but I couldn't stop staring at the blotter, at my name. I didn't recognise it. It didn't look like it belonged to me.

'I left.'

'Where did you go?'

'To Juliet's house.'

'Why?'

My eyes lost focus as I remembered walking through the side gate to find Mike there, smoking a cigarette. He frowned when he saw me. 'What are you doing here? Aren't you supposed to be at the Beastie Boys gig with Nancy?'

I didn't answer, just licked my lips. He watched me, his eyes suddenly black. When he edged closer, I licked my lips again. 'Give me that,' I told him, taking the cigarette and making sure our fingers touched when I did.

'I went to finish what I'd started,' I told Doctor Gilyard.

Through the blur, I could see wet dots appearing on the blotter and I stared at them. I guess that was our tipping point – mine and Juliet's – that moment with Mike. The moment I'd had enough of flicking matches at her and finally set light to everything she had.

I woke up the next morning in my make-up with the taste of cigarettes in my mouth.

For a moment, I didn't know where I was. The air was still sweet with perfume from when I got ready the night before, so I thought I was at St Jude's. When I opened my eyes, I half expected to find Olivia on the other side of the room face down on her bed, her pillow streaked with eyeliner and one leg poking out from under the duvet. But when my eyes adjusted, I saw my wardrobe and realised I was in London and it came back to me all at once.

That happens every morning, even now. There's a minute when I first wake up where everything is watery and edgeless, like the Monet postcard Juliet had taped to the inside of her locker at college. My head is empty, I guess. Clean. And in that minute everything is quiet again. Nothing is broken. My life is as it should be; I'm at St Jude's; Dad is at home, eating a fry-up and reading the paper; Uncle Alex is listening to the football results in his car and swearing at the radio; Duck is asleep on the suit Dad has laid out on his bed.

I could quite happily lose the other twenty-three hours and fifty-nine minutes of the day if I could just keep that one minute. I could live a whole life in that minute. That's where Emily Koll is right now, in that minute. But I can't and as soon as it passes, it all comes back in a rush. I remember. The cracks reappear. And it's so cruel, having that reprieve, because of all the things I want to forget, it isn't what I've done, it's what I had. Who I was.

No one else remembers Emily Koll with any fondness, so why should I?

That morning was worse, though, because I didn't just remember what Juliet did, I remembered what *I* did – with Mike – and the weight of it pinned me to the bed. I tried to get up, but I couldn't. My bones felt as thick as branches, my heart like a rock. I didn't think I'd ever have the strength, that I'd have to live there for ever, on that bed, in that room, with the smell of perfume in the air.

I tried again and managed to lift my head off the pillow to check the clock on my bedside table. I had to blink a couple of times before the red lines on the digital display came back into focus, but when they realigned I realised it was 11:11. *Make a wish*, I thought, but gave in to the weight of my head before I could.

When I opened my eyes again, it was almost one in the afternoon and I felt worse. Every part of me ached, even my fingernails. And my head – oh my head – felt full of something, like that yellow sponge they used to stuff sofas with. I hadn't shut the curtains before I went to bed so the sunlight spilled through the window, making my eyes sting. I went to pull the duvet over my head but realised it wasn't there; I wasn't underneath it, I was curled up on top of it in the clothes I'd worn the day before.

I hadn't even taken my shoes off.

I groaned and sat up, blindly reaching for the bottle of water on my bedside table. I drained it in a few desperate gulps as I turned my phone on and waited. After a second or two, it sprang to life, the screen flashing with a list of text messages and voicemails. I jumped as it started ringing and jumped again as I realised it was Mike. Then, as if I wasn't already a wreck, someone started pounding on my front door.

My whole body went rigid, my fingers curling around my phone. I waited, hoping it was just someone coming to check the meter or to shake a charity tin at me. But the knocking got more and more persistent until I was sure the door was going to give way.

I crept down the hallway, my heart on my tongue, and peered through the peephole.

Juliet.

'Alright,' I muttered, the muscles in my shoulders softening as I opened the door.

When I did, she was standing on my doormat, looking at me

with utter contempt. 'So you're alive.' She crossed her arms. 'What happened to you last night?'

'I wasn't well,' I said. It didn't take much effort to sound pathetic.

'We missed the gig looking for you. Why aren't you answering your phone?'

'I lost it.'

She nodded at my right hand. 'Isn't that it?'

'It was under the sofa,' I told her, tucking it into the back pocket of my jeans in case Mike called again and she saw. 'I just found it.'

'Sid's mum's in the hospital,' she said with a sigh, throwing it at me like a rock. My legs almost gave way. I reached for the door and realised I was already holding it.

'What?'

'She tried to kill herself.'

'What?'

'He came home to find her last night.'

It was like a succession of slaps. I stared at her. 'Last night?'

My stomach lurched so suddenly, I was sure I was about to vomit at her feet.

'This is my fault,' I murmured.

I didn't think she'd heard me, but when I lifted my eyelashes to look at her, she looked so angry, I thought she was going to hit me. 'Can you not, Rose?'

'Not what?'

'Can you not make this about you?' she said with a sneer.

'Don't get me wrong, Rose, it's quite a gift, how you can turn every conversation, every situation, back around to yourself. Even Sid's mother trying to kill herself is about you.'

She stopped to roll her eyes and I wanted to fly at her, tell her that I wasn't being melodramatic; it *was* about me, if Sid hadn't been looking for me, he would have been at home and he might have been able to stop his mum, to talk to her. But Juliet had obviously been practising her little speech, so I let her have the stage.

'When you change a light bulb, Rose, do you just hold it up' – she pointed at the ceiling – 'and wait for the world to revolve around you?'

I've never wanted to kill her more than at that moment. I wanted to bite the smirk off her face. But I straightened up. I was only a couple of inches taller than she was, but it was enough.

'Feel better?'

'Not really.' She crossed her arms again. 'Sid's mum's in intensive care, but he's out of his mind worrying about you. So can you let him know you're okay so he can focus on his mum for a while? I think she needs his attention more, what with her nearly dying.'

I had to close the door on her then, otherwise I would have punched her.

Mercifully, she wasn't at the hospital when I got there.

'Ro!' Sid gasped when he saw me. I suppose it should have been awkward after I'd disappeared during the gig, but standing in the waiting room of the ITU, surrounded by sobbing, shaking families, it all seemed so juvenile.

He scooped me up into a hug and when he put me back on my feet, I smiled softly and asked him if he was okay.

'Are *you* okay?' he asked.

I looked around, half expecting Juliet to come flying at me. 'Where's Nance?'

'She had to go home for a sec; Eve needed to talk to her about something.'

I wanted to ask why, but the word got caught in my throat as my cheeks started to burn. So I tried to change the subject. 'I brought you something.'

I held up a plastic bag and he peered into it. 'There'd better be some Smarties in here.'

''Course. I drank all the Stella on the bus, though.'

He tipped his head back and laughed. I don't think I've ever been so relieved to hear someone laugh. The sound was so warm, so *bright* that, for a moment, it made me giggle too.

'Only you would joke about that here, Ro.'

I realised what I'd said and gasped. 'Sorry. I didn't think.'

'Don't apologise,' he said, draping an arm across my shoulders and kissing the top of my head. 'I don't want to think for a while, either.'

'Fag?' I suggested and his face lit up.

'Quick. Before Nance gets back.'

'Is she alright? Your mum?' I asked, while we were waiting for the lift. There was a Christmas tree in the corner, its coloured

272

lights blinking merrily. I remember how strange it looked – vulgar, almost – next to a poster reminding visitors to use the hand gel in the dispenser provided before they went into the ITU.

Sid slipped his hands into the back pockets of his jeans and shrugged. 'She's better. They're moving her out of intensive care, but she tried to kill herself so I don't think so.'

It knocked the air right out of me and I just looked at him for a moment.

'I'm so sorry, Sid. I don't know what to say,' I admitted, looking at my feet.

'That's okay, 'cos I don't want to talk about it.'

Thankfully, the lift arrived then and he held the door open so that I could get in. It was full, so we had to squeeze in, but as soon as the doors closed, I reached for his hand like I had at the cemetery. I didn't look at him and he didn't look at me, I just squeezed it and he squeezed mine back, so hard I felt my ring dig into my knuckle.

When we got outside, I didn't push him. I didn't ask how he was feeling or tell him that everything was going to be okay, I just lit a cigarette and handed it to him. We passed it back and forth and when it was finished, he sat on the railing and peered at me from under his eyelashes.

'Come here,' he said, and he looked exhausted, like his mother had at that wedding, like he hadn't slept for years and years.

I stood between his legs, and when he put his arms around my waist and pulled me to him, I shivered. I shivered again when he dipped his head, resting his forehead on my shoulder. I didn't know what to do. I suppose I should have said something comforting, held him and spun him a line about how everything was going to be okay, but I just stood there, my hands fisted in the front of his jacket, so I wouldn't touch him.

I never did, you know. Touch him, I mean. I read what they said in the papers, that I threw myself at him, that I led him on. SHAMELESS, the *Mirror* wrote in capital letters under a picture of me once, but I never laid a finger on him.

I won't lie, I wanted to. There were days when we were in the park, eating chips and bickering about our dream Glastonbury line-up, when the urge to touch him was unbearable. The number of times I almost reached a hand up to twirl a wave of his hair around my finger or I wanted to run my thumb along his bottom lip. But I didn't. And I didn't that afternoon outside the hospital, either. I just waited for him to lift his head again and look at me.

'Thanks, Ro,' he said with a long sigh.

I told myself to let go of his jacket. 'For what?'

'For this.'

'For what? I didn't do anything.'

'Exactly,' he said with a tired smile. 'Nance is amazing, she hasn't left my side, but she's so *practical*. So far today she's brought me two sandwiches, five cups of tea and made me read a load of leaflets about depression.' He stopped to rub his face in his hands. 'She's even been looking up local AA meetings.'

'Yeah, but you need that stuff. I brought you a tube of Smarties and twenty B&H, how's that gonna help?'

'It does.' He reached for my hand and when he pressed a kiss to my palm, the shock of it made me take a step back.

'We should get back inside. I'm freezing,' I told him, my nerves rattling.

But he didn't move. 'This is my fault, isn't it, Ro? What happened to Mum.'

'What?' I took a step towards him again. 'No.'

He shook his head. 'I should have done something when I found the bottles.'

'What were you supposed to do?' I waited until he looked at me again. 'It was her choice. It was a *bad* one, but we're the kids and they're the grown-ups, they're supposed to know what they're doing. Why do we always blame ourselves for *their* mistakes?'

He nodded and he looked so sad I couldn't bear it. So I raised my hand and smoothed the crease between his eyebrows with my finger. He smiled, but before I could smile back, I was aware of someone standing behind me.

'She knew?' I heard someone say and turned to find Juliet watching us.

'You told *her* about your mum,' she looked at Sid, but pointed at me, 'not me?'

'Nance,' he said, jumping down from the railing with a sigh, but she wasn't listening.

'You bitch,' I heard her say before she flew at me.

It happened so quickly that I didn't have time to raise my hands before she slapped me across the face. I'd never been slapped before. It knocked my eyes out of focus and I fell against the railing. It's a strange thing to remember, but I remember how cold the metal was as I reached out for it to steady myself. It was so cold I almost let go of it again.

'Nance! What are you doing?' Sid grabbed her wrist as she tried to slap me a second time, so she tried to slap me with her left hand, but he grabbed that wrist too. 'Stop it!'

'She's a whore, Sid!'

'What?'

'She shagged Mike!'

Sid let go of her then. 'What?'

'She shagged Mike.' She stopped to blow a curl out of her eyes, her fists clenched at her sides. 'That's why I had to go home; Eve wanted to tell me they're getting a divorce!'

Sid stared at me. 'I didn't,' I breathed, shaking my head. 'We just kissed.'

'Like it matters! I thought you were my friend!' Juliet came at me again, grabbing my hair and pulling so hard I yelped. 'You ruined everything. I have to live with another family.'

Sid grabbed her wrists again and looked at her. 'What? Why?'

She stopped then. I suppose I could have told him; because they're not her aunt and uncle, they're her foster parents and if Mike leaves, who'll protect poor, precious Juliet? Perhaps I should have. Perhaps I should have reached up and pushed her off that high horse. Then she would have seen what it was like down in the gutter with me.

But then a woman in a dressing-gown looked at us as a nurse in a Santa hat pushed her wheelchair up the ramp towards the hospital and I remembered where we were.

'Can we not do this now?' I said, lowering my voice. 'I think Sid—'

'Don't tell me what's best for Sid,' Juliet interrupted with a filthy glare.

I tried again. 'I don't think now is the best time to—'

'No. I want to do this now. I want Sid to know who he's confiding in.'

'Well, can we do it somewhere we're not disturbing a load of sick people?'

'You're the sick one, Rose. I know your type.'

I shouldn't have, but I bit back. 'My type?'

'Your family's broken up, so break up mine. Can't find a boyfriend? Take mine!'

I saw the tears in her eyes, the way her hand shook as she pointed at me, and my heart. She knew what I'd done. I didn't even have to tell her and she knew.

Juliet Shaw is a lot of things, but she's not stupid.

'I thought we were friends, Rose. I told you everything.'

I stepped forward then, an eyebrow raised. 'Everything?'

'That's *enough*!' Sid barked, standing between us before I could say it, *scream* her name until my lungs burned. 'Enough!'

'Sid—' she started to say, but he shook his head.

'No, Nancy. I don't want to hear any more.'

'But, Sid!'

'*But, Sid* nothing. Do you know that my mother is in intensive care right now?'

She stepped back, but she still looked livid. 'Of course I do!'

'So why are you bringing this drama to me right now?'

She laughed and pointed at me. 'She behaves like a whore and it's *my* fault?'

'Stop calling her a whore,' he said and my heart doubled in size.

'I knew you'd defend her.' Juliet shook her head, but he was unmoved.

'I don't know what happened, but you only have to look at Rose to know she's messed up. I mean, look at the state of her. She's a wreck.'

Juliet looked me up and down. 'We all have problems, Sid, but most of us can deal with them without drinking ourselves stupid.'

He crossed his arms and titled his head. 'What? Like my mum?'

There was a painful silence after he'd said it. Juliet's jaw clenched.

'All I'm saying,' Sid continued, 'is that Rose needs help and I don't care if she threw herself at Mike, he didn't have to catch her. She's *sixteen*. She needs someone to be there for her, she doesn't need some dirty old man trying to get his leg over.'

Juliet slapped him then, so hard he staggered back.

Then I was between them. 'Go back to your mum, Sid. I'll deal with this.'

He didn't move, so I nudged him back with my elbow. 'Go. It's okay.'

He did and as soon as Juliet and I were alone, I stepped forward. She stepped back into the railing. 'Touch him again and I'll cut your heart out,' I told her, and I'd never sounded more like a Koll.

Dad would've been proud.

She lifted her chin to look at me, her eyes wild and bright and there she was at last, Juliet Shaw, not Nancy Wells. The Juliet Shaw who stabbed my father in the back and brought my whole world crashing down around me. And I knew then that was it.

I was ready.

'Shut up,' I told her. As soon as I did, she opened her mouth to say something. I lifted my finger. 'I said shut up. That's enough. *Enough*. We'll talk about this later.'

She nodded, and I looked at her, really looked at her for the first time, right in the eye. And I didn't care what she saw, if she saw Rose or Emily.

I wanted her to see.

Val killed herself this morning. When they found her, they made us go to our rooms and wouldn't let us out until we'd spoken to Doctor Gilyard.

I didn't have anything to say. I mean, it's shit, but Val was obviously miserable. Maybe she's better off. So what Doctor Gilyard wanted to talk about, I don't know, but she sat in my room for an hour. I know it was an hour because the door was open so I listened to the whole of the one o'clock news before I kicked off my blanket and sat up.

'Val killed herself. So what?' I shrugged. 'Can I have a fag now?'

She looked at me for a long time, then she wrote something in her notebook.

I rolled my eyes and went to stand by the window, looking

through the bars at the sad roll of the clouds. The weather had turned again; the sky was pale blue and there was no chill from the glass, no frost gathering at the corners of the window like cobwebs.

'Maybe it's you who needs to talk to someone,' I told her with another shrug.

She looked up then. 'Why's that, Emily?'

'You couldn't help her. You're not helping me.'

She looked down again, but she didn't write anything. 'What makes you say that?'

'This isn't working.'

'What isn't working, Emily?'

'This, *this* whatever you're supposed to be doing, isn't working.'

'In what way isn't it working, Emily?'

'I'm not—' I stopped, my eyes following a bird as it dipped then soared again.

'You're not what, Emily?'

'Better.'

It was very quiet after I'd said it. I could feel the silence between us, thick as smoke, touching the walls, filling the corners.

'Do you want to get better, Emily?'

I do. I used to be able to do this. I used to be able to put food in my mouth and taste it. I used to be able to close my eyes and sleep. Do normal things like paint my nails. When I think of those September afternoons in the park with Sid and Juliet, eating crisps and squabbling over what film to see as the sun melted behind the trees, it feels like for ever ago. Will I ever do anything that normal again? Will I forget? Forget the chill of sitting on damp grass? Will I ever look up at an endless blue sky, or will I only see it in strips from now?

I heard Doctor Gilyard writing and turned towards her again.

'You look worn out, Emily. I'm going to give you something to help you sleep—' she started to say, but I wouldn't let her finish.

'No!' I hissed, my fists clenched. 'No more pills!'

'Emily—'

I lunged towards her. 'No more pills! Is that your answer to everything? Talk. Take a pill. Talk. Take a pill. Talk. Take a pill. Talk. Take a pill.'

When she didn't flinch, I snapped. 'Do something! Will you just *do something*!'

'Do what, Emily?' she asked, and when she took her glasses off to look at me, I wanted to reach for her shoulders and shake her. But I was so rigid with anger, I couldn't move; I was sure my spine would snap if I did.

'Help me!' I said. Begged. 'Help me!'

She stood up then, turning to put her notebook on the chair, and the shock of it made me take a step back.

'Okay, Emily. Come with me.'

'Where?' I asked, my cheeks stinging.

She didn't wait for me to respond, just walked out of my room.

When I followed her on to the mezzanine I could smell chips. That's all this place smells of: chips. Chips, rolling tobacco and something else, something metallic. Whatever the doors and keys are made of, I guess. That smell you get on your fingers when you've been holding a handful of pennies.

I listened to the tap of Doctor Gilyard's shoes on the steel stairs as she walked down them and when she got to the bottom, I peered over the railing. I watched her go into the TV Room, but before I could tell myself not to give her the satisfaction of doing what she said, I ran down the stairs and followed her in.

When I saw the cello, I took a step back.

'No.' I shook my head. I knew she was going to do that.

I knew it.

'Emily—' she started to say, but I shook my head at her again.

'No.'

'Emily—'

'No.' My heart was beating so hard, I thought I might fall over. 'No. Not here.'

She frowned. 'Why not here?'

I pointed at the cello. My hand was shaking, but I didn't care if she saw it. 'Not here. Don't bring that in here. You can't bring that in here.'

'Why not, Emily?'

'I won't play it. I won't. I won't go near it.'

I stepped back into the doorway to prove the point. We stared at each other for a moment, me with my arms crossed, her with the cello standing next to her like a faithful dog.

'It might help, Emily.'

'How?' I roared, so loud I'm sure I felt my bones rattle.

'I know what you think of music therapy, Emily, but—'

'No! I won't play that here!'

'Why not, Emily?'

'Because it's beautiful!' I told her, charging back into the room to stand opposite her. 'It's beautiful and I won't let you ruin it!'

'Why would playing it here ruin it, Emily?'

'Because it's miserable here! Miserable and grey and hopeless and that is so, so beautiful.' I pointed at the cello again. 'It can make sounds that will lift you right out of your shoes. I won't let you ruin it. I won't.'

She nodded. 'And because when you played it, you were at your most happy; when you were at St Jude's; when you were with Sid.'

'Stop.'

'You can be happy again, Emily. You will be happy again, Emily.'

She held the bow out to me and I shook my head. 'No.'

We stared at each other, the bow between us. When I heard my heart beating in my ears, I realised how quiet it was. It was strange. The television was off, I realised, and it made my heart beat harder. I thought of Val then, pictured her hanging from that pipe in her cell, her feet not quite touching the floor and something in me finally gave way.

I snatched the bow from Doctor Gilyard. 'Fine.' I felt my blood bubbling – burning – as I reached for the cello, too. 'But we need an audience.'

I paced out of the room, the rubber endpin of the cello bouncing on the lino as I swept into the mess. Doctor Gilyard followed me in as fourteen heads looked up from their plastic plates of chips and over-cooked sausages.

I dragged a chair into the middle of the floor and sat on it. I didn't touch the cello the way I did that afternoon in the music shop in Camden, with awe – with *longing* – I just parted my knees and put it on the floor, my hand grabbing at the neck as I dragged the bow across it. It made the most awful sound, nails-on-a-chalk-board awful, and I felt everyone in the room wince. I looked up at Doctor Gilyard then, Doctor Gilyard in her neat black heels and her neat black pencil skirt, and I did it again and again until the cello was screaming out. The sound was so painful – so *vicious* – and when my eyes darted over to the table to find no one looking at me any more, I realised *that* is what I do to people, I make them look away, as though I'm a mad man who has stumbled on to their carriage on the tube ranting about God.

So I stared at the table, at the fourteen heads dipped, staring at their half-eaten dinners, and played harder and harder until I could feel tears spilling off my jaw. I wanted to hurt them, to make them listen to the sound I heard in my head all the time, the battle between the Emily I was and the Emily I actually am so they could know what it's like.

So they could hear how it's killing me.

But from nowhere, my bow grazed the strings at just the right point to produce a sound so clear – so sweet – it made me shiver. So I tried to find it again and when I did, I shivered once more. I can't remember the last time I shivered like that, the last time I felt so light. It wasn't happiness, I know, at least not the happiness

I felt at St Jude's or when I was with Sid, but it was enough to make me play until the cello sang, until I was breathless and everyone looked up from their dinner. Until Doctor Gilyard stepped closer and nurses began to hover in the doorway. Until I lifted each one of them out of their shoes.

This is why I didn't want to play the cello, because I knew this would happen, that I wouldn't sleep, that playing again would make my whole body hum with heat and hope, like it did that afternoon at the music shop in Camden when I thought I could do anything. That I could fly.

I have so much I want to say; I can't write it quickly enough. There's a dent in my finger from holding the pen so hard. I know we're getting to the good stuff. This is what you want, right? You don't care about who I was and how I felt and my inane conversations about tattoos. You just want to know what happened, why I did it. That's why you're reading this, right?

So okay, this is why I did it.

Sid came to my flat after I had had the fight with Juliet.

He'd never been to my flat before – I didn't think he knew

where I lived – but there he was when I opened the front door, pale and exhausted, his hands in his pockets.

'I can't go home,' he said before I could say hello, and he sounded out of breath, as though he'd run all the way from the hospital.

'You shouldn't be here,' I told him, but I stepped back to let him in and he followed me, peeling off his jacket as he kicked the door shut behind him.

'You okay?'

'What are you doing here, Sid?' I asked, walking into the living room. But I knew. As soon as I saw him, I knew.

I waited for him to say it, my hands shaking as I leaned down and picked my box of cigarettes off the coffee table. When I turned to face him again he was watching me as I lit one. I don't know if he was waiting for me to take a drag then hand it to him, but I didn't.

'I came to see if you were alright,' he said, taking a step towards me.

He was staring at the heart-shaped bruise darkening on my cheek, so I turned my face away. 'I'm fine.'

'Are you?'

I took a drag on my cigarette and blew the smoke towards the television. I remember that there was an ad on for a furniture shop or a supermarket, or something. I remember this little boy in red tartan pyjamas ripping open a Christmas present. When 'Rockin' Around the Christmas Tree' started playing, I snatched the remote off the sofa and turned it off. Then the flat was too quiet – too *still*. It made my heart pounding in my ears sound even louder. It was so loud that I half expected my neighbour to start banging on the wall, telling me to shut up. So loud that I almost didn't hear him say, 'You didn't, did you?'

'Do what?' I said, and I don't know why. I wanted to hear him say it, I guess.

'Sleep with Mike.'

'What's it to you?' I leaned down and stubbed my cigarette out in the ashtray on the coffee table. 'I can sleep with whomever I like.'

I made a point of looking at him then, made myself look him in the eye.

'No.' He shook his head. 'No. You wouldn't.'

'Wouldn't I?'

He lifted his chin, adamant. 'No. The Rose I know wouldn't do that.'

I almost laughed.

Rose.

We stared at each other across the living room for a moment and looking back on it now, I think he might have loved me. I'd catch him looking at me sometimes, not like he looked at Juliet, I admit, but we'd be walking through the park, arguing about song lyrics and he'd look at me like he was trying to decide, like he was waiting for me to make him laugh one more time or to mock him for his weakness for Springsteen and then he'd know for sure. And I could have loved him too. That wild, uncontainable kind of love. Let's-pack-a-bag-and-run kind of love. The sort of love that starts wars and brings down governments.

So Doctor Gilyard's right; I could have let myself be Rose. He would never have known. I could have grabbed him and kissed him until he couldn't breathe, until he forgot every word he knew except for my name. But he wasn't looking at me, was he? He was looking at Rose Glass. And I'm not Rose Glass. I'm not sixteen. I've never lived in Barnsbury. My hair isn't even red.

'I wish I could be who you think I am,' I told him and he frowned.

'But you are.'

I thought of Juliet then, of what she had done, of what I wanted to do to her, and something in me reignited.

'You don't know me, Sid. You don't know what I've done. What I'm capable of.'

He took a step towards me. 'I don't care. It doesn't matter.'

'It does. It has to. It's who I am. It's made me who I am.'

'Don't say that. You can be whoever you want to be, Rose,' he said, and I smiled.

That was the last time I let anyone call me Rose.

He didn't want me, that's why I did it. That's what they say in the papers, isn't it? Hell hath no fury, and all that. But the truth is: I chose her not him. Emily not Rose. I know what I did to Juliet. I hold my hands up to it, sign my name across it. I know what she lost, but I lost something too, you know. I could have been happy.

I could have been happy.

But that doesn't sell newspapers, does it?

You know the rest: how it ended, under that tree in Brighton. I don't how Juliet got there; I think she ran all the way from London. When she found me at the top of the hill, she sounded so out of breath that she could have. I don't know how she found me, either, under that tree, the one by the cottage with the red-

293

painted shutters. I don't even remember giving her the address when I called.

But there she was.

'Rose!' she gasped, running towards me.

It was what I wanted, her wide eyed and terrified and me ready, at last. When I called her sobbing, I knew she'd come. I'm going to kill myself, I told her, I'm going to drag a knife across my wrists and bleed out into the grass. Earth to earth. But when I saw her, I was furious. She came. Even after everything I'd done, she came. She shouldn't have. She should have told me to fuck off, told me that we weren't friends any more, told me to call Mike. But she didn't and I hated her so much then.

Have you ever met someone like that? Someone so good – not perfect, but *good* – that they make you feel rotten? If Sid made me feel like I could fly, then Juliet made me feel like I'd never leave the ground, that I'd live out the rest of my days in the gutter.

'Rose,' she gasped again when she got to me.

When I'd left London, the weather was foul, the sky grey and the clouds so thick you couldn't tell if it was night or day. But suddenly, the sun punched through the clouds and I could see for miles. Miles and miles. All I could see was her, her lips parted and the sunlight catching on her eyelashes, and I was ready at last – at last – but then I saw Sid.

He looked terrified. 'Ro,' he called out as he ran towards me.

'What are you doing here?' I wanted to roar, but it came out as a whisper.

He wasn't supposed to be there. See? I told you not to believe everything you read, it was just supposed to be me and Juliet. But there he was.

I turned to Juliet. I thought of her sitting on the floor of that bookshop with a copy of *To Kill a Mockingbird* between her fingers and I felt my resolve harden.

'Why did you bring him?' She didn't answer, but I knew and I was giddy. 'You need him,' I told her with a slow smile. I'd always known she loved him, but she *needed* him. As long as I'd known her, she'd never needed anyone, but then she did.

I tipped my head back and laughed, so loud that the birds fled from the branches over my head. I looked up as they wheeled past, then turned to look at the tree. 'I haven't been here since I was eight. Not since my gramps died. My nan wouldn't come back without him,' I told them, pressing a hand to its dark trunk. 'It isn't how I remember.'

I remember how my heart sagged when I got there that day. The tree wasn't as tall as I remembered and I was sure it was closer to the sea. I could see it – on the horizon – and I could smell it, the tang of salt in the air, but it was too far away.

'Rose, come on,' Juliet said carefully. Despite the sunshine, it must have been cold because when I turned to look at her, her curls were whipping back and forth, but I couldn't feel a thing. 'There's a café at the bottom of the hill. Let's go get a cup of tea and talk.'

I knew that café. Dad used to take me there for ice cream whenever we came here. When I was tiny, he would walk me up and down the hill on his shoulders. 'Are you holding on, little one?' he'd ask, then he'd bounce me up and down and I would laugh and laugh.

'Rose, please,' Sid said, stepping forward. 'You're scaring me.'

I turned to face the tree again. 'When I was eight, I climbed this tree. It was the bravest thing I've ever done. I thought I was on top of the world.'

I turned to Sid as he lifted his eyelashes to look up at the sky, and I knew he was thinking about that afternoon at the park.

'But after a few minutes I realised that I was all alone,' I breathed and he looked at me again, his forehead creased. 'I'd never been alone. There was always someone downstairs or watching me scramble across the monkey bars at the park. But here, up this tree, I was alone. I knew if something happened to me no one would know. No one would find me because, for the first time, I hadn't told anyone where I was going, I just went.'

Sid nodded. 'There was this awful moment when I thought I'd never see anyone again, my dad, my uncle, my nan, Gramps. I thought that was it.' My heart tensed at the memory. 'It's horrible, to be eight and to know it's *just you*, that your parents won't always be there. I wanted to climb this tree so bad, as soon as I saw it, but then I wished I hadn't.'

The wind blew my hair into my face and when it stuck to my cheeks, I realised I was crying. 'Curiosity will break your heart,' I told him with a shiver.

He stepped forward and I think he was going to say something, but I'll never know what it was because Juliet interrupted. 'If this is about yesterday, about our argument, don't worry. It'll be okay,' she said, coming to stand next to me. 'I promise.'

I stared at her, suddenly livid. 'You broke my heart, too.'

'What?'

'You ruined my life.'

She looked stunned. 'What? How?'

'You stabbed my father.'

I said it so smoothly. After months of swallowing down the words every time she smiled at me or Sid kissed her, they finally flew out of my mouth. BANGBANGBANG.

I heard her breath catch in her throat, then she took a step back. 'Who are you?'

'Who am I? Who are you? That's the question.'

Sid looked between us. 'What's going on?'

'Tell him, Juliet.' I said her name with a smile. Sang it like a fucking aria.

She took another step back. 'Who are you?'

'Well, you're Juliet Shaw and you stabbed my father so that would make me . . .' I tilted my head and pretended to think about it.

'Emily Koll,' she breathed and I looked at her with a wide smile.

No one had ever been scared of me before then, like really, truly *scared*. I can't say I enjoyed it, even though it was what I wanted. And it's funny that, how you can want something for so long, then when you get it, it doesn't feel like you expected it to feel.

Sid stood between us. 'What's going on? What are you talking about?'

'Sid, be careful. Stay away from her.' She took another step back and then it was so quiet that all I could hear was my heart in my ears as I took the knife out of my pocket and held it up. It looked beautiful in the sunlight, like it was made of gold.

As soon as Sid saw it, the colour fled from his cheeks. 'Rose, what are you doing?'

'Don't call me that.'

'Call you what?'

'Sid, don't. Get away from her,' Juliet said, reaching for the sleeve of his jacket and tugging him back. 'You can't reason with her. She's dangerous.'

But still he tried. 'Rose, stop it. What are you doing? Give me the knife.'

'An eye for an eye,' I told him. 'A heart for a heart.'

I smiled and drew a heart in the air with the knife.

'Rose, you're scaring me.'

'Stop calling me that!' I hissed.

'Sid, please,' Juliet sobbed, grabbing at his sleeve again. 'Get away from her.'

I pointed the knife at her. 'I lost everything because of you!'

'I lost everything because of your father!' she roared back.

'But you got it all back, didn't you? Mike and Eve, Sid.'

'It's not the same!' She was crying then and it was beautiful. So beautiful.

'Better than being Emily Koll, the gangster's daughter. I didn't do anything wrong!'

'How is it *my* fault that your father is a criminal?'

I shook my head. 'He wasn't. Not until you stabbed him.' I looked at Sid then. I wanted to grab him and shake him. 'I didn't know. About any of it. Before she stabbed him, he was just my dad. You know?' Sid nodded. 'I didn't know.'

I looked back at Juliet. 'Then you stabbed him and everything fell apart and I had nothing. *Nothing*. Everything I knew was a lie. How does it feel?' I stepped towards her. She looked down at the knife. 'Everything about you is a lie. Sid doesn't love you, he loves Nancy Wells. Your aunt and uncle aren't your aunt and uncle, they're just some random couple you were sent to live with. You weren't even born in February, your birthday is in October. It's all a lie. Everything. I've said it out loud now so it's all gone. *POOF*. Gone. How does it feel?' I laughed and pointed the knife at her. 'How does it feel, Juliet?'

Sid stood in front of me before I could take another step forward. 'Ro, don't do this.'

'I love you so much, Sid.' I looked up at him and I could hear my voice shaking. Shaking and shaking. 'You know that, right? I'm out of my mind in love with you.'

'I know. Rose, please. *Please* don't do this.'

'But I hate her more.'

'Don't, Rose.'

'Please don't call me that,' I told him with sob.

Then I stabbed him.

I have ten minutes before the guard gets here to take me to the Old Bailey, so I'm writing this as quickly as I can. Sorry if you can't read it.

This morning has been strange. Quiet. I'm wearing a suit. I haven't worn this suit since that Open Day at St Jude's when I played the prelude from Bach's Cello Suite No. 1 and everyone in the auditorium clapped so hard I couldn't hear my heart in my ears any more.

I kind of look like Emily. I can't remember the last time I looked like Emily. Naomi helped me get ready; she brushed my hair and filed my nails with an emery board she borrowed from one of the nurses. She didn't say a word while she did it; she didn't ask how I was feeling or tell me that everything was going to be okay, and I was glad. I know what people think of girls like

301

us, of girls who end up in a place like this, but despite our misdemeanours and the colourful array of pills we live on, we don't lie to each other.

Doctor Gilyard just called me into her office. I thought she was going to sit me down, ask me again if I'm sorry, but she just nodded at the phone on her desk.

'I've arranged for you to speak to someone, Emily.'

I looked at her, then at the phone. 'No.' I shook my head. 'I'm not talking to her.'

'Please, Emily.'

I stepped back from the desk. 'I have nothing to say to her. I'll say it all in court.'

She picked up the receiver and held it out to me like she did with the bow that afternoon in the TV Room. It made me think of Val, of her feet not quite touching the floor.

My legs shook as I took the phone from her and sat down. 'Hello?'

'Emily,' a voice said, and my heart started to throb.

I think it knew before I did.

'Dad?'

'Hello, little one.'

Everything in me relaxed all at once. I felt my bones soften like warm wax.

'Daddy.'

'You alright, little one?'

I had to wait a second or two before I could speak, but even when I'd caught my breath, it still came out as a whisper. 'Yeah.'

The line was quiet after that. I heard the scrape of a chair leg on lino, then he sighed. 'I'm sorry, Em. I wanted to be there today, but it turns out it's a bit late to try to be a dad.'

'That's okay.'

'No.' He sounded tense. I imagined him shaking his head, perhaps running a hand across his forehead. 'No, it isn't. You shouldn't have to do this on your own.'

'I'm not on my own.'

'Who's with you? That doctor?'

'Yeah.' I lifted my eyelashes to look at her. She was in her chair. 'Doctor Gilyard.'

'She sorted it so I could speak to you.'

I wanted to tell him that was nice of her, that it was so good to hear his voice again, but I could feel the tears gathering at the corners of my eyes and I couldn't let them out. I wanted to be brave. I wanted him to see how strong I was.

But he knew.

'You alright, little one?'

I tried to blink the tears away, but I couldn't, so I squeezed my eyes shut. 'Yeah.'

'You giving them hell?'

That made me chuckle. It felt all warm and soft in my chest. 'Yeah.'

I opened my eyes again and looked over at Doctor Gilyard. She was flicking through her notebook and bouncing the rubber end of her pencil against her bottom lip.

'Good girl. You ready for today?'

I tugged on the hem of my jacket. 'I'm wearing a suit.'

'The black one?'

'Yeah, it smells weird. Like home.'

'Yeah?'

I sniffed the lapel. 'It smells of that perfume you bought me in Paris for my sixteenth birthday. Do you remember?'

''Course I remember. What was that place we went to afterwards?'

'Ladurée.'

'Yeah, Ladurée. Twenty-five euro for a cup of tea and a bit of cake and you didn't even eat it!'

'I did!' I chuckled again and as I did, I felt something in me stir, something under my skin, like when you cut yourself and a couple of days later, the ache becomes an itch.

Dad chuckled, too. 'You didn't! You just took photos of it on your phone.'

'But it was so pretty.'

'And what was that mad bookshop called?'

'Shakespeare and Company.'

'I don't know how you found so many books in there. It was a mess.'

'At least they spoke English.'

'True. We would never have found that crêpe place otherwise.'

There was a long moment when we just laughed and for that moment I forgot – where he was, where I am. It was like I was ringing him from St Jude's. I wanted to ask about Duck, to curse Arsène Wenger and whinge about homework. But then I heard a door – the cold click of a key in a lock at his end or mine, I'm still not sure – and my shoulders fell.

'I'm so sorry, Daddy,' I said with a defeated sob as the tears finally found a way out.

He listened to me cry for a moment or two – not just cry, wild *ugly* sobs – but when my breathing settled, he didn't hush me like he did when I was little, he didn't tell me not to be silly, that everything was going to be okay, he just told me to stop.

'Don't, Emily,' he said, and I could just see the look on his face, the look he gives me whenever I tell him that I can't do something. I knew he was pointing at the phone. 'Don't you dare apologise to me. You're my baby girl; I should have been looking out for you.'

'Yeah, but—' I started to say with another broken sob, but he stopped me.

'No, Emily. This is my fault. Look what I made you do.'

I shook my head. 'You didn't make me do anything.'

'Of course I did! This isn't you, all this anger, this bravado. What've I done to you?'

There was a tremor in his voice when he said it and nothing in my life – not Juliet, not this place, not whatever will happen to me today – has scared me more than that tremor, than that moment of helplessness.

He'd never sounded so human.

'Daddy—'

'Emily, don't.'

'Don't what?'

'Just stop it.'

'Stop what, Daddy?'

'Stop trying to be me.'

My hands were shaking. I wondered if his were, too.

'You're better than that, Em. Better than this.'

I looked out of the window, at the rolls of razor wire and the grey, grey sky and it was like waking up from a Sunday afternoon nap; I suddenly didn't know where I was.

'I thought I was doing the right thing,' he said, almost to himself. 'I thought I was protecting you, sending you to boarding school, not telling you about your mum.'

He stopped. I think he was waiting for me to catch my breath, waiting for me to ask.

'What happened to her?' I said it so quietly I thought I'd have to say it again, like that time I broke the Chinese vase in the dining room.

'I don't know, Em. She just left.'

I smiled at that. A strange reaction, I know, but it made something in me realign.

He hadn't lied to me.

'Em?' he said when the silence lingered a moment too long.

I didn't think I could breathe, but I managed to ask, 'Why didn't you tell me?'

'I don't know,' he said with a long sigh. 'It was selfish. It just hurt so much to talk about, you know?' I nodded, even though he couldn't see me. 'I couldn't make her happy so all I wanted to do was make you happy. I wanted you to be so happy, Em.' I heard his chair scrape through the phone again. 'I love you so much, you know that, don't you?'

I wiped my cheek with the heel of my palm. 'Of course I do, Daddy.'

'Then you need to get better,' he told me, and he sounded like him again, like Superman. 'You need to do everything that doctor tells you to do so that you get out of there and not go to Cambridge like I want you to, but run off to Paris or start a band or marry a broke writer or any of those other things you'd swore you'd do whenever you were mad at me.'

I tried to laugh, but it came out more like a hiccup. 'I will.'

'No, you *have to* 'cos you're the only thing I've ever done right, kid. The only thing.'

'Yes, Daddy,' I breathed, my cheeks burning as the shame finally flooded through me. I looked away from the window down at the blotter on Doctor Gilyard's desk. My scribbles were gone, the sheet clean, but as I ran my fingers over it, I could still feel the deep grooves in the paper, as though it remembered me.

'Promise me, Emily.'

'I promise.'

The line was quiet for a second or two. I heard another door open then shut. A key in a lock.

'You're gonna be alright, you know.'

'Am I?'

''Course you will, Emily. You're a Koll, ain't you?' he said, and even through the phone I knew he was smiling. And I smiled, too, because he's right, I am.

I guess I forgot that isn't always a bad thing.

The following loose pages were tucked into the back of the notebook.

DERIVATIVES **sorrowfully** adv.

sorry – adj. (**sorrier, sorriest**) 1 feeling sympathy for someone's misfortune. 2 feeling or expressing pity. 3 in a regretful state. 4 uncomfortable and unfortunate: *I said nothing of the whole sorry affair*.
ORIGIN Old English, 'distressed'.

sort – n. 1 a group of people or things distinguished by a common nature or feature. 2

ORIGIN Old French *luvesche*.

love – n. 1 a profound feeling of affection. 2 sexual passion or desire. 3 a deep interest and enjoyment of something. 4 someone to whom love it felt. 5 (in tennis, squash, etc.) a score of zero.
v. (**loves, loving, loved**) 1 feel love for. 2 like very much.

I loved you less, I might be able to talk about it more.

'I've dreamt in my life dreams that have stayed with me ever after, and changed my ideas: they've gone through and through me, like wine through water, and altered the colour of my mind. And this is one: I'm going to tell it - but take care not to smile at any part of it.'

~~CHAPTER XXVII~~

So, throughout life, our worst weaknesses and meannesses are usually committed for the sake of the people whom we most despise.

girls are so queer you never know what they mean. They
say no when they mean yes, and drive a man out of his wits just for the fun of it,

Is ~~Emily~~ ~~Koll Evil?~~

this

it

Let it

be.

the

laughed

little girl

Acknowledgements

This book may have been written, but it certainly wouldn't have left the confines of my hard drive were it not for the support and guidance of the following people. First, Cristin Moor, not only for encouraging me to write, but for making me fall in love with books again. Liz de Jager and her Red Boots of Awesome for feeding me tea and holding my hand through this whole process. Dawn Klehr and Kathryne Del Sesto for reading the various drafts of this story and making sure that I wrote the best book that I could. Kelly Bignall, Sarah Genever, Jade Bell, Fiona Hodge, Martha Close and Ros Lawler for telling me I could do it, then crying when I did. Jo Burton, Sarah Platt and Debbie Kilbride for cheering me on when I left a perfectly decent job at the BBC to write a book. Sue Hyams and all my friends at the SCBWI. John and Kerry at La Muse for giving me the time and space to write this book. Camille Gooderham Campbell at Every Day Fiction for taking a chance on me and publishing my first short story. Tracy Marchini for telling me that the first draft needed more tension. Without her, Emily's story would never have been told. My wonderful and ceaselessly patient agent, Claire Wilson at Rogers, Coleridge & White, for never dropping olives on slate floors. Jane Morpeth, Hannah Sheppard, Sam Eades, Vicky Cowell, Lucy Foley and the rest of the team at

Headline who are brilliant and seem to love this book as much as I do. My mother, who loves me in a boundless and incorruptible way, whatever I do or want to be. And finally, my brother Martin, who knew I could do this before I did. Okay. You can read it now, bro.

Author Q&A with Tanya Byrne

Have you always wanted to be a writer?

Oh dear. My first author interview and I'm already contemplating lying. This does not bode well.

The truth is, I haven't always wanted to be a writer. I've always been creative. I loved Art at school and seemed to permanently have paint under my fingernails or be peeling PVA glue off my fingers, but I didn't read much as a child. I grew up in a house without books and don't remember ever being read a bedtime story or being encouraged to read for fun at school. In fairness, I think the teachers struggled to get us to read the books we had to read and if they did suggest anything else, I was more concerned with split ends and the fine art of applying eyeliner to listen.

But then I got Miss Briggs for English Lit. Miss Briggs used to act, so when she read aloud in class we were rapt. (Her Lennie from *Of Mice and Men* was particularly good, if I recall.) I had no idea books could be so entertaining, so *exciting*, and when she took us to the theatre (it was the first time I'd been to the theatre to see something other than a pantomime), all of a sudden, the stuff we were reading in class was being played out in front of me and it began to make sense.

But as much as I enjoyed seeing the play of *Jane Eyre*, reading the book was still arduous. That sounds awful given what I now do for a living, but, to me, books were written by solemn – usually *dead* – people who said things like *ergo* and *methinks*. Girls from East London who get detention for wearing DMs don't say things like *ergo* and *methinks*. So watching a play was one thing, but spending weeks reading a thick book with tiny writing was quite another.

Then someone brought a copy of *Forever*, by Judy Blume, into class and when we heard what it was about, we were hysterical. I had to wait my turn, but when it was finally passed onto me, I *devoured* it. Obviously, the subject matter held some appeal, but more than that, it was about teenagers, teenagers who spoke like me and talked about things my friends talked about. I didn't think books could be like that. Some people will say that they shouldn't, that teenagers should be reading the classics, but I think there's room for both. After all, if I hadn't read *Forever*, I don't think you would be holding my book right now. So read. Read everything you can get your hands on. And if it makes you happy, read it again.

How did Emily's voice develop?

I've been asked this *a lot* by writerly friends and I wish I could say that I did this, or I did that, but really, I just wrote and wrote. It's a bit like trying to tune in an old radio; for a long time all I heard was staticstaticstatic then *this voice*. I had the plot, so I knew what was going to happen to her, and I kept asking myself, How would Emily react to that? How would Emily react to that?

The friends who read early drafts would sometimes say to me, *Emily wouldn't do that* and I'd raise an eyebrow and think, *Um. Excuse you. I created Emily, I think I'd know what she'd do.* But then I'd read it back and realise they were absolutely right. By the time I was done, they knew Emily as well as I did. I hope readers will too.

What were your influences when writing *Heart-Shaped Bruise?*

Hamlet is one of my favourite plays so, with hindsight, it's no surprise to find so many of its themes in *Heart-Shaped Bruise* — morality, corruption, betrayal. Emily's need for revenge, her procrastination, her madness, for want of a better word. I think it influenced me more than I realised, as did all the books I love. Characters like Scout Finch, Briony Tallis, Lyra Belacqua, Will Parry, Katniss Everdeen, Holden Caulfield, Alaska Young and so many others, all shaped Emily in some way.

What was the inspiration behind the novel?

Initially, I wanted to write a novel about a girl who has to join the witness protection program when her father is murdered, so *Heart-Shaped Bruise* was originally from Juliet's point of view. But then, in an effort to create more tension, I introduced Emily, Juliet's new friend at college who wasn't quite what she seemed.

I quickly realised that Emily's version of events was more interesting, so I started again.

How do you want your readers to feel about Emily?

This is such a hard question. I want readers to love her, to see that she's broken, that what she did isn't *who* she is. And while I'm sure most people will see that, not everyone will love her for it. After all, Emily did a terrible thing – lots of terrible things, actually – I don't expect anyone to be TEAM EMILY, but I hope no one just dismisses her as evil.

What do you want your readers to most remember about *Heart-Shaped Bruise*?

People ask me all the time why I write about young adults and I tell them it's because they feel things so *intensely*. The first time their best friend betrays them, the first time a boy doesn't love them back and, even deeper than that, the first time they realise their parents are human, which is what triggers Emily's downfall in *Heart-Shaped Bruise*. I hope readers remember how that felt and understand how it was enough to make Emily do what she did. I also hope *Heart-Shaped Bruise* reminds readers that bad things happen to everyone, but it's how we react to those things that matters. Whether we overcome them and move on – like Juliet did – or if we let them fester and infect everything in our lives, like Emily did.

What advice would you give to aspiring novelists?

Read, read and read some more. Read everything, not just books in your genre, not just *books*, read newspapers, magazines, graffiti. Inspiration comes when you least expect it. You don't even have to finish a book if you're not enjoying it, just remember why you abandoned it and don't make the same mistake with yours.

Most of all, be honest. If you're not proud enough to stand on a chair, hold your book up and say, I WROTE THIS, then start again. Don't write what you think will sell. Don't write what you think readers will like. Don't write what other authors write. Just write. Write until your hands shake, until the words begin to weigh on those bruised parts of you that no one else knows about and when they do, keep writing.

Which writers do you most admire, past and present?

I read pretty widely. I didn't do a creative writing degree, so I learned to write from reading other people's books. I read everything. I'm not sure if it shows in my writing, but if *Heart-Shaped Bruise* has even a little of Kurt Vonnegut's honesty, Suzanne Collins' energy, John Green's humour or Nabokov's bone-meltingly beautiful prose, I'd be happy. I've also recently become besotted with Melina Marchetta. I love the way she writes boys. They're such, well, *boys*. I hope people will say the same of Sid.

Music has an important place in the novel. Do you listen to music when you're writing, and if so, what?

Definitely. I used to work for BBC Radio, so music, especially live music, is in my blood, my marrow. I had different playlists for different parts of *Heart-Shaped Bruise*. I listened to Yo-Yo Ma whenever I wrote about St Jude's or when Emily played the cello, and to a lot of Radiohead and Martha Wainwright when she was at Archway, not forgetting Sinatra when I wrote the scene between Sid and Emily at the wedding. I've been asked if that's their song, I suppose it would be, but for me, 'Rolling in the Deep' by Adele always will be. I listened to it on repeat while writing most of their scenes. But if Emily had a song of her own, it would be 'You Know I'm No Good' by Amy Winehouse. Amy died as I was nearing the end of the final draft. I was writing the scene in the music shop when I found out and I sobbed and sobbed. I had to read the final paragraph of that chapter aloud recently, where Emily says that she would be better if she could be the girl she was when she was with Sid all of the time, and I still got a lump in my throat, even after all these months.

Is there hope for Emily at the end of *Heart-Shaped Bruise*?

The ending certainly isn't a happy one for Emily, but it's an honest one. I struggled with it, to be honest, with what note to end it on. I wrote several versions before I found one that rang true, because the truth is no one is going to sweep in and save her, Emily has to save herself. But that's where the hope is, I think, she sees the line at last and has taken a step back from it.

How does it feel to see your debut novel in print?

I can't begin to tell you how exciting it is, just seeing these words, these words I've spent hours agonising over, held to paper forever. It's a remarkable thing.

What are you writing next?

My next book is about a seventeen-year-old girl called Scarlett Milton, who is very different from Emily, but I'd like to think, if they ever met, they'd be mates.

Reading Group Questions

1. Doctor Gilyard asks Emily: 'Do you think you could have been friends, if this hadn't happened?' (p. 244)

   Do you believe that Emily and Juliet could have been friends in other circumstances?

2. To what extent is 'Emily Koll' just as much of a fiction as 'Rose Glass'?

3. Is Emily's revenge on Juliet also a sacrifice? How?

4. Are there similarities between Emily and Juliet, and do you think, if so, that Emily is herself aware of them?

5. Does Emily want us to forgive her, even if she isn't asking us directly?

6. Who do you think Sid is better suited to: Emily or Juliet?

7. Emily feels that Juliet took away her father by stabbing him and revealing the fact that he was a criminal. To what extent do you agree with Emily that her relationship with her father prior to the stabbing was an illusion?

8. '"Can you not make this about you?" she said with a sneer. "Don't get me wrong, Rose, it's quite a gift, how you can turn every conversation, every situation, back around to yourself."' (p. 270)

    Is Emily self-centred, as Juliet implies?

9. Is Emily a reliable narrator?

10. In her letter to Juliet, Emily says that she 'is not sorry'. Do you think this is true?

11. 'Rose Glass felt more whole than Emily Koll sometimes.' (p. 118)

    Why do you think Emily enjoys being Rose Glass for a while?

12. Do you like Emily?

13. 'After what you've read in the papers, you were expecting something awful, blood even, a few broken bones. But that would have been too easy. It was the little things, I knew, that would unpick her – slowly, slowly.' (p. 144)

Why do you think 'blood' and 'broken bones' would have been 'too easy' for Emily's revenge upon Juliet?

14. Is there hope for Emily at the end of the novel?